LIVE-IN COUPLE. Handyman and housekeeper. Maintain Blakely Beach estate. 40-hr. week, benefits. Refs. reqd. Contact: Miss Feinstein, 555-1244.

Donovan had to figure out where to find a wife in a hurry, or forget about getting an insider's view of Jon Blakely's motives for murder. One of the housekeeping services, perhaps. Glamorous detective work, he thought, laughing, often began with the judicious use of the Yellow Pages.

Moving toward the inner office, he heard rather than saw the outer door open. He swung around, but it wasn't his new client standing on the threshold.

The white ruffled cap and apron, and the little black dress looked like hand-me-downs from "Upstairs, Downstairs," and the duster glowed with orange feathers that had never touched furniture.

"Don't say anything." Francesca strolled toward him, eyes dancing. "Let the effect sink in."

ABOUT THE AUTHOR

Jacqueline Diamond lives in Brea, California. Her house is stuffed with one hundred and one pasta recipes and populated by her husband and two young sons. She spends her spare time chasing raccoons out of the tomatoes, scaring birds off the apple tree and dreaming up weird ideas to write about.

Books by Jacqueline Diamond

HARLEQUIN AMERICAN ROMANCE

218—UNLIKELY PARTNERS
239—THE CINDERELLA DARE
270—CAPERS AND RAINBOWS
279—A GHOST OF A CHANCE
315—FLIGHT OF MAGIC
351—BY LEAPS AND BOUNDS
406—OLD DREAMS, NEW DREAMS
446—THE TROUBLE WITH TERRY

Jacqueline Diamond

A DANGEROUS GUY

Harlequin Books

TORONTO • NEW YORK • LONDON
AMSTERDAM • PARIS • SYDNEY • HAMBURG
STOCKHOLM • ATHENS • TOKYO • MILAN
MADRID • WARSAW • BUDAPEST • AUCKLAND

Published June 1993

ISBN 0-373-16491-2

A DANGEROUS GUY

Chapter One

From his vantage point on the balcony, Donovan Lewis watched a Rolls-Royce prowl down the flagstone driveway, feeling its way in the near-darkness through a jungle of Ferraris and Jaguars.

The sprawling house, tucked into a hillside overlooking Laguna Beach, was illuminated by jewellike Malibu lights that lent it a fairy-tale air. As far as Donovan was concerned, the tiny pricks of light might have been invented by burglars for their own convenience.

In the faint light, shadows twitched and danced. So far, he'd apprehended one trash bag blowing in the breeze and one waiter sneaking a smoke.

This whole evening wasn't to Donovan's liking, he reflected as he watched the Rolls-Royce approach the front portico. He'd known when he started his own agency that the private-eye business was cyclical. He'd realized that he'd have to moonlight as a security guard once in a while.

But he hadn't featured himself nursemaiding a bunch of society party-goers for an eccentric dowager like Mrs. Farthington Cornsworth.

Item: Mrs. Cornsworth loved to show off her collection of jewelry. No object was worth less than fifty thousand dollars, and most were small enough for a thief to hide in his pocket.

Item: Mrs. Cornsworth had grumblingly agreed to lock her latest acquisition, a five-million-dollar necklace, in a shatterproof glass case, but refused to install any kind of sensing device. Earthquakes were too frequent in southern California, she contended, and she didn't want to be troubling the police with false alarms.

Item: Her rambling modern house was a maze of oddly placed rooms, unexpected nooks and other ideal spots to cloak an intruder.

Item: Mrs. Cornsworth refused to insult the guests at her annual Halloween charity ball by hiring uniformed guards—or even disguising undercover guards as waiters, because she claimed they would be too obvious. She had only engaged Donovan at the insistence of her insurance agency, and because, she said, a former lawyer with a degree from Harvard was classy enough to pass as a guest.

So here stood Donovan, would-be righter of society's wrongs and rescuer of damsels in distress, patrolling the premises dressed like an escapee from an Errol Flynn movie.

Mrs. Cornsworth had rented the costume herself: a broad-brimmed pirate's hat, a scarlet coat that strained to cover Donovan's chest, and fawn-colored breeches so tight they'd split if he sat down. It had taken all his powers to persuade his client that a hook and eye patch were not terrific ideas when it came to security work.

Below, in the driveway, the driver's door of the Rolls-Royce flew open, and a uniformed chauffeur stepped to the rear door.

In the dim light, Donovan caught only an impression of the couple that emerged: a woman too plump for her antebellum hoop skirts and cinched waist, and a reedy man in a cutaway coat and fake mustache. Scarlett and Rhett, a few decades past their prime.

Donovan was about to continue his patrol when a flicker of motion caught his eye. He turned back toward the driveway.

Something was moving through the overgrown acacias that shielded one side of the property. Donovan reached instinctively toward his shoulder holster, then pulled his hand away. It was probably a dog, or one of the chauffeurs.

On the other hand, he wasn't being paid to make assumptions.

Donovan swung over the railing. The house was set into a hillside with a balcony wrapped behind, three stories above a canyon. This lip, however, extended toward the front, only one story above the drive.

Donovan's gymnastics days were long gone, but it was a simple matter to grip the bars and lower himself within striking distance of a patch of soft Thai grass.

Or it would have been a simple matter, if not for his costume.

Donovan hung from the railing, the red jacket bunching up around his armpits and the hat sliding to the back of his head. He dropped, slipped, and scrambled for balance. As he landed, he felt a few stitches give way in the seat of his pants.

Well, that little problem was between Mrs. Cornsworth and the rental company, wasn't it?

Donovan jammed the hat into place and crouched in the darkness. All he heard was a sudden blare of big-band music as someone opened the door for Rhett and Scarlett.

In the blinding patch of light, he thought he saw a slim figure slip inside, half hidden by Scarlett's billowing skirt.

Was it a trick wrought by glare and tired eyes? Or had an intruder just gained access to the house? If so, he had to be stopped, and quickly.

Donovan hurried across the flagstones and yanked on the door. It rattled and held. The bloody thing was locked.

He jabbed the doorbell. Once, twice. Finally it swung open, and a paunchy Batman waved him inside, spilling a martini in the process.

"Yo-ho, Pirate King!" cried the masked man. "Avast, and all that good stuff!"

Good lord, where was the maid? This drunken party-goer would have let anyone in! "Where did they go?"

"Who go? Say what?"

Donovan gripped Batman's shoulder. "That couple from *Gone With the Wind*. And whoever came in with them. Did you see him?"

"See who?" sputtered the impromptu doorman. "Bar's back that way. Ballroom's upstairs. Durn cocka-mamie house. Built upside down and backwards."

"I said, did you see..." A blast of big-band music drowned out Donovan's words, and, with a wiggle of his empty glass, Batman departed.

Donovan paused to take his bearings.

The couple might have headed straight back to the buffet, or climbed the staircase to the living room. Besides, by now the interloper—if there had really been one—had probably left their company and begun mingling on his own. With more than a hundred and fifty guests on the premises, Donovan would have no way of identifying the newcomer.

He went to find Mrs. Cornsworth.

The hostess stood near the buffet, refilling her plate with crab cakes. Almost as plump as she was tall, she had attempted to disguise herself as a bird of paradise. A green feathered cape fell from her shoulders, and orange and purple plumes jutted at odd angles from her hair. She looked like a papier-mâché centerpiece come to life.

Her eyes twinkled as Donovan approached. "My favorite pirate. Goodness, what a scowl! Have you made someone walk the plank?"

He fought the urge to smile. Donovan couldn't help liking this jolly lady, but he was here to protect her, not to make idle conversation. "I believe an uninvited guest is on the premises. I'll need your help to identify him."

"Oh, pooh..." Mrs. Cornsworth waved her hand, setting the feathers to trembling. "Probably one of those society reporters. They're always sneaking about. I don't mind. Really, I like reading what they write. I'd invite them myself, but that would destroy all their fun, wouldn't it?"

"Nevertheless, I think he should be identified."

"But it's so much more intriguing this way, don't you think? A mystery guest!"

In the face of such obstinacy, Donovan felt a wave of frustration. By nature he was direct, a man of action. That was why he'd first given up his law practice to become a deputy district attorney and then given that up to go into the investigative business.

He'd grown tired of half measures, of technicalities and twists in the evidence. Most of all, Donovan hated seeing the guilty go free, and he certainly didn't intend to have that happen tonight.

This fellow needed to learn a lesson in respect for other people's property. Reporters had no business crashing private parties, particularly not when there were millions of dollars' worth of jewels lying about.

Donovan reviewed his vague impression of the intruder: average height, thin figure, black hair. A dark costume, or one of a neutral color—nothing that stuck in the memory.

Not much to go on, except that most of the crowd tended toward ostentation. With all these sequins, feathers and eye-catching colors, the intruder would stand out by his simplicity.

Or her simplicity, Donovan amended. He preferred the old-fashioned ideal of women as noble souls entitled to a man's protection, but he did keep up with the times.

He saw no one fitting the interloper's description in the buffet room, but in a nook to one side he spotted the antebellum couple. He strode toward them.

Before he could question them, however, a hand touched his wrist, and he stopped abruptly, his head snapping around in surprise. He hadn't noticed anyone nearby.

"Oh, I'm sorry." But she didn't sound sorry, the possessor of those lively dark eyes that were so close to his. How had she managed to catch him off guard?

"Where'd you come from?" Donovan couldn't suppress a gruff tone. He hated being one-upped.

"I've been standing right here. I'm not used to being overlooked, I assure you."

He made a quick mental catalog: long dark hair, olive skin, a tan body giving tantalizing shape to a golden halter top and gauzy harem pants; slender feet displayed in golden sandals with a single thong between the toes.

Then Donovan's organized thought processes hit a stumbling block. He didn't usually notice perfume, and especially not scents as subtle as this one. Exotic—he couldn't place it. And her skin—the costume exposed plenty of it—where did that sheen come from? She was just standing there, breathing, yet she seemed to be undulating. Must be the effect of the semitransparent material rippling in a draft.

Donovan tried to guess her age. Twenty-seven, maybe twenty-eight. Old enough to understand the effect that low-cut halter would have on a man standing close enough to notice the gold sparkles that dusted her softly rounded breasts.

"See anything you like?" the woman asked.

"What's not to like?" he said, and realized he hadn't breathed in a long time.

"I brought you something." Her hand brushed his, and he felt something hard and cold. He tensed, then recognized it as a drink. "Boy, you're jumpy."

"I don't care for any—"

"Ginger ale." She pressed the glass into his palm. He had to take it to keep it from falling. "I knew you wouldn't drink on duty."

"How did you...?" Donovan hated being recognized, in private investigator's terminology, being "made."

Laughter teased his ear. "You're so straight, they could paint lines on the freeway with you."

"Now wait a minute!"

"I'll catch you later. Unless you catch me first." Her hand slipped under his coat, the fingers dancing across the silken shirt. He wasn't prepared for the intimacy of her touch, and before he could react she was gone.

Donovan stood there, with the drink icy in his hand, his body burning in unexpected and inappropriate places. Inappropriate for a man who was halfway certain he'd just been confronted by the very intruder he sought.

The woman was so clever she'd bedazzled him while letting him know that to her this encounter was a game. But he didn't think she was some party girl amusing herself. More likely the most dangerous kind of criminal, the kind who enjoyed the work.

Now where the bloody hell had she gone?

Donovan set the glass on a table and went upstairs.

In the living room, he found the band taking a break and the air filled with the buzz of conversation. The room looked like a hotel lobby, an enormous octagon sparsely furnished with low white couches and glass tables. At the back, French doors opened onto the balcony.

Donovan's gaze went automatically to the glass display cases interspersed among ferns and African carvings. Spotlights picked out huge rubies, amethysts and emeralds set with diamonds in a wealth of bracelets, earrings, rings and chokers. Some were modern designs; others dated back to the eighteenth century. Their total value would have made a big dent in the national debt.

At the far side of the room, beside the bandstand, stood the tallest of the cases. So new that it had not yet scuffed the hardwood floor, it was lined with black velvet that set off the elaborate necklace and huge crystalline stone inside.

The Sakahara diamond. Its origins were shrouded in legend. Some said it had belonged to the last czar of all the Russias; others, to an Indian rajah. Wherever it came from, the immense stone had found its way to Hong Kong and been set into a blaze of emeralds and smaller diamonds, then purchased by a Hollywood producer for his paramour during the golden age of silent films. Later, it had been acquired at auction by a Japanese tycoon, who had sold it to Mrs. Cornsworth.

Frankly, Donovan found the thing gaudy. His family in Boston might not be wealthy by Mrs. Cornsworth's standards, but the Lewis money had the patina of age. His mother preferred simple designs of plain gold with a few small diamonds tucked into them. His grandmother swore by pearls.

But he hadn't come here to critique the jewelry.

Donovan surveyed the room for the mysterious woman. It would be hard to find her at this costume party run amok. He noted a Big Bad Wolf and a Little Red Riding Hood, someone dressed like the creature from *Alien,* a couple of beach bums in Hawaiian shirts, two robots, a Klingon and a uniformed Star Fleet officer from *Star Trek.* He saw Marie Antoinette and Louis XIV, and a lot of costumes he couldn't place, everyone shifting and strolling and darting to and fro.

On the bandstand, musicians filtered back to their positions. They'd brightened their tuxedos with red-and-orange cummerbunds, and the drummer began chinging a south-of-the-border beat.

Swaying to the Latin tempo, people converged on the dance floor. Donovan couldn't keep track of who was who. A slender woman could conceal herself behind a plant stand or simply disappear behind cover of all the bodies.

Donovan knew he had to start thinking like a thief.

The woman wouldn't have a chance of emptying one of the cases in front of all these people, even if they weren't locked. Still, Mrs. Cornsworth wasn't particular about the quality of her locks, and some of them had aged. A few of the smaller cases could be easily pried, although the woman would have to stage a diversion.

That raised the possibility of an accomplice. Donovan took a deep breath. If she had help, he, too, might need an assistant. He would have preferred to hire someone in advance, but Mrs. Cornsworth had refused, so he'd have to make do with what was available.

He stepped toward a blond young man serving hors d'oeuvres from a silver platter. Donovan had checked out the hired help in advance. The young man, Greg, was a college student with a clean record.

"Greg." Donovan pretended to be selecting a canapé. "Someone may try to draw my attention—break something, spill something, whatever. Keep your eye on the jewelry. Don't be afraid to yell if you see anything suspicious."

Greg's expression of polite boredom yielded to one of enthusiasm. "Really? Wow, great! I'm your man, Mr. Lewis!"

"That's the right stuff." Actually, Donovan didn't intend to allow himself to be lulled, but he preferred not to take chances. A good detective arranged for backup when he needed it. If Mrs. Cornsworth wouldn't let him hire guards as waiters, he'd turn her waiters into guards instead.

By now, the room had filled with a seductive samba beat—or maybe it was reggae. Donovan had survived a ballroom dancing class as a youngster, but he didn't keep up with trends in music.

"You will help, won't you?" The woman's voice was deep and breathy, inches from his ear. Donovan flinched. He hadn't noticed anyone approaching. Had she overheard him talking to Greg?

The dark eyes peered mischievously into his. "Daydreaming, detective? That's twice I've caught you."

His hand clamped on her upper arm. It was slender and firm, and the bare skin was golden. "I need to have a word with you, miss."

"There's someone following me." Her eyes widened. "A man—he's wearing a Napoleon costume. I think he's got a gun."

"Oh, does he?" He didn't believe her, yet he couldn't dismiss her claim without checking it out. "What's your name?"

"Francesca." She gave it the Italian pronunciation, the first *c* sounding like "ch." "Francesca Adamo. I'm a friend of Mrs. Cornsworth's daughter." That would be Cheryl, a socialite who was vacationing in Hawaii.

"And where is Napoleon now?"

The young woman gazed around the room. "I don't see him."

"It would be hard to miss a man in a Napoleon costume."

"Not really. Napoleon was short."

"And was this man short?"

"I said he looked like Napoleon, didn't I?"

"Just because a man wears a costume, it doesn't mean he actually looks like— Forget it." Donovan felt as if he'd become entangled in a conversational maze and had to hack his way out. "Let's go and see our hostess, shall we? I'd like her to vouch for your identity."

"There he is!" Her full lips pursed, Francesca nodded toward the dance floor. "He's with Marie Antoinette."

She hadn't been kidding. There really was a short man in a French uniform half-hidden behind a woman's voluminous gown. They were shaking to the Latin beat, both slightly off the rhythm.

"I'll talk to him." Donovan released her shoulder, and then, on the verge of walking away, recognized his near-mistake. He took Francesca by the wrist. "And you're coming with me."

"Of course," she said.

He caught a whiff of that exotic perfume again. It hinted of jungle flowers that reveal themselves only once in a century. Flowers nestled deep in forgotten tangles, waiting to be discovered, waiting to be plundered . . .

What had gotten into him? Donovan frowned and caught Francesca's amused smile. It annoyed him no end.

His first impulse was to march right up to Napoleon and demand to see some ID, but Mrs. Cornsworth had given strict instructions to avoid making a scene. Besides, Napoleon might turn out to be the mayor of Laguna Beach, or even the chief of police.

Donovan needed to observe the man without calling attention to himself. He particularly needed to observe whether Napoleon was paying undue attention to Francesca. He wondered why that possibility irked him, and decided it was his sense of professional responsibility.

"You're going to dance with me, aren't you?" Francesca took his hand and placed it on her bare waist.

He couldn't resist answering, "If duty requires."

"I thought private eyes were supposed to be dashing and heroic."

"You've been reading the wrong books," he said. "Don't you know we're grouchy, sarcastic and in perpetual need of a cup of coffee?"

"I make wonderful espresso," she said.

"Can't stand the stuff. I like mine the old-fashioned way. Boiled."

"Why don't you shut up and dance?"

They eased into the mass of bodies, letting the rhythm overtake them. Francesca's eyes half closed, as if the music were lifting her into another realm.

Donovan could feel the curve of her hip through her satiny skin, could trace every ripple of her muscles as she swayed. He'd never felt a woman move like this outside a bedroom. And that had been much too long ago.

"You'd better keep dancing," she murmured. "People are staring."

"Let them," he said, but he'd already been swept up by her swinging motions.

The insistent beat seeped inside Donovan's joints, and it took no effort at all to match Francesca quiver for quiver.

It was Donovan's style to hold himself in reserve, on and off duty—to watch, to catalog, to stay in control. He couldn't explain the languid feeling that had invaded his joints, or the way he kept forgetting about everything except Francesca, this laughing woman with her arching body, her winking exposed navel, and the sway of transparent fabric around her slender legs. Her hair kept flicking against his neck; her skin burned beneath his hand.

"Better, better..." She drew his free hand to the other side of her waist. "Let yourself go. Throw yourself into it."

Donovan tried to check on Napoleon's whereabouts and stumbled against Francesca. "This isn't working."

"And whose fault is that?" She lifted her hands overhead and clapped lightly in time with the music. The gesture thrust her breasts into clear definition against the silky fabric, but she showed no trace of self-consciousness.

Donovan wasn't going to let her defeat him at this game. Two could play as well as one.

With his thumbs, he traced her waist to the lower rim of the halter. At the same time, he took control of their direction, dipping her to one side and letting their legs tangle lightly.

Was it only his imagination, or did Francesca's breath come faster? Long, dark lashes fluttered against her cheek; she wasn't meeting his gaze. Well, he could fix that, too.

Donovan cupped both her hands, lifted them overhead and clapped them for her in imitation of her earlier gesture. In the process, her body stretched against his, touching point for point. He thought he felt her nipples tighten beneath the soft fabric, and he smiled to himself.

"So you do know how to dance," she murmured.

Instead of replying, he caught her in a lift—one hand beneath her thigh, the other under her arm—and whirled her around until she was balanced against his shoulder. She followed his lead like an acrobat.

Her thigh was yielding in his grip; her lips grazed his neck. Donovan relaxed his grip for an instant, then flipped her overhead, swiveling and catching her as she slid down. He couldn't quite believe he'd done that, and yet it had seemed natural, even inevitable, so finely were their bodies attuned to one another.

It was as if they'd rehearsed this. Or was this the rehearsal? Donovan wanted the real thing. He wanted to be alone with her. . . .

"He's gone," Francesca said.

"Who?" Even as he spoke, Donovan understood. "Oh. Napoleon."

"Maybe he went to Waterloo." Francesca chuckled.

Donovan released her abruptly, not caring that she landed with a thump. Talk about a diversion! And he'd believed he was taking control.

"I've had about enough of this," he said tightly, and went in search of Greg.

The waiter hadn't noticed anything amiss with the jewelry cases, and he didn't recall seeing a man in a Napoleon costume doing anything suspicious. "I think the guy went downstairs a while ago, actually."

"Thanks." Donovan clapped him on the shoulder. "Good work."

He turned back toward the dance floor. The band had shifted into a waltz, and Francesca was dancing demurely with the Phantom of the Opera. If she noticed Donovan, she gave no sign.

What the hell had come over him? Donovan never let a woman get to him like that, not when he was working. Even in private life, his preference was for self-contained professional women in tailored suits, women who wouldn't intrude in his work.

Or in his life, either, for that matter. Donovan never consciously decided to keep people at arm's length, but he realized he liked ladies who didn't ruffle his composure. He cherished the ideal of romantic love, but the reality tended to be inconvenient.

He made the rounds of the jewelry cases. Nothing was missing, and he saw no signs of prying.

As he finished his inspection, Donovan noticed Mrs. Cornsworth talking with Minnie Mouse on the balcony. He sauntered outside and waited until there was a break in the conversation.

"Excuse me." Donovan gave Minnie a polite nod and caught Mrs. Cornsworth's eye. "Have you seen a man dressed as Napoleon?"

"That one?" She pointed to two figures farther along the balcony.

That was Napoleon, all right, smoking a cigarette and talking to Darth Vader. "Yes. Know who he his?"

"Of course," she said. "He's my lawyer. In fact, I've been meaning to introduce you. You two have so much in common. You could discuss torts or writs, or whatever you people chat about."

"Not just now, thanks." Lawyers usually talked about their investments, and Donovan had sold all his to start the agency.

Minnie piped up. "You're a lawyer? Gee, I've been wanting to ask somebody. I've got this neighbor who lets his dog dig up my rosebushes—"

"I'm afraid I'm no longer a member of the bar, so I can't give legal advice," Donovan said. "Why don't you talk to Napoleon?"

"Oh, good idea!" squealed Minnie, and headed for the diminutive emperor.

"One more question," Donovan said as Mrs. Cornsworth's attention wandered back toward the living room. "Do you know a friend of your daughter's named Francesca?"

"Francesca?" repeated his client. "She isn't a little blond with a lisp, is she?"

"Slim, dark hair, dressed as a harem girl," he said.

"You mean she's here?" The hostess quirked an eyebrow. "Goodness. I never invite Cheryl's friends. They're too rowdy."

"That's what I thought." It gave Donovan no satisfaction to discover that he'd been right all along: The woman was a liar and a fraud. "I'd better go talk to her."

"She sounds intriguing," said Mrs. Cornsworth as he spun to leave. "I'd like to meet her."

"I'll bring her over."

In the living room, the band was playing "Fly Me to the Moon," or maybe it was "Begin the Beguine"; Donovan never could tell them apart. The dancing had spilled over onto the carpet, and some of the Fred Astaire and Ginger Rogers wannabes were circling dangerously close to the ferns. Near the bandstand the Phantom of the Opera was leering at Little Bo Peep.

Mentally Donovan divided the room into sections and visually combed each one, trying to match his memory of flying dark hair and laughing eyes. There were orange wigs and Morticia tresses, piles of white fluff and Raggedy Ann braids, but nothing and no one who bore any resemblance to Francesca Adamo.

She'd vanished. He could only wonder which of Mrs. Cornsworth's prized possessions might have vanished with her.

Chapter Two

It didn't improve Donovan's mood when he couldn't find any items missing. It would be just like that scheming female to have taken something he wouldn't be watching for: a small painting, or even some valuable toiletry item.

At his insistence, Mrs. Cornsworth went downstairs and peeked into her bedroom. She reported that her silver comb and brush set remained intact, and added wryly that her toothbrush hadn't been stolen, either.

Donovan refrained from pointing out that something could be missing from one of the guests' purses. No point in causing unnecessary alarm.

Besides, he didn't think Francesca Adamo—or whatever her real name might be—was a petty thief. Stealing jewels carried a certain cachet; swiping loose change from purses was mean-spirited. And he didn't see Francesca Adamo as mean-spirited.

Or was he letting his physical response affect his judgment?

Donovan still couldn't quite understand what had happened. He felt as if he'd had too much to drink, though of course he never drank on duty. What had he been thinking of, dancing with Francesca in such sensuous abandon?

Even now, his memories of her focused on intimate details—the satiny smoothness of her skin, her habit of cocking one eyebrow as if constantly amused, the moist whisper of her breath against his neck.

He would have been hard put to describe the whole woman for a police report. Donovan could just imagine the response if, under Identifying Marks he wrote "A small dimple on the left cheek that only flashes when she's about to say something mischievous."

Donovan couldn't shake the embarrassing suspicion that for once his masculine nature had overwhelmed his detective's instincts. The whole situation filled him with rage. He was going to find out what that minx had been up to.

Maybe she was a reporter, as Mrs. Cornsworth believed. If so, her byline would show up tomorrow on some story, and Donovan would find himself impaled on her pen. But there were ways of turning the tables on reporters, particularly if they had anything disreputable in their past that a detective could dig up.

For the rest of the evening, he partnered various ladies on the dance floor, made surreptitious rounds of the premises and questioned the chauffeurs waiting outside, none of whom admitted to having seen Francesca. He didn't see how they could have missed her.

Donovan tried to keep his mind on his surroundings. That was the first requirement of a good detective, to be alert to what was around him.

Fortunately, the rest of the guests behaved more or less normally. A few inebriated individuals had to be discreetly ushered out to their cars, or into taxis, if they hadn't brought designated drivers. One man made a pass at a woman and was challenged to a duel by her husband, Zorro; a lady lost her contact lens, and the geography of the living room was briefly reshaped as the guests dropped to their knees and joined the search. The missing lens was finally located clinging to the lady's shoulder.

At last the house was empty, save for Mrs. Cornsworth and a live-in maid.

"You can go home now." The dowager yawned as she tried to shoo Donovan out the door. "I'll set the alarm."

Donovan stood his ground. "Mrs. Cornsworth, at the risk of repeating myself, that security system of yours wouldn't stop a professional for five minutes, especially if he'd had a chance to case the place...."

He stopped right there. Of course. Francesca had been spying out the weaknesses in the security system. If she or an accomplice knew how to pick locks in a hurry, they could break in and disable the thing before it went off.

Moreover, Mrs. Cornsworth, with her unwillingness to trouble the police, had bought the kind of alarm that simply rings loudly on the premises. Even if it sounded, the police might not be summoned until it was too late to prevent a major robbery.

"This alarm is perfectly adequate. I've never had a problem with it before."

"I'm sure that's true, but just to be on the safe side, I think I'll stick around," Donovan said.

She leveled a sharp gaze at him. "Now look here..."

"No extra charge."

"That isn't the issue." Mrs. Cornsworth folded her arms across her chest. "I'm not such a helpless old woman as you think. I've got a gun."

"Where?" Donovan eyed her empty hands meaningfully.

"Next to my bed, of course!" The orange and purple feathers in her hair shook defiantly.

"Loaded?"

"I assume so."

"You assume?"

"It belonged to my late husband," Mrs. Cornsworth said.

After a startled moment, Donovan snapped his mouth shut. There was no use in arguing with a woman who believed herself protected by a pistol that had lain unused and uninspected since her husband's death—some five years before.

She'd obviously never fired the thing, wouldn't know if it had a safety or how many bullets might be in the chamber. "Well, if anyone comes in through your bedroom window, you dispatch him for me, will you, Mrs. Cornsworth? In the meantime, I'll just hang around for a while, if you don't mind."

She heaved an exasperated sigh. "Well, you're too big for me to throw you out, and I certainly wouldn't want to call the police just to get rid of you. Mind you don't knock anything over!" With a flip of her green cape, the dowager turned away. Then she swung back. "I've tucked some hors d'oeuvres in the fridge."

"Thank you." Donovan had no interest in food right now, particularly not the vegetable crudité's and shrimp-and-caviar delicacies that the caterer had provided. He preferred corned-beef sandwiches, potatoes fixed almost any way, and, when his conscience forced him to consider a nominally green vegetable, cabbage, boiled or chopped into coleslaw. "Sleep well."

"Make sure *you* don't set off the alarm!" Mrs. Cornsworth finished, and marched away.

Silence closed around Donovan, broken only by the faint hum of a distant refrigerator. A dim light from recessed fixtures bathed the rooms with a cool, unwavering glow that seemed to Donovan to take on an unearthly quality.

He paused by the front door, on the middle level of the house. From here he could see the open stairway leading up to the living room, the buffet room straight ahead, and, through etched sidelights, part of the front drive.

He checked to make sure the alarm was set, then began his rounds.

All went well for the first hour. The doors and windows—of which there were a ridiculous number—had been securely fastened and nothing appeared to be amiss. Donovan passed the time by grumbling to himself about the absence of a motion sensor that could have provided the jewelry with high-grade security.

Then, on his third patrol, Donovan discovered a new room on the top floor. He had passed the door several times, assuming it to be a broom closet; it was of substandard width, and set near an outer wall.

This time he turned the knob and found himself in a small office. Not much here: a delicate cherrywood desk, two Regency-style chairs, a glassed-in bookcase containing leatherbound volumes that looked as if they had never been opened.

Nothing much, except for the disturbing fact that, set into the far wall, was a French door that opened onto the balcony. A door that stood ajar, letting a cool October breeze whisper through the room.

How long had it stood that way? All the French doors required keys, so Mrs. Cornsworth or her maid must have opened it at the start of the evening. If so, why hadn't they remembered to close it?

Or had someone picked the lock during the party and left it open, meaning to return later? But that made no sense; the lock could be jimmied as easily from outside as inside, so why bother to open it in advance?

Donovan could think of only two explanations. Either the person coming to burglarize the house was not the same person who'd picked the lock, or someone had left a clue on purpose.

Was he being set up, or simply mocked?

Outside, the canyon lay three stories below, only faintly visible in the gloom. Donovan paced onto the balcony and studied the shrubbery below. Pale moonlight picked out shadows that shivered in the breeze, and from far off came the aching cry of a coyote, but he saw no sliver of movement that spoke of a human presence.

Donovan continued along the balcony to the lip that wrapped toward the front. He peered at the clumps of acacia trees that edged the driveway, but caught no hint of a disturbance. A car grunted up the steep grade of the road, out of sight behind the trees. It coughed past the property and groaned onward until its noise blended with the rustle of branches.

Donovan inhaled the mingled smells of pine, automobile exhaust and eucalyptus, and wished he had a bloodhound's ability to lock on to a specific scent.

Such as a gossamer perfume that hinted of secrets and steamy hideaways.

Donovan thought of Francesca, and knew that if he ever saw her again he would teach her a little respect. And caution. She was daring, all right—he admired her for that—but she flaunted herself with the recklessness of an amateur.

Something nagged at Donovan's awareness, interrupting the flow of thoughts. It took a moment to fix on the faint sound from within the house. A footstep, light and quick, nearly inaudible.

Mrs. Cornsworth was a heavy woman who moved with dignified stiffness. Her maid walked with a pronounced limp.

His heart rate shifted into second gear. So far, Donovan had tantalized himself with suspicions, but there'd been no proof. Even the open door might have been an accident.

He drew his gun. He didn't know if the burglar was Francesca or not, but it was a safe bet he—or she—wasn't going to give Donovan any leeway.

He wasn't overly concerned about the possible theft of the Sakahara necklace; the damn thing was insured, and Donovan wasted no sentiment on stones. But Mrs. Cornsworth and her maid lay sleeping below. For all he knew, they might be in danger.

Moving quietly in his rubber-soled boots, he returned to the small office. As he paused to listen, an all-too-familiar scent nudged at Donovan's nostrils.

He could never mistake that exotic fragrance. His heart slammed into high gear.

Donovan realized he'd been hoping Francesca really would turn out to be a reporter or some party-crashing friend of Cheryl's. He didn't want her to be his enemy. He didn't want her to be one of the hundreds of lowlifes a detective ran into as part of the job. He wanted her to be someone special.

She was special, all right. He'd send her a dozen roses in jail.

Donovan edged out of the office, flattening himself against the wall. His senses were honed to a fine point, ready for the faintest click of a gun being cocked or the slightest rustle of a footstep.

Nothing.

The living room hulked with shadows. Without taking his eyes from the expanse, Donovan felt along the wall for the light switch. Brightness flung itself into his eyes. In that instant, he had to rely on his ears, but there was no sound.

The living room was empty.

Leaving the lights on, Donovan proceeded down the steps to the front hall. Although he'd expected it, he felt an adrenaline surge when he saw that the alarm had been turned off. The front door stood ajar.

The intruder had been quick, expert, and well prepared.

Donovan intended to go straight to Mrs. Cornsworth's bedroom, make sure she was safe and then call the police, but a faint whuffing sound from beyond the buffet room stopped him. It could have come from the kitchen or the bar nook.

Francesca was here, on this floor. If he went downstairs, it would mean letting her escape. And he had no intention of doing that.

He still hoped for the advantage of surprise. After all, she couldn't be sure he was still on the premises. Donovan had parked his nondescript van half a block up the street, where anyone might have claimed it.

On the other hand, Francesca had known who he was when they first met. He realized now that she hadn't "made" him as a detective—she'd come prepared. If so, she probably knew what his vehicle looked like, too.

Donovan considered what he could do next. He could head upstairs and guard the living room, but he'd be setting himself up as a target. Besides, he didn't intend to leave the next move to Francesca. He'd catch her before she even got near those jewels.

He could already feel those slender wrists in his grip, or maybe he'd catch her by her delicate shoulders, or around her bare waist. Was she still wearing the harem costume? He hoped so.

What was he thinking of?

Donovan realized he'd passed through the buffet room in a daze. Now he had to choose: bar to the left, kitchen straight ahead, a hallway to the right. He hadn't heard another sound to indicate Francesca's whereabouts.

She wouldn't have gone into the bar nook; too easy to get trapped. The kitchen had a side service entrance, but the hinges were rusty. When opened, the thing squealed like an angry sea gull.

Her best bet would be the hallway. There was a powder room, he recalled, and a little-used game room and . . . in a maze like this, who knew what else?

As he advanced into the hall, Donovan's foot brushed something on the floor. Without taking his eyes off the passageway ahead, he knelt and scooped it up.

It was a sandal with a golden thong. A trace of scent floated tantalizingly upward.

She even wore perfume on her feet?

Donovan gripped the sandal, feeling the indentation of her toes. Had she lost it in her flight? He doubted it. She'd had no reason to panic. No, Francesca had left it here on purpose.

He hated the feeling that swept over him, that he was being led when he'd believed himself in pursuit. It took all his self-control to keep from shouting with fury, snapping on all the lights and raging through the house until he cornered her.

But rage, like panic, blurred the senses—and led to fatal mistakes.

The thought brought Donovan up short. This wasn't like him. He might be a man of action, but he'd always taken pride in his self-control. He never flew off the handle. He never made foolish mistakes in a frenzy.

He wasn't going to let that scheming vixen get to him.

Neither was he going to prowl around like a blind man, stumbling over whatever clues she'd deliberately tossed in his way. By now she'd probably gone back upstairs and was picking a lock.

Donovan didn't take the main staircase this time. He twisted along the hallway away from the entrance until he reached a niche that he would normally have passed without a second glance. There he pressed a button recessed into the wall.

When she'd first showed him around, Mrs. Cornsworth had explained that during her late husband's illness they'd had to install an elevator. Neither of them had liked the high-tech industrial effect, so they'd tucked it away out of sight.

Donovan was almost sure it hadn't been used that evening. Even if Francesca had somehow obtained the original architect's plans for the house, the elevator wouldn't appear on them.

It would take him up to a secluded alcove from which he'd have a perfect view of the living room, without being visible himself. He was smiling as the door glided open.

In the center of the elevator, nearly filling the small space, sat an oak TV table topped with a silver tray. It held two English china dishes and two crystal goblets. One dish displayed a neat array of hors d'oeuvres; the goblet sparkled with champagne. The other plate contained only a few crumbs, with a trace of liquid remaining in the second glass.

She might as well have left a calling card that read, "Gotcha!"

Donovan ignored the wrath that threatened to obscure his thought processes. There was no time for petty personal emotions. He had to concentrate.

Usually he could keep one step ahead of his target. If he was tailing someone and lost him in a crowd, he'd figure out where the guy was likely to turn up next and, sure enough, there he'd be. When it came to an uncooperative witness, Donovan would ferret out the person's pet hobby, or pet peeve, or pet anxiety, and get his questions answered.

He'd drawn a blank with Francesca. Was she simply too clever, or was her incredible physical appeal muddling his thoughts? He could still feel the soft leather of her sandal, even though he'd left it behind in the hall. The shoe had a cushiony feel, yielding beneath his fingers like firm but tender flesh inviting his caress...

He shook his head fiercely. Where was she? Where—

In that instant, he knew without a doubt that Francesca Adamo had come here for only one reason. She'd be satisfied with nothing less than the Sakahara necklace. She wanted his ultimate and complete humiliation.

He didn't even dare take the elevator. For all he knew, she might have booby-trapped it.

No longer concerned about being heard, Donovan ran back along the hallway and up the stairs. The pirate hat flew off his head. The tight jacket pressed against his chest as his breath came hard.

His boots thudded across the polished floor of the living room. Something about the jewelry cabinet looked wrong.

Donovan halted in front of the display case, blood pounding in his head so hard it misted his vision. He caught a deep, shuddering breath.

The Sakahara necklace was gone. In its place sat a fresh-flower lei with a note that read "Aloha, hello and goodbye."

She couldn't have gone far. Donovan knew it hadn't been more than a few minutes since he'd heard that noise back in the kitchen area.

The one good thing about this crazy house was its isolated location on a narrow, winding street. Even Francesca couldn't pull off a nighttime escape through the treacherous canyon. She'd have to keep a car parked somewhere nearby, and there was only one route down the hill.

She might even still be visible from the balcony.

Donovan ran to the nearest door, then remembered it was key-locked. His heart kicking against his ribs, he raced back to the small office.

The French door was closed, just as he'd left it. He grabbed the knob and wrenched it open.

As he did so, the jangling of a dozen alarm bells screamed through the house. The floor vibrated; adrenaline shocked Donovan's system even as his brain identified what had happened.

Francesca Adamo, master thief, had gone back downstairs and reset the alarm before making her escape through the front door. She'd left Donovan to give notice of his failure to the world.

She'd hoodwinked him, bamboozled him, flim-flammed him and made a monkey out of him.

He was going to pay that scheming wench back if it was the last thing he ever did.

WRAPPED IN A SILK KIMONO, her thin hair rumpled from sleep, Mrs. Farthington Cornsworth stood beside Donovan, staring at the lei.

"I suppose, if it's any satisfaction, you were right," she said. "And I was having such a nice dream. I was on a sailboat with Tyrone Power."

"I'll get it back," Donovan said. "She can't just walk into a pawnshop and fence a thing like that. She'll have to find a buyer, someone very unusual, someone willing to pay a fortune for a necklace that can't be shown in public. Or she could break down the stones, but even so... Unless she's got a buyer already, of course."

"I never thought of that." Mrs. Cornsworth perked up. "Really, who do you suppose it is? An Arab sheik? How interesting!"

Donovan tried to keep his thoughts focused on ways to recover the Sakahara diamond. He tried not to think about what a scandal there would be, or how bad this would look for the already struggling Donovan Lewis Detective Agency.

"We'll have to notify the police," he muttered through his teeth, wishing he could chew up the words and swallow them before his client heard. "At least we've got a description of the suspect."

"Oh, I do hate all that fuss." Mrs. Cornsworth retrieved the lei and touched the flowers to her nose. "How lovely. Where do you suppose she got it?"

"I don't think they sell them around here."

"You'd have to go to Hawaii," said the dowager. "Like my daughter. But of course she didn't do this. She isn't smart enough. Besides, why would she steal her own inheritance?"

"You may want to get dressed before the police arrive," Donovan reminded her.

"Not tonight!" Mrs. Cornsworth stared at him in dismay. "I'm so tired, and the place is a mess."

"We don't want to leave them a cold trail."

"But you said you could get it back!" she reminded him. "I do wish you would. This whole thing is so inconvenient."

"Well..."

"And all the newspaper headlines!" She shook her head. "Really, Mr. Lewis. I'll give you twenty-four hours to find it."

"Done," he said, and wondered if there was any coffee left from the party. Preferably very black and very strong.

He was going to need it.

BY NOON THE NEXT DAY, Donovan had come to realize that foolish bravado must have vanquished his better judgment when he'd promised to recover the necklace.

He'd spent the morning on the telephone with jewelers, pawnshops, even underground newspapers where Francesca might place an ad for a buyer. He'd talked to a friend at Customs, and realized that, with a practically unsecured border with Mexico less than two hours away, there was no way to stop Francesca from taking the thing out of the country.

She'd probably drive out wearing it in full view. Just to get a last laugh.

He'd talked to auction houses about potential buyers of fabulous jewelry, and been reminded that people rich enough and unscrupulous enough to trade in this kind of stolen goods would never bid under their own names even for a legitimate purchase. They'd go through an intermediary, or two or three.

Donovan had even tried to track down the origin of Francesca's dropped sandal, only to learn that it was of a brand sold at discount outlets across the country. Now it sat atop his desk, flaunting itself, just as its owner had done.

Donovan had also batted zero trying to locate Francesca Adamo. There were a dozen Adamos in the Orange County phone book, but no one who was home had ever heard of her. He had a couple of numbers to call back, including an Adamo Gallery right here in Laguna Beach, but like most art galleries, the place was probably closed on Mondays.

He'd reached Cheryl Cornsworth in Hawaii, hoping against hope for some link regarding the lei, only to learn that she'd wired several dozen of the flowered specialties to friends around the country. She didn't recognize either Francesca's name or her description.

Perhaps the woman could be located by painstakingly interviewing all of Cheryl's gift recipients, but most of them didn't answer their phones, or had unlisted numbers.

Donovan had about as much chance of locating the necklace in one day as he did of finding the Loch Ness monster.

He tipped his chair back, rested his aching head against the wall and closed his eyes. His body throbbed with fatigue and his skin felt like it was crusting over.

The worst of it was, he could still smell her perfume.

He could smell it even through the dust collecting around his battered office. He could smell it even through the noxiously cheery odor of bubble gum left by his twenty-two-year-old receptionist before she'd gone to lunch. He could smell it as if Francesca Adamo were right here in the room with—

Donovan opened his eyes and started so sharply that he bumped his head on the wall. Flecks of plaster from the ceiling showered onto his shoulders like dandruff, adding insult to injury.

"Hi, sucker," Francesca Adamo said, and set the Sakahara necklace atop the pile of phone books on his desk.

Chapter Three

"There! You see?" Francesca announced, as if presenting him with the necklace should make the whole situation crystal-clear.

Donovan's first thought was that there must be something wrong with anyone who could look so crisp and perky at this hour of the morning. Then he remembered it was noon.

He'd never seen so much pink in one place at one time. A short-brimmed pink straw hat sat jauntily atop her dark hair. She wore a pink linen suit with a short jacket over a white-and-pink patterned blouse. She even wore— and he had to twist his neck at an awkward angle to observe this—pink-and-white sandals with straps around the ankles.

The whole effect made Donovan doubly aware of how grimy he felt. He had to fight the impulse to rub one hand across his chin to check the depth of his stubble.

"You're damn lucky I haven't called the police." He leaned forward with a glower intended to intimidate. A ray of painfully bright light roared through the window into Donovan's eyes, forcing him to squint. He tried to tell himself it made him look like John Wayne.

"But I gave it back!" She blew some dust off a chair and sat down.

"It's still burglary," he growled. "Not to mention trespassing, destruction of private property..."

An eyebrow went up. "Destruction?"

Now that he thought about it, Francesca hadn't actually broken anything. "Eating the hors d'oeuvres," was the best he could do.

Her merry laughter grated across his nerves. "Oh, honestly! You'll have to do better than that. Now look—I'm here to make you a proposition."

The only kind of proposition he would be interested in wasn't what she had in mind, Donovan felt quite sure. Even in his exhausted condition, he couldn't help noticing that her slim legs were bare of stockings, that tiny pink stones glowed in her velvety earlobes, that the fingernails tapping lightly on the desk had been painted a rich shade of magenta and set with stars.

What the hell? She'd gone out this morning and had her nails decorated while he was spending an amount of money on phone bills that could have underwritten a congressional campaign?

"This better be good." He reached for his coffee cup and nearly choked on the condensed wad of grounds in the bottom.

"I've always wanted to be a detective," Francesca said. "I love those old movies. *The Thin Man,* that sort of thing."

"If you're looking for Hollywood, it's twenty-five miles up the freeway."

"I expect a little more courtesy than that!" she snapped. "I've just done you a favor."

"A favor? You call stealing a necklace a favor?"

"You can look like a hero to Mrs. Cornsworth. By the way, say hello to Cheryl for me, will you?" It was indecent how innocent those dark eyes appeared beneath the pink hat. Donovan knew that looks were supposed to be deceiving, but this was carrying things too far.

"You weren't on Cheryl's list," he said.

"Oh, she sent the lei to my sister Belle, under her married name," Francesca said. "Belle was afraid her children would tear it apart, so she gave it to me. I thought Mrs. Cornsworth might like to have it."

"Very considerate." How did this conversation keep getting off track? "As for the necklace, I think I can persuade my client not to press charges."

"Honestly! I only borrowed it," Francesca said. "To prove a point. Admit it. Have you ever seen anyone pick a lock that fast? Not to mention how I outfoxed you!"

"Impressive." Donovan refused to let her see that every word was like salt shaken into a wound. He hated to lose at anything. He'd hated it as a high-school gymnast and, after he'd grown too tall, as a track star. He'd hated losing when he was a lawyer, and he'd hated it even more as a prosecutor.

It was one of the things that had attracted him to detective work: With persistence and a little luck, he could usually find the information he sought. And whatever eluded his hard work generally yielded to charm and the occasional bribe.

Donovan liked facing new challenges while upholding his ideals. What other job gave a man such freedom while allowing him to help people in distress, to tip the balance of justice a little in the right direction?

Once he took a case, he let nothing and no one defeat him. Until now.

Francesca Adamo was a spoiled socialite. She hadn't embarrassed him because she needed money; she hadn't done it for some high principle. She'd done it for kicks. She might have the jauntiest chin west of the Rockies, and a tiny curl of hair on her temple that made Donovan want to brush it into place, but...

"Don't you think I'd make a terrific gumshoe?" Francesca was saying.

"Gumshoe?"

"Private eye," she said. "Sleuth. I want to work for you. Okay?"

"Not okay." He stood up wearily. "Door's over there."

"No way!" She stood up, never taking her gaze from his. She barely reached his shoulder, but then, Donovan was a six-footer. "You can't believe how much trouble I went to! I spent weeks planning that little caper!"

"Maybe you should have spent them making the rounds of employment offices." He didn't relish the prospect of throwing Francesca out bodily. For one thing, it went against his chivalrous instincts. For another, he suspected she'd turn out to be a secret master of the martial arts.

"An employment office wouldn't do me a bit of good!" All trace of smugness had vanished beneath a blaze of fury. "First I thought I'd take classes, but then I found out that's not how you get to be a detective. You have to have three years' experience working for somebody else!"

"Correct. And then pass the state exam," Donovan finished for her. "Most people get their experience as police officers in the detective division."

"You didn't," she said.

"You've done your research."

"I read a newspaper article about you, how you found an adopted woman's birth parents so she could have a bone marrow transplant that saved her life," Francesca said. "It said you got so angry at one case you lost when you were a prosecutor that you quit, and one of the detectives you used to hire returned the favor."

Donovan shrugged. "What goes around, comes around." It hadn't been easy, starting his career over at the age of thirty, working for peanuts while he learned a new profession. But it had been worth it.

"Well, I don't have those kinds of connections." Francesca gripped the edge of his desk. "I've called every detective agency in the Yellow Pages, and nobody would give me a chance. So I decided to prove myself to you. And I did!"

The woman had a lot to learn. "Sit down." Donovan assumed his most commanding power stance, feet apart and hands on hips, and waited until she'd complied. "Look, being an investigator is nothing like those old movies. There's a lot of drudge work. A lot of digging through paperwork. A lot of sitting in a parked car watching a house and trying not to fall asleep. You have to be patient, you have to be able to distance yourself emotionally, and you have to be able to blend into the background."

"I can do that." Her hands clenched and unclenched in her lap.

Her quiet determination touched him, but Donovan knew he'd better be ruthless, for both their sakes. "Francesca, you're too flamboyant."

Her mouth twisted stubbornly. "But I got the jewels!"

"I'm not hiring a jewel thief, I'm hiring a detective." Donovan caught himself. "Cancel that. I'm not hiring anybody. I can't afford to."

Francesca jumped to her feet. "That's just the problem! Look at this place. You haven't the foggiest idea how to do public relations!" Her elegant fingers flipped dismissively across a sagging venetian blind.

She gestured at the walls, which, now that he noticed, had aged from beige to a streaky yellowish tan. It had never occurred to him before, but no two of the room's four chairs were even made of the same kind of wood, let alone of the same design. As for the linoleum, it was good solid stuff, except in the few spots where it had been worn down to the backing.

Donovan didn't see what the condition of his office had to do with public relations, anyway. He'd been attracted to this discreetly shabby Victorian on a quiet Santa Ana side street because of the low rent. Besides, his upbringing in history-steeped Boston had made him suspicious of too much newness.

"Nothing wrong with this place," he said.

"It's musty! It's rusty! And it's dusty!" Francesca snatched up a yardstick and poked at a spiderweb festooning one corner near the ceiling. "Doesn't anybody ever clean?"

"A custodian comes in once a week." Donovan frowned. "Don't you know spiders eat other insects? They're ecologically desirable."

"You've got to spiff this place up—or, better yet, rent some decent digs in Newport Center!" Francesca went on. "That dinky little ad in the Yellow Pages has got to go. You need to get your name in some of those glossy magazines around L.A. Think trendy! Think high-tech! I'll help you make this place a going concern!"

Donovan took her elbow and led her toward the exit. "You have great ideas. I think you'd be a big success in the advertising business."

"That's not what I want!" She jerked her arm away and snatched up the golden sandal from Donovan's desk. "I'm offering you a good deal. You won't even have to pay me much. Help me get the experience I need, and I'll drag you out of the Dark Ages. You'll be surprised how useful I can be."

"You'll just have to be useful somewhere else." He refused to acknowledge a faint knock of regret in the vicinity of his ribs as he gestured her into the outer office.

"If money's the problem, I'll take an IOU!" She stopped abruptly as the door opened and his secretary, Tammi Simms, swooped in, balancing two boxes of fried chicken and—bless her—two paper cups of coffee.

"Oh!" Tammi dumped the load on her desk. "Sorry. Am I interrupting?"

"Francesca's not a client," Donovan said. "Just a job applicant."

"It's taken," Tammi told Francesca. "I've been here two months, and I just love it! The pay's lousy, but wow! My friends are so jealous! And I can wear anything I want, too."

He had to admit that his generous policy regarding personal appearance might be a mistake. His last secretary hadn't been much of a problem, and he could hardly object to fraying tweeds and runs in her stockings when he was paying a tuna-fish-and-thrift-store salary.

But Tammi had apparently worn her only suit to the interview; or maybe the suit had been borrowed. Since then, she'd given her body over entirely to Spandex. He wondered if chopped-off waistlines and abbreviated, skintight pants were flattering even to fashion models.

They certainly didn't do much for Tammi's lanky figure. Nor did the limp way her hair fell over her chipmunk cheeks; she'd worn it in a bun at her interview.

Still, he instinctively defended her against Francesca's quirked brow. "Tammi took a secretarial course and got off welfare. She's doing a terrific job."

Francesca didn't miss a beat. "The pay's lousy, huh?"

"Well..." Tammi bit her lip. "I mean, my sister watches my kid."

Francesca turned to Donovan and held out her hand. "When you decide you're ready to upgrade your image, give me a call."

Her grip was firm when they shook, but Donovan could feel the fineness of her bones. He held her hand a moment longer than he should have, and released it reluctantly.

"You're a good jewel thief," he said. "Too bad there's no future in it."

She slipped a small pink card into his hand. "There's my number. For when you change your mind."

Then, to Donovan's astonishment, she stood on tiptoe and kissed the corner of his mouth. Her touch was so light it tickled, but the pressure of her lips sent sweet sensations shivering down into his core.

"Call me," she said, and then she was gone.

THE ENCOUNTER with Francesca left Donovan too keyed up to concentrate. He fiddled away the rest of the afternoon, telephoning a couple of former clients who hadn't paid their bills, running by his gym for a shower and shave, and then returning the necklace to Mrs. Cornsworth.

She beamed at him above the lei, which she wore with a Hawaiian-print sundress, and said she'd never doubted he would find the diamond. And, now that he mentioned it, the dowager said, she did recall a friend of Cheryl's named Belle who had a sister named Francesca.

"Their father is Bruno Adamo, the sculptor. He has a studio on Coast Highway. Oh, he's marvelous. I wish he worked in gemstones!" Mrs. Cornsworth said. "I'd collect him."

Laguna Beach was known as an art colony, although the summer arts festivals were only a distant memory this time of year. Still, some of the residents maintained year-round galleries, and after he left Mrs. Cornsworth's house Donovan found himself easing into traffic on busy Coast Highway instead of taking the more sensible freeway route back to the office.

Bruno Adamo's gallery was tucked into a small row of shops on the cliff side of the highway, away from the ocean. As he drove by, Donovan noticed that the display window was dominated by a twisted mound of metal studded with spikes. It looked dangerous.

Like father, like daughter, he thought.

It was nearly three o'clock by the time Donovan got back to the office. In the small parking lot behind the Victorian, a rented Cadillac had been wedged between Tammi's aging Honda and the red sports car owned by the proprietor of the costume shop on the ground floor.

A white fur jacket had been tossed carelessly into the Cadillac's back seat. October nights tended to be nippy, but daytime temperatures still hovered in the upper seventies.

Donovan wondered if the coat was an affectation, or a sign that the driver planned to continue on to some evening destination. Or maybe it, and the car, were stolen.

One problem with being a detective was an inability to turn off one's curiosity. Donovan wished he didn't so often find himself playing guessing games about objects that other people would pass without a second thought.

Still, he rarely saw expensive cars or fur coats in this neighborhood. Could it be another trick of Francesca's? After last night's caper, he didn't expect her to give up her job quest easily.

Walking up the stairs to his office, he sniffed the air, but there was no trace of Francesca's perfume. Regret burned in Donovan's stomach along with the remains of his chicken lunch.

Damn it, he'd sent her away, and that was the end of it. No more driving by art galleries like a moonstruck teenager, and no more anticipating her perfume, Donovan told himself as he opened the glass-paned door that bore the faded legend Donovan Lewis Detective Agency.

Instantly he knew something was wrong.

The characteristic clutter of papers and candy wrappers had vanished from Tammi's desk. A spray bottle of cleanser and a rag had replaced them atop the pitted wooden surface. Tammi herself was nowhere in sight.

An acrid plume of cigarette smoke wafted from the inner office. Tammi didn't smoke, and besides, Donovan identified the scent as cigarillos. The kind that had to be smuggled in from Cuba.

An illegal immigrant with an obsession for cleanliness? It didn't track.

And what had he—or she—done with Tammi?

Donovan edged along the wall toward the inner door, keeping out of a direct line of fire. He could hear someone breathing inside, a smoker's wheeze.

Tap-tap. High heels on linoleum. A woman.

Relaxing slightly, Donovan nudged the inner door open with one foot.

"Yes?" The voice was feminine and brittle, with a slight rasp. "Who's there?"

Donovan assumed a casual slouch as he entered the room. "Seen my secretary anywhere?"

"I believe she went to get some furniture polish." The woman turned from the window and flipped cigarillo ashes into one of the aging paper cups on Donovan's desk.

His first impression was that his visitor had been carved from ice. A silver cloche hat covered neatly waved white-blond hair; her eyes were a cold blue against pale skin; a shimmery satin gown draped to the floor. The only contrast was a slash of scarlet on her thin lips.

"You're Donovan Lewis?" Elegant nostrils flared as she examined him. Donovan wondered what she would have thought had she seen him unshaven and unwashed, and remembered, irrelevantly, that Francesca hadn't seemed to mind. "My name is Amanda Carruthers." She didn't offer her hand.

"What can I do for you?" He hoped she was a client. She looked like she could pay her bills.

"My sister's been murdered." The words came out clipped and stiff, without a trace of the emotions usually associated with the words *sister* and *murdered*.

Donovan was familiar with shock, and he forgave Amanda Carruthers for her chilly manner. This was clearly a woman in distress. "I'm sorry to hear it. You're trying to find her killer?"

"I know who killed her." Amanda tapped out more ashes. "I want you to prove it."

"Please sit down." Donovan held a chair for her, choosing the same one Francesca had occupied earlier, since it had incidentally been wiped of its dust. "I assume you've contacted the police?"

"Indeed." Amanda didn't bother to look at him as he circled toward his own seat. "But the evidence is purely circumstantial. And Jon is a powerful man. Jon Blakely. Perhaps you've heard of him."

"The soap heir?" Who hadn't heard of him? Jon Blakely's mansion dominated a hill overlooking Newport Bay. He gave vast parties on his yacht; he served as honorary chairman of half a dozen prestigious charities; he bought and sold brokerage firms, radio stations and, according to some accounts, politicians.

"He murdered your sister?" Donovan echoed. "And who might that be?"

"Cindy Blakely. His wife." Amanda stared out the window, as if fascinated by the taco stand across the street.

Donovan began to put the pieces together. He'd read about Cindy Blakely's disappearance two weeks ago. Her car had been found near a cliff overlooking the ocean, with her purse and some torn clothing in the back seat. No sign of her body, but if she'd fallen onto the rocks below she could easily have been washed out to sea.

Rumors were circulating about a divorce, but Jon Blakely publicly maintained that he loved his wife and wanted her back.

The evening news had aired a photograph of Cindy, her flaming red hair restrained by a designer scarf. It was hard to say without having seen Cindy in person, but Donovan thought he detected a family resemblance to her sister.

At the time, Cindy had sounded to him like a party girl who'd married for love and gotten in over her head. And Jon Blakely seemed to be the kind of man Donovan disliked instinctively, the kind of man who used his money to manipulate people. Possessing a fortune was no substitute for good character.

"I told her to leave him," Amanda went on. "Cindy was such a sweet girl. She really loved that bastard. He's the worst kind of abuser. He never actually laid a finger on her, but he was always putting her down, making her feel inadequate. She reached the point where she had no self-confidence at all. They were fighting constantly, yet she couldn't bring herself to leave."

"Then why kill her?" Donovan suspected that Amanda's emotions had run a roller-coaster ride as she watched Cindy's suffering. All the more reason for her to maintain such a stony front now.

"I think he'd found someone else," Amanda said. "You see, Jon made one big mistake. He never drew up a prenuptial agreement. They were married for five years, and he bought and sold a lot of property and stocks, moved bank accounts around and so forth. His inheritance was commingled with current income, and, as you know, this is a community property state."

So Cindy would have been entitled to half Jon's fortune. That was more than enough motive for murder.

"He wouldn't have killed her himself," Amanda went on. "He would have hired someone. Even if the police catch the actual murderer, they'll never pin it on Jon. He's too clever."

Donovan forced himself to rein in his instinctive desire to help this damsel in distress. "I prefer not to interfere in a police investigation. For one thing, they won't like it. For another, you'd be wasting your money. I don't have the kind of resources that law enforcement does, the crime lab, and so forth."

"You won't need it." Amanda Carruthers stubbed out her cigarillo and pulled a newspaper clipping from her purse. "Look at this."

A classified ad had been circled in purple ink. It read:

Live-in Couple. Handyman and housekeeper. Maintain Newport Beach estate. 40-hr. week, bene- fits. Refs. req'd. Contact: Miss Feinstein 555-1244.

"That's Jon's assistant," Amanda said. "Sort of a glorified secretary."

"Handyman and housekeeper?" Donovan wondered where he was going to find a female to accompany him. "What happened to the last couple?"

"He fired them. Cindy engaged them, and they were loyal to her. So of course he detested them." Amanda stood up. "Working from the inside, you ought to be able to come up with something, don't you think?"

"Eventually he'll slip," Donovan agreed. "Are there other servants?"

"He had a driver and groundsman named Thomas," Amanda said. "But he quit recently. I suppose they'll be replacing him next. There's Miss Feinstein, and a cook, and some day maids and gardeners."

"About my fee . . ."

"I've checked you out. You're competitive." Amanda dismissed the subject as if she had plenty of money. Donovan liked her style. "And you're smart. You do know how to fix things?"

"Sure." Donovan's handyman experience was limited to hanging a few paintings in his condo and shooting the breeze with the plumber when his sink overflowed, but he figured he could pick up a book on home repair.

"Good. He'll have a lot of applicants, but you should outclass them. He's such a snob. As for references, here..." From her purse, Amanda produced three sheets of triple-folded stationery.

Donovan took them carefully, noting the expensive paper and the engraving. The addresses were impressive: Park Avenue in New York, Chevy Chase, Maryland, and Palm Beach, Florida.

Each stated that Mr. and Mrs. Donovan Lewis had worked for the family for a period of three to five years, that they would be sorely missed, and that they were recommended without reservation.

Mr. and Mrs., he reflected. Tammi wasn't old enough to have worked that many years. Besides, she had a small child who needed Mommy home at night.

Well, he'd figure out something. He didn't have much choice. Now that the Cornsworth job was done, he needed Amanda's fee to cover the rent.

"How come Mr. and Mrs. Lewis move around so much?" he asked, since Amanda seemed to have figured out the whole cover story.

"You love the arts," she said. "You haven't much formal education, but you like art, theater, music, whatever you have time for and can afford. You feel there are gaps in your knowledge that only southern California can fill. Jon will appreciate your interest. He loves that stuff."

"Sounds easy enough." Donovan hoped he'd be able to wrap the case up quickly. He'd have to put most of his business on hold while he was living at the mansion. And he wasn't sure how well he could pretend interest if Blakely decided to tutor them about Wagnerian operas. But, hell, it was a job.

Amanda handed him a cashier's check for five thousand dollars. "I thought you'd want a retainer," she said. "Is that enough?"

"That will be fine." Donovan swallowed an urge to throw back his head and laugh. He didn't suppose Amanda Carruthers would be impressed if he jumped up and clicked his heels, either. "I'll get on this right away."

"Yes. The job won't stay open long." She stood up. "I want my sister's murderer to pay for his crime. It won't bring her back, but at least I'll be able to sleep nights."

"Where can I contact you?" Donovan asked as he walked her to the door.

"I'll get in touch with your office," Amanda said. "I'm staying at a hotel right now, and I may be moving in with a friend. I'll leave messages with your secretary."

They emerged to find Tammi back at her desk, scrubbing the scarred surface with lemon oil. After seeing Amanda out, Donovan turned back, puzzled.

"What are you doing?"

Tammi brightened. "That friend of yours called. Francesca. She had a few suggestions, and you know, she's right. People like to see a cheery decor. It gives them confidence."

"Blot that oil up and put the mess back," Donovan instructed. "This is a detective agency, not *Better Homes and Gardens.*"

"But Mr. Lewis!"

He overrode her protest. "I don't want any decor around here. Got that?"

He was trying to figure out where to find a wife in a hurry. One of the housekeeping services, perhaps. Detective work often began with the judicious use of the Yellow Pages.

Moving toward the inner office, Donovan heard rather than saw the outer door open. "Forget something?" he asked, swinging around—but it wasn't Amanda Carruthers standing on the threshold.

The white ruffled cap and apron looked like hand-me-downs from *Upstairs, Downstairs* and the duster glowed with orange feathers that had never touched furniture. The dark blouse and skirt might have passed inspection, but no maid in her right mind would wear those tiny sandals.

"Don't say anything. Let the effect sink in." Francesca strolled toward him, lips twitching, eyes dancing. She reminded Donovan of a little girl playing dress-up, except that little girls weren't shaped like Francesca.

"How the—" But there was only one way she could have known. "You bugged my office!"

"This was the best I could do on short notice. That costume shop downstairs is terrific." Francesca twirled, and the skirt flared to reveal lean, tanned thighs.

"I'm going to find a real cleaning lady," Donovan said.

"You don't have time." She noticed Tammi dumping papers back on the desk. "Don't do that!"

"But he said—"

"He's going to change his mind. About a lot of things." Francesca reached up and ran her thumb across Donovan's jaw. For some reason, her touch rendered him momentarily speechless. "Good—you shaved. We can call Mr. Blakely from your car phone and be on our way right now. I won't even charge you for my time. I'll settle for whatever he's paying."

"I—" Donovan's voice got stuck somewhere in his chest. He figured it must be due to the infamous southern California smog, or to all the pollen in the air.

"By the way," Francesca said as she steered him toward the outer hallway, "I'm sure by now you've reached the same conclusion I have."

"Which is?" Donovan managed to ask.

"Jon Blakely's innocent, of course," she said, and scampered ahead of him down the hall.

Chapter Four

Jon Blakely's assistant agreed over the phone—with some reluctance—that they could come that afternoon. She gave them the address in Newport Beach, an upper-crust coastal community.

"Mr. Blakely's conducting interviews right now," said the assistant, Tenley Feinstein. "Do you have experience? We require at least three years."

"Absolutely. And references." Donovan, who was using a hands-free speakerphone, accelerated his blue van up a ramp and onto the Santa Ana Freeway. He could hear Francesca's motorcycle rattle in the back, where they'd hoisted it outside Donovan's office.

"Well," said Miss Feinstein. "We'll see you shortly, then."

He pressed the End button. "You don't happen to live near here, do you?" he asked Francesca. "I think a change of clothing is in order."

"This is perfect!" Her mouth tightened as she glanced down at her ruffled apron, but then she shrugged. "Oh, all right."

As she provided the address, Donovan allowed himself a pleasurable glance at his passenger, enjoying the play of sunshine across her cheekbones. It was the first time he'd seen her in full daylight, and her light olive skin had taken on a glowing richness. "What makes you think Jon Blakely is innocent?"

"Everything." Her generous lips pressed together as she considered. "Most of all, Jon Blakely himself."

"You know him?"

Dark hair tumbled as she shook her head. "Not personally. But do you realize he heads a charity that has raised five million dollars for disabled children?"

Donovan was surprised she didn't see through the man. "He's just a figurehead. He couldn't care less about disabled children."

"Wrong!" Fire glinted in Francesca's eyes. "The newspaper ran a picture of him visiting Children's Hospital, and then at the charity carnival there was a shot of him helping this little girl onto a pony...."

"I thought you were the expert on public relations." Donovan sighed. "Francesca, he only shows up for photo opportunities like that so people will buy more Blakely Flakes. And maybe for his ego."

"That's the most cynical thing I've ever heard! You know, some rich people really do have hearts." Francesca curled her legs on the seat. She had slim, rounded knees that looked fragile, but could probably do a lot of damage at close quarters. "That's my exit up there."

"I still haven't heard any reasons why I should believe he's innocent." Donovan angled the car toward the off ramp. "You've jumped to a conclusion based on nothing more than the fact that he poses for cameras at charity parties. If you're going to be a detective—"

"That doesn't mean I have to turn into a cynic! Go left here, then right at the next signal," Francesca said without missing a beat. "I also remember when companies were laying off workers left and right and taking their operations overseas. Jon Blakely bought back the public stock offerings, went private, and took a cut in profits to keep his factories open."

"So nominate him for sainthood." Donovan despised hypocrisy, and he hated to see her taken in by it. "You'll recall he was running for the county board of supervisors at the time. Then, after he lost, he merged two plants and cut his staff by several hundred."

"By attrition!" Francesca snapped. "And he couldn't help it. The air quality board passed those new regulations, and it was more than he could afford."

"Yeah, he might have had to drink beer instead of champagne," Donovan muttered. It sounded like Francesca had spent a lot of time reading about Jon Blakely. The millionaire, a former playboy with patrician good looks, was reputed to have a devoted female following. He hoped she wasn't among them.

Was she going to let her emotional response get in the way of the facts? Had he made a mistake in letting her accompany him?

And why did it annoy him so intensely that she seemed to admire the jerk?

As Francesca pointed the rest of the way to her apartment complex, Donovan said, "Let's get a few things straight."

"Okay, boss." Francesca tilted her chin. He couldn't tell whether the gesture indicated defiance or capitulation.

Donovan pulled into a parking space and killed the motor. He swung around in his seat and caught Francesca by the shoulders, commanding her full attention. "Point number one. We're not working for Jon Blakely, we're working for Amanda Carruthers."

"Aren't we working for the truth?" Her gaze searched his. "Don't you think Cindy's sister would want to know what really happened? Can't you admit the possibility that Jon isn't at fault?"

"That's for us to find out." Donovan kept a firm hold on her. He had to be sure of her cooperation before they met Jon Blakely; once Francesca was established as "Mrs. Lewis," he'd be stuck. "Point number two. We have to proceed on the assumption of guilt. We have to look for anything to support that. Protecting Jon Blakely isn't our problem. He can afford the best defense attorneys in the country."

"I won't railroad him!" Her jaw was quivering.

"We're not the police. We don't have to be fair," Donovan said. "We work for Amanda Carruthers. If you can't accept that, you have no business trying to become a detective."

"I thought you were an idealist!" At these close quarters, he could feel the heat rising from her skin. "In that article, you talked about—oh, something about slaying dragons. I guess that was just a load of beeswax, huh?"

"And when Sir Galahad went out to slay a dragon for a fair maiden, do you think he asked for the dragon's side of the story?" Donovan stopped. He couldn't believe he'd said that. "We're both spouting nonsense. Forget it, Francesca. This will never work."

He could feel the fury seep from her muscles. Dark lashes lowered against her cheek. "I'm sorry." Her voice came out so low it was almost inaudible. "I really do want to go with you. You're right. We have to try to prove him guilty, even though I hope we can't."

Donovan knew he ought to send her packing anyway. He needed someone less volatile and definitely someone less likely to get under his skin. Little things kept distracting him—the way the ruffled cap had slipped to one side, giving her a jaunty air, the way her curled legs brushed against his—

"Do you own anything even vaguely resembling a suit?" he asked.

"Let's go see." A smile transformed her face as she flung open the van door.

They unloaded her lightweight motorcycle. Donovan couldn't imagine why anyone would want to whiz around Orange County's crowded freeways on such a flimsy vehicle. It bothered him to think of Francesca running such a risk.

They left it at the curb. "By the way," he said as they strolled between stuccoed buildings and overstuffed flowerbeds. "If you're going to be tailing people, you'll need something more discreet than that bike."

"Really?" Francesca led the way up a flight of exterior steps and unlocked the door at the top. "I love my cycle. It's the closest thing to flying without a plane."

When she opened the door, the first thing Donovan saw was— No, he couldn't believe it, he must be thinking about what Francesca had just said. But, yes, it really was an airplane, hanging from the cathedral ceiling inside the living room.

"Is this how you get around when the bike's not working?" he cracked as he followed her in. "How did you get that thing in here?"

"Piece by piece." Francesca walked past him. "Make yourself comfortable. I've got a suit and jacket that ought to do." As she disappeared into the hallway, she called, "There's beer in the fridge."

Donovan didn't want a beer. He wanted to know why she had a Cessna hanging from her ceiling. He circled the room, inspecting the thing.

One wing sported red and white stripes, the other white stars on a blue background. The underbody had been painted in green and yellow spirals, the nose was purple and orange plaid, and the wheels glowed yellow-green.

The stark white living room walls featured two enormous photographs of similarly gaudy airplanes—one in flight, the other tied down at an airport.

"Is there some kind of significance to these planes?" he called.

Francesca's voice floated from the recesses of a bedroom. "My mother made them."

"Ailerons and all?" It seemed like a strange thing for someone's mother to do, even Francesca's.

"No, just the paint. Mom went through an airplane-painting period. Then she started flying the things as a kind of performance art. When she decided she liked flying better than painting, she moved to Alaska and started her own air service. Dad stayed here and went on with his sculpture. It was kind of sad when they split up."

"Do you ever see her?"

"I worked for her for a couple of years—I love to fly. But I wanted to be a detective more."

These last words emerged along with Francesca. She'd put on a skirt and jacket in a striking shade of aquamarine. The silky fabric clung to her body, and the jacket, with no blouse underneath, revealed a tantalizing hint of black lace against the swell of her breasts.

"Is this what you had in mind?" she asked.

"You look . . . great." He cleared his throat. "But not much like a housekeeper."

Laughter sang through the air. "I'm not going like this, Donovan! I've got to put on a blouse, but first I wanted to know if it was okay."

"Yeah. Yeah, it's fine." He wished like hell she'd go finish dressing. Otherwise, Donovan didn't know if he could resist finding out just how that silky fabric would feel in his hands, and how the rest of that black lace garment underneath the jacket looked.

Francesca showed no signs of leaving. "Would you like anything to drink? A snack? I mean, it's almost dinnertime."

"Detectives are like camels. We can go indefinitely without food or water." But not, Donovan couldn't help thinking, without undoing that jacket.

"Really? I get headachy if I don't eat." She sneaked a longing glance toward the kitchen.

Almost subliminally, he heard a metallic rumble like a glass door sliding open. From within the apartment came a shallow, raspy intake of breath.

"Someone's in there. Get back!" Donovan said, pulling Francesca against the wall. He clapped his hand over her mouth as a precaution and felt her moist breath tickle his fingers.

His muscular body covered hers, and even as he listened for the intruder his chest registered the yielding softness of her breasts. She was shivering with fear. Or was she reacting to the pressure of his thighs against her hips? Donovan felt a soft rhythmic thudding and recognized it as his own heartbeat.

Damn it, he had to protect Francesca, not make love to her. "Expecting anyone?" He drew his gun and turned toward the hall.

Francesca eyed the automatic. "What caliber is that?"

"A .38." He wished she'd keep quiet. He couldn't hear if the burglar was moving around.

"Doesn't a .45 have more stopping power?"

"It puts a bulge in my jacket." He gave a quick shake of the head, hoping she'd take the hint.

"But if you ran into someone on PCP—you know, with superhuman strength—you might need that extra power."

"Would you be quiet?"

"It could be a matter of life or death." Francesca said. "According to one of the books I read—"

He glimpsed a large blur launching itself at them from the doorway. Donovan flipped off the safety and was on the point of firing when his brain registered that the intruder had ginger-colored fur and was wagging its tail at near light speed.

Donovan peppered the air with a string of imprecations. "Why didn't you tell me you had a dog?"

Francesca dropped to her knees and fussed over her pet—some kind of terrier, possibly an Airedale. Donovan preferred bigger dogs, Labradors and German Shepherds. The smaller breeds tended to be nervous. Or maybe they just made *him* nervous with their high-pitched yapping.

"I thought it was obvious." Francesca tousled the pointy ears. "He likes to snooze on the balcony. Did you really think somebody would walk right in while we were talking? Not to mention that we're on the second floor!"

"Don't you know I nearly shot him?" he snapped.

"You mean that's loaded?" Francesca glared up at him. "Donovan! With all the publicity about the dangers of guns! I mean, what if you dropped it and it went off and a child was walking by?"

"Automatics don't discharge by accident. They've got built-in safety devices." He holstered the gun. "As for its being loaded, I wouldn't carry the damn thing if it weren't. I'm not playacting at this job, Francesca."

"I didn't mean that." She stood up, brushing at her skirt. "You're right. I'm sorry. I really did put Asta in danger, didn't I? I was just interested in seeing how you work."

"If you're going to keep playing games, I think you'd better find another job."

"I'm not." It was hard to stay angry when she looked so contrite. "That was a stupid thing for me to do. My apartment seems like such a safe place, I just couldn't visualize you shooting anybody."

"There is no safe place," Donovan said.

Sadness touched her face. "I hope I never get that pessimistic."

"Not pessimistic. Realistic." He checked his watch. "It's nearly five. We'd better get moving."

Francesca finished dressing and set out some food for the dog, and they headed for Jon Blakely's mansion.

THE WORD that came into Donovan's head as the van drove up the curving driveway was *overkill*.

Nobody needed a house like this—ten thousand square feet if it was an inch. Nobody needed wing after wing of fake-Tudor splendor or a six-car garage with parking spaces for a dozen more. Nor a stand of imposing cypress trees that screened the front entrance as if to protect it from prying eyes.

Donovan grumbled to himself as he parked next to a modest sedan that probably belonged to another job applicant. "With all the homeless in the world, you'd think he could make do with half this and give the rest away."

"Oh, really!" Francesca said. "He *does* give away a lot, hundreds of thousands a year. I think he has a right to enjoy his money a little."

"You call this a little?" Donovan ran a comb through his hair and wondered if he looked handy enough.

"It's a matter of aesthetics." Francesca ruffled her hair and slipped on the imitation gold ring they'd picked up at a discount store. "Why shouldn't he be surrounded by beautiful things? It's not as if he stole the money!"

The high-necked white blouse that she'd put on did, Donovan had to admit, make her look more business-like. On the other hand, he'd never understand how a woman could project such natural lustiness even under the starchiest clothing.

Given the man-about-town reputation Jon Blakely had rung up in his single days, it was a good thing Francesca was arriving with a husband to protect her. Only who was going to protect her from Donovan?

As they followed a walkway formed of fanned semicircles of brick, Donovan felt his senses coming alert. The job really began now.

He imagined Cindy leaving from one of these garages on the day of her death. Had she been alone? He needed to check out the police report, but he recalled reading that she'd last been seen about nine o'clock at night.

On the street below, barely visible through the trees, a few cars hummed past. Had anyone staked out the road at that hour and queried drivers? People tended to travel the same route each day, and one of them might have noticed Cindy leaving. Donovan hoped he'd have time to do that, but he couldn't afford to arouse Blakely's suspicion.

There was nothing else useful to be seen, certainly not in the huge fountain with its cherubic marble angel, and not in the fleur-de-lis pattern carved into the double oak doors.

"Everything seems so peaceful," Francesca said. "It's hard to imagine violence touching this place."

Donovan resisted the impulse to point out that the potential for violence lurked everywhere. In a way, he envied the optimistic side of Francesca's spirit. Donovan sometimes wished he didn't know how easily paradise could turn to purgatory.

The doorbell sent "Greensleeves" echoing through a cavernous space. A few moments later, a small, rotund woman opened the door. She pushed bifocals down from atop her head and inspected them.

"Mr. and Mrs. Lewis? I'm Tenley Feinstein." She snatched her hand away after the briefest of shakes. "You certainly took your time. Mr. Blakely has to leave for an engagement in a few minutes."

The vast entryway felt cool from the marble that faced the floor. The walls, discreetly covered with textured paper, displayed paintings of varying sizes all the way up two stories to an immense chandelier. At the back, twin stairways curved to the second floor.

Several glass cases revealed a collection of Oriental carvings. The only other furnishings were two elaborately worked mahogany side tables.

"It's beautiful." Francesca grinned impishly. "Wouldn't you love to Rollerblade in here?"

Donovan shot her a quelling look. They followed Ms. Feinstein through an enormous peach-colored room that in any other house would have been the main parlor, but in this one probably served as a spare den. Massive couches barely made a dent in the space, while an entire wall of glass overlooked a sprawling swimming pool, a pool house of more than a thousand square feet, double tennis courts and a lawn broad enough to play polo on.

Here again, artwork dominated: a large painted wood sculpture in one corner, open shelves displaying miniature portraits, a hanging piece worked with multicolored hanks of yarn, macramé rope, feathers and mirrors.

Nothing hinted at a personal touch. There was no sign that Cindy had ever lived here.

Donovan wondered if Blakely had done an equally thorough job of eradicating her from his memory.

Anger quivered through him. He hadn't had time to reflect since Amanda had walked into his office, but now he remembered his slow burning anger on reading about Cindy's demise. One police officer had speculated that "we may never find the truth about this," which Donovan had translated to mean that if the killer had enough money, and if his victim had been trusting enough to walk into a trap, he could get away with murder.

Men as rich as Jon Blakely, men who had never been forced to take the consequences of their own actions, often held themselves above the law. Above kindness or honor. Above justice.

But Amanda Carruthers didn't hold Jon Blakely above justice. And neither did Donovan.

They passed through a parquet-floored court and into an oversize office. From the floor-length draperies to the custom-woven carpet, the room hummed with sunrise colors of peach, pink and aqua.

"Have a seat," Miss Feinstein said. "Mr. Blakely will be with you in a minute."

She sat down at the broad blond desk, and Donovan realized that this was only the outer office. He noticed a photograph on the desk of two laughing children, a boy and a girl who resembled Miss Feinstein.

Beside him, Francesca was studying the room as if preparing to be cross-examined about it.

"See anything?" Donovan murmured.

"Spiderwebs." She indicated a corner of the ceiling.

Miss Feinstein must have been listening. "Goodness! You're right!"

Donovan knew he ought to add something equally appropriate, and was grateful when he spotted a discolored patch on the ceiling. "Must be a leak in the roof."

"Hardly," the assistant said with a sniff. "We're on the first floor."

"Plumbing problems," said Francesca. "Have they been taken care of?"

Tenley nodded. "We'll be redecorating in here one of these days. Mr. Blakely has been distracted, as you can imagine."

A rear door opened. Donovan jumped to his feet as an elderly couple walked out, their faces roughened by time and molded by hard work into nearly identical patterns of wrinkles.

Guilt twinged through Donovan as he watched the pair plod out. Other people needed this job, and deserved it. Well, they'd get their chance in a few days, when he and Francesca were finished.

A moment later, Jon Blakely emerged.

He'd always appeared tall on television, but in person the man didn't exceed five-foot-nine. His face was thinner than Donovan had expected, and dark circles underlined his sand-hued eyes. His gray silk suit sagged on his shoulders, an indication he'd lost weight so recently that he hadn't even had time to visit his tailor.

Could it be that Cindy's death was troubling her husband? Or was it guilt that dogged Jon Blakely?

"Hi." Francesca thrust out her hand. "I'm Francesca Lewis, and this is my husband, Donovan."

The man blinked as if a bright light had hit his eyes, then shook her hand cautiously. ''Jon Blakely.''

Donovan found Blakely's grip firm, but not hearty. Cool, he thought. Restrained.

They followed the gray silk suit into Blakely's office.

If the sun rose in Miss Feinstein's chamber, it set in this one. Gold and rose streaked the walls, the colors picked up by a triptych of paintings. It seemed only fitting that the broad window to their left admitted equally vivid hues from the real setting sun, as if Blakely's wealth were so vast it could even coordinate nature with his decor.

''Nice office,'' Francesca said.

''My wife designed it.'' Blakely waved them onto one of a pair of couches covered with hand-painted aqua-on-white fabric. On a glass coffee table lay a pile of oversize art books.

Someone transplanted here by magic wouldn't have taken it for an office at all; only a small scrollwork desk in one corner hinted at the room's true function.

Atop the desk sat a large framed photograph of Cindy, caught in a moment of vulnerability. Despite her red hair, she bore a strong resemblance to her sister, and yet there was an indelible difference, a softness that Donovan couldn't imagine touching Amanda's fierce eyes.

Atop a rear cabinet, Donovan noticed a rack of pipes. They appeared to be hand-carved, some old-fashioned, some quite intricate and probably foreign.

Blakely picked up a pipe and tamped tobacco into it as he described the job—long hours, modest pay—and emphasized a requirement that employees agree not to talk to the press or to write any articles or books about their experiences here.

''Certainly not,'' Francesca said.

Realizing he needed to speak, as well, Donovan added, "Mostly we like to spend our spare time going to art galleries and theater. We're kind of self-taught, you know. That's why we came out here to the West Coast. There's so much to see." He hoped he sounded sufficiently handyman-like.

"Well, if I get any tickets I don't need, I'll toss them your way. If I hire you, of course." The thin man set his unlit pipe aside and flipped through their letters of recommendation. "This is impressive. Most of the people I've talked to are misfits. I consider domestic service a respectable profession, not something people fall into if they can't make it in the so-called real world."

"We like our work," Francesca volunteered. "It lets us spend time together, and it's satisfying. You don't have children, do you, Mr. Blakely? We love children."

Donovan gritted his teeth. If she ran on this way, she was certain to trip herself up sooner or later.

Jon Blakely's mouth pinched. "Children? No. That's neither here nor there. Look, there's a new requirement that wasn't mentioned in the ad. Do you know anything about car repairs?" He regarded Donovan impatiently.

"Car repairs?" This was more than he'd bargained for. "Well . . ."

"What seems to be the problem?" Francesca asked.

"My chauffeur's quit. Until we can replace him, I'm perfectly capable of driving myself." Blakely drifted around the room, his pipe forgotten. "However, my Mercedes is having the engine retooled and right now I'm down to the housekeeper's station wagon. Aside from my antique car collection, which I don't want to risk on everyday driving. Now I'm having problems with the station wagon, as well."

"Broken, huh?" Donovan realized that didn't sound much like a mechanic. "I mean, you've lost power?"

"Oh, it runs." Blakely stared out the window as if Donovan were too insignificant to notice. "But the left front wheel makes a groaning sound, like metal on metal. It's not the brakes—they were just relined. I'm concerned the damn thing might get me in an accident. Think you could take a look at it?"

Anything more than washing the windshield lay outside Donovan's experience, but he heard himself say, "Sure," and hoped the automotive fairy would tap him with her magic wand. Or that at least he'd be able to make up a convincing speech about gaskets and carburetors until he could get the thing to a mechanic.

Blakely led them outside onto a tiled patio, where yellowish light bathed a large enough assembly of tables and chairs to furnish a café. As they passed a built-in barbecue and wet bar, Francesca ran one finger across it and sniffed disapprovingly at the dust. She was really getting into her role, but Blakely didn't seem to notice.

They entered the garages through a rear access door. The place was enormous, with gleaming stalls housing classic automobiles from a Model A to an early Corvette convertible. Off to their right, in an extra-large space, Donovan spotted a hulking Bugatti that looked big enough to pull a freight train.

On the far left, in the maintenance garage, Donovan groped along one wall and flipped on the light. He felt as if he'd just used up his entire repertoire of vehicular expertise.

The light washed over a hydraulic lift, diagnostic equipment and walls lined with tools whose functions he could only guess at.

"Excellent," Francesca said. "You ought to be able to fix anything in here, darling."

If she weren't a woman, Donovan might have slugged her.

The station wagon squatted humbly in the middle, pocked with parking-lot dents. "Not much to look at," Blakely said. "If they don't get the Mercedes finished soon, I may have to buy a new one. But in the meantime, I need wheels."

"Let's see." Francesca strode forward. "Where did you say the noise was coming from?"

"Left side." Blakely jerked his head toward the wheel.

Francesca stuck her hand behind the tire. "I thought so. You've got a torn CV boot. Don't you think so, dear?" To Blakely, she said, "He's been teaching me."

Repressing a grimace, Donovan shoved his hand in the same place and encountered a grease-laden piece of rubber. "Absolutely," he said. "Very good, honey."

"It's the—you know—the gizmo that holds the lubrication where the tire meets the axle," Francesca told Blakely. "We'll have to get a replacement part. It's not a big deal."

"Very good." Blakely nodded shortly. "I like competence. I insist on it."

"Oh, so do we." Francesca wiped her hand on a rag and tossed it to Donovan.

For one nanosecond, Donovan's deep-down masculine instincts rebelled at the realization that this golden-skinned woman could probably reengineer the space shuttle while he was still trying to figure out how to change a tire.

Then he realized that if she was equally skilled at home repairs, he'd have a lot more time to snoop. Maybe she hadn't been such a poor choice after all.

"Frankly, I think I'll drop the car at a garage and pick up a rental tomorrow," Jon said. "I'm not taking any chances on breaking an axle."

Back in the office, he gave them papers to sign and arranged for them to move in the following day. Apparently Francesca's wizardry with the station wagon had done the trick.

As they departed, Blakely didn't offer to shake their still-smeared hands. Donovan couldn't blame him.

"We did it!" Francesca exulted when they were back in the van. She propped her feet up on the dashboard, oblivious to the way her skirt slid down her upraised thighs. Very tan, very shapely thighs. Donovan could imagine how buttery they'd feel beneath his touch. He forced his thoughts away.

"It occurred to me that if you could take over the repair side of things, as well as the housekeeping, I'd be able to get a lot more work done," he said. "There have to be clues somewhere. It's amazing how much evidence people leave."

"Oh, honestly." Francesca straightened. "You haven't figured it out yet?"

"Figure what out?"

"Cindy wasn't murdered," she said. "She was kidnapped. And I wouldn't be surprised if that client of yours did it."

Chapter Five

"And what brilliant observation led you to that conclusion?" Donovan couldn't believe he'd missed some obvious clue.

"Jon Blakely's not wearing black," Francesca said.

"That's it? That's your evidence?"

"Now listen." Her hand cupped his, stopping him from turning on the ignition. His skin prickled where they touched. "Donovan, sometimes what people don't do or say is as important as what they do."

"Possibly." He stared out into the gathering twilight. "Well?"

"Your theory is that Jon Blakely wanted Cindy dead so he can keep all the money for himself." Francesca's dark eyes penetrated his thoughts. "Right?"

"It's not my theory, it's Amanda's, but that's right."

"Now, assuming he had her killed, he has no reason to pretend she's still alive. If he knows she's dead, and he wants other people to believe she's dead, why isn't he dressed in mourning?"

Donovan couldn't believe she'd formed a kidnapping theory based on such thin speculation. "Because the natural thing for a loving husband to do in a case like this is to cling to hope. Which is what he wants the police to believe he's doing. And how did you arrive at a kidnapping?"

"If she wasn't murdered, *something* had to happen to her," Francesca protested.

"Wouldn't there be a ransom note?"

"Maybe it got lost, or maybe Jon's afraid to tell the police because he doesn't want her killed."

"Why suspect her sister?" Donovan pressed.

"She's hiding something, I just know it," Francesca said. "And she doesn't have a heart. I could hear it in her voice. The woman's a walking ice cube."

"Could be grief," he said. "Some people act cold when they're crumbling inside."

Francesca made a face. "That's a preposterous way to act. If that's what Amanda's doing, she needs a psychiatrist, not a detective."

"You've drawn all these conclusions on the basis of Jon Blakely's wearing a gray suit?" Donovan reached for the key. "Francesca, you haven't even begun to learn the basics of detective work—let alone common sense!"

"Think what you like, but I trust my intuition! I don't suppose you believe in intuition, do you?"

He stiffened, eyes fixed on the rearview mirror.

"Donovan?"

"Can it, would you?"

"How rude!"

In the dim light he thought he'd seen a man slipping across the estate grounds toward the garages. Whoever it was would be hidden now behind the large building.

"We've got a visitor," he said. "Stay here."

"Like hell!"

"I can't catch him and protect you at the same time!"

"It ever occur to you I might actually be able to help?"

As he eased out of the van and crossed the parking lot, Francesca followed. This was no time for a fight, so Donovan kept his peace.

As they sidled along the garage building, his mind worked rapidly. The only people who were supposed to be on the premises at this hour were Jon Blakely, Miss Feinstein, and the cook he'd heard rattling pans in the kitchen.

He doubted Blakely employed a guard; few people did in the relatively safe confines of Newport Beach. A sign in front indicated the grounds were protected by a security system, but Francesca had demonstrated how easily one of those could be disabled.

Yet, if their man was a garden-variety burglar, why head for the garage? And why come here at the dinner hour, when people were likely to be awake?

"What do you think he wants?" Francesca whispered. "Something incriminating? Maybe in one of the cars?"

Right on target. Donovan had to give her points.

"He knows this place," he murmured back. "There must be a sensing device that gets turned on at night. This would be the best time to break in—nearly dark, deserted, but not yet protected."

That possibility suggested a disgruntled former employee, perhaps the departed chauffeur or the former handyman. Or anyone else who knew Blakely's habits.

"The hired killer," Donovan muttered.

"What?" Francesca trod on his heel. "Sorry."

"He could have come back for more money. Blakely's put himself in a position to be blackmailed." Donovan was thinking out loud now. "Or maybe the guy left something behind, something that could lead the police to him."

"Like he might have dropped it when—" Francesca gasped. "Do you suppose he was hiding in the back of Cindy's car? How awful. Maybe he forced her to drive to that cliff."

"You're conceding she was murdered?"

"Maybe he's one of the kidnappers and he's trying to find out what happened to the ransom note," Francesca offered.

"Discussion to be continued later." Donovan gestured to her to be silent as they turned a corner and approached the rear entrance. The door stood slightly ajar.

"Shouldn't we call the police?" Francesca asked.

"Good idea." Donovan seized the excuse to put her out of harm's way. "Go back to the van and call on my car phone."

She flipped him a smile. "Not without you."

"Suit yourself." He led the way into the dark interior, stepping quickly aside to avoid being silhouetted against the open door. He wished he'd thought to grab a flashlight from the glove compartment. It was as inky as midnight in here.

He stood motionless, listening. He could hear Francesca's uneven breathing close behind, and imagined he felt it nestle against his neck. "Don't breathe," he whispered.

"What?"

"Hold your breath."

She sucked in air with an angry hiss, then held still.

Donovan focused on the silence. He catalogued a faint electrical hum from the air-conditioning system, the scratchy scurrying of a rodent, and—there it was—the unmistakable shuffling sound of a shoe on cement.

What kind of hired killer was too careless to wear rubber soles?

As his eyes adjusted, Donovan began to make out the shapes around them. They stood in a corridor separated from the row of stalls by six-foot partitions. The repair facility lay off to their left.

The noise came from one of the stalls to the right. Just when Donovan thought he could tell which one, footsteps chuffed impatiently across the cement. Whatever the man was looking for, he hadn't found it.

A white circle of light moved toward them. Donovan held out his arm and forced Francesca against the wall. The prowler might not notice them in the shadows.

But the man didn't turn toward the exit. He headed straight toward them, still unaware of their presence, probably intending to search the repair facility.

Donovan tensed to attack. The man was about a stride too far away when, beside him, Francesca uttered a ragged gasp, as if stricken with pleurisy, and staggered forward.

He realized two things simultaneously. First, that she'd been holding her breath this whole time and had finally run out of air. Second, that the man was rushing her.

"Whoa!" Donovan shoved her aside and shouldered the man into the back of a stall. He heard the crunch of a head hitting the hardwood partition, and expected to feel the figure go slack.

Instead, the man struck back with such force that Donovan realized he must have been braced against the wall. As Donovan gasped from the impact, he registered the man's build—stocky and powerful.

Powerful enough to pummel Donovan until his teeth rattled. Powerful enough to crunch him in a wrestling hold and twist him under an armpit that smelled of Brut and two days' worth of sweat. Powerful enough to send little bursts of flame along his neck as if someone had set off firecrackers.

"Stop it!" The shrill voice was Francesca's. The man arched backward, as if she were pulling his hair, and Donovan sucked in a painful but welcome gasp of air.

A deep grunt welled out of the man's gut—a sound that expressed something like irritation at a fly—and he turned to deal with this new attacker.

With a thump, Donovan landed on the floor. His every instinct screamed at him to tackle the intruder before Francesca got hurt. He ordered himself to rise. His joints refused to move. He tried to twist around to see what was happening, but his neck had frozen. Finally it occurred to Donovan that he wasn't sure which direction would be considered up.

Then he heard her scream.

It wasn't one of those high shrieks they dubbed into horror flicks. It was a throaty roar of rage mixed with fear that could only have come from Francesca.

Donovan considered, and rejected, drawing his gun. It was too dark and there was too great a risk of hitting Francesca by mistake.

His muscles finally yielded, just enough for him to push up onto his knees. His hand scrabbled across the fallen flashlight. It was as long as his forearm, solid and heavy, and under the circumstances it was a lot more practical than a gun.

Grasping it, he rocked onto his heels and felt Roman candles flare above his collarbone. But they weren't state fair quality anymore, just bright enough for, say, your hometown Fourth of July picnic.

Donovan couldn't make it all the way to his feet, not yet. But a thick leg encased in cuffed jeans brushed by, and Donovan took the hardest swing he could, every

ounce of low-fat, high-fiber breakfasts and weight lifting at the gym funnelled into that one metallic thrust to
the back of the knee.

With a groan, the man collapsed on top of Donovan
like a felled tree. It felt as if someone were squeezing all
the air out of his chest with a vise. He tried to cough, and
only managed a thin huff. The lug must have weighed
two hundred pounds stripped, which was not an appe-
tizing thought.

A high, keening wail burst from somewhere overhead; no, a chorus of howls from two throats. Francesca
and the burglar were screaming at each other at a fre-
quency that throbbed directly into Donovan's tortured
brain. He wished he could breathe so that he could tell
them to shut up.

With a gasp of relief that reverberated through his
synapses, he felt the great weight lift from his back and
heard the shoes stumble out the door. At that moment,
he hardly cared that the intruder was escaping.

"Francesca?" Donovan wished she'd scream again so
that he could find her. "Are you all right?"

"Mmmph," came the reply.

"I'll, uh, be right with you." He realized he was still
holding the flashlight, and he switched it on.

She sat against the partition, hugging her knees. "He's
getting away." She made no move to follow.

"Did he hurt you?"

"I'm fine." But her voice was trembling.

"You're not fine. You're in shock. You aren't used to
this kind of violence."

"And you are?"

He shrugged, and sparklers sizzled along his verte-
brae. "It goes with the territory."

"For me, too," Francesca said. "Don't you think we should get up?"

"Is this a rhetorical question?" he asked hopefully.

"I was suggesting a course of action."

"That's what I was afraid of." He sighed. "Both together, then. One, two, three . . ."

They staggered to their feet like drunkards, leaning on each other. "Just a minute," Donovan said. "I need to check something out."

Francesca held his arm. "Don't go."

"Stay here. Yell if he comes back. I need you to keep lookout." He didn't like to leave her, but he needed to concentrate.

Donovan found what he was seeking on the oil-stained floor, a cigarillo butt rimmed with pink lipstick. When he returned, he said, "That's where Cindy parked. Our friend must have been looking for her car."

"How can you be sure that's Cindy's?"

"Not many women smoke cigarillos. Her sister does, so she probably does, too."

"Unless Amanda dropped it while she was kidnapping her."

"Cindy was last seen by the cliff. Alone."

That seemed to end the argument. Francesca kept quiet as they wobbled outside until she asked, "So where is it?"

"Where is what?"

"Cindy's car."

"Police impound lot. Material evidence." They winced across the parking lot. There was no sign of the intruder, not even the sound of a nearby motor.

"Don't you think we'd better find it?"

"I'll check on it tomorrow." He swung around to face Francesca. In the twilight, her eyes looked even darker than usual. "Aren't you exhausted?"

"Actually, it was kind of exciting." She stood on tiptoe, smoothing back a wisp of hair from his forehead. "Aren't you all keyed up?"

"Hungry, mostly."

"Then let's go eat."

They stopped at a burger drive-in, where Francesca asked for a salad, then changed her mind and made it the biggest cheeseburger on the menu, with fries and a shake. That sounded good to Donovan, too.

Despite her insistence that the incident hadn't shaken her, he thought Francesca looked pale. She sat slouched in her seat, her face blank, not even reacting to the tantalizing aroma of French fries wafting from the sack. He knew that her adrenaline rush had ebbed by now and her body was paying a price for its burst of energy.

As he drove, he wished he knew what to say to her. Or to ask. He didn't think she'd been seriously traumatized, but she needed to talk about her feelings. Or at least he supposed she did. He wished he knew how to draw her out.

She sat staring out the windshield, lost in thought. What did she think about, anyway, when she wasn't cooking up schemes to complicate his life?

He wanted to let her know that he understood her turmoil. He wanted to come up with something profound and sensitive, clever and probing.

"You sure you're okay?" he said.

She nodded and hugged the bag of hamburgers.

They reached her apartment complex. Donovan supposed he ought to depart with his meal, but Francesca's skin looked so translucent and her eyes so shadowed that he followed her upstairs.

The airplane didn't startle him this time, but it hadn't grown on him, either. The ginger-colored dog lay sleeping on a cream sofa; otherwise, he realized, the room was devoid of color. Cream furniture, curtains, carpet. As if Francesca had held back from committing herself even to an apartment. Maybe someday she'd just dismantle her airplane, pack her dog and go, leaving no trace.

He didn't like the image of this room without her. Of any room without her.

They sat at the kitchen table, eating their burgers. Several times Donovan tried to start a conversation about the day's events, but he gave up after receiving only monosyllabic responses.

Finally he said, "I'll pick you up about noon tomorrow."

That got her attention. "Noon? Shouldn't we report for work first thing?"

"I want to check with the police first," Donovan reminded her. "I'm sure even Jon Blakely doesn't expect us to pack and move in the blink of an eye."

Her jaw tightened. "What do you mean, 'even Jon Blakely'?"

It was a relief to see Francesca recover her old combative self. "What was it he said? That he considers service an honorable profession? I'll bet he wouldn't consider it an honorable profession for himself. The man's a snob. He considers servants a lower life-form."

Baiting her into a quarrel might not be the approved method of banishing the blues, but Donovan was willing to try.

Francesca jabbed her fork into a French fry. "Jon Blakely isn't really arrogant. Just—maybe a little sheltered."

"If you consider King Louis the Fourteenth 'sheltered.'"

Francesca waved the French fry in midair as if debating whether to whack him with it. "You're exaggerating on purpose. I think you're actually beginning to enjoy fighting with me."

"Not fighting. Debating," he said. "If you're not going to eat that potato, could I have it?"

A chuckle forced its way up her throat. Francesca managed to transform it into a cough, but she couldn't hide the curve of her lips. "You're impossible."

"I'm glad you weren't injured. You were lucky." Donovan leaned back, trying to ignore his own twinges and aches. "That guy was built like a bulldog."

"He sure did a job on you. Don't you at least need an aspirin?" She balled up the paper sack and tossed it toward the trash. A perfect hit.

"My bruises are well distributed. They kind of cancel each other out," he said.

Francesca struggled against a yawn. "We could go use the hot tub downstairs."

As she stretched, Donovan's eye was drawn to the V of her jacket and he remembered that earlier glimpse of lace, now hidden beneath the blouse. "Go to bed before we both do something we'll regret." He pushed back his chair.

She caught his sleeve. "Stay a little while."

"You should rest." Even as he said it, he couldn't help wishing she'd keep tugging at his shirt. Maybe her fingers could work their way along his chest and then down . . .

"Wait." She pulled her hand away. Darn it. "I—I'd appreciate it if you'd hang around. Until I'm asleep, I mean. I'm trying not to think about what happened today, but I can't help it." She picked up a paper napkin and tore little strips around the edges.

Of all the women Donovan had ever met, Francesca seemed the least in need of a knight in shining armor. He could picture himself riding up to rescue her only to find she'd already slain the dragon herself.

But there was something vulnerable about her tonight. The fortress walls had crumbled, and the drawbridge was down.

"You should go to bed," he suggested. "Get some sleep."

"I think I'll stay up. Watch TV. The truth is, I'm not sure I can walk very well right now."

So he did the only thing a red-blooded male could do under the circumstances. He walked over to her chair, scooped her up in his arms, and carried her into the bedroom. It hurt like hell. It was the most idiotic thing he'd ever done. But it felt great.

"Hey." Francesca cuddled against him. A trace of her voluptuous perfume curled around his senses. "What do you think you're doing?"

"Shall I read you a bedtime story?"

"Not on your life!" But she didn't resist as he settled her onto the comforter.

"I'll watch TV in the living room till I hear you snore," he said. "Doesn't happen to be a sports section around here, does there?"

"In the recycling bin." Her eyelids drifted down. "Thanks."

"You're not going to sleep in that suit." He didn't know why the thought bothered him. He'd slept in his own suits plenty of times.

"I'll have to dry-clean it anyway."

"You could at least take your shoes off."

"My feet will get cold." The consonants were slurring. Definitely the effects of posttraumatic something-or-other, Donovan decided.

"You're going to wake up crabby tomorrow and you're going to take it out on me," he said. "Your feet will hurt, your panty hose will itch—"

"I beg your pardon!" She tried to sit up, and one shoe dropped from a slender foot.

"You'll be sore from lying on your buttons, and there'll be makeup smeared on your pillow." He wasn't guessing about the last part; Donovan had had his share of girlfriends. He'd always considered a dab of spot remover a small price to pay, but Francesca might not take the same attitude tomorrow, and he wanted her in a good mood. "At least brush your teeth."

"Too tired. I'll be all right."

"Whatever you say." One thing troubled him, though. Her shoes. One on and one off.

He crossed to the bed and removed the remaining one.

Francesca had beautiful feet, long and fine. Donovan couldn't forget his first glimpse of those thong sandals she'd worn at Mrs. Cornsworth's party. They'd made her look brazenly bare.

"Going to stop there?" she murmured.

Donovan unbuttoned her jacket and tossed it over a chair. When he turned back, the picture of her lying there stunned him. Light from the bedside lamp played across her velvety skin, highlighting her smooth jawline and full lips. The dark hair flowing across her pillow was right out of his dreams.

That high collar must be rubbing against her neck, Donovan decided, and unbuttoned the top of her blouse.

"You have gentle hands," Francesca said. "I wouldn't have expected it."

He undid the rest of her buttons, to demonstrate just how gentle his hands could be. He felt a breath shudder through her as he brushed her flat stomach, laying the fabric aside.

Now he had come to the secret of the black lace, a garment that probably boasted some fancy French name. Donovan had seen women at some of L.A.'s trendier bars wear them openly, without blouses. They'd never appealed to them that way; he liked a mystery. He particularly liked this mystery.

Fingers played across his own shirt. Donovan looked down to see Francesca working a button, starting in the middle. "Not very efficient," he said. "I've still got my coat on."

"Take it off."

"I ought to go." He didn't move.

"We shouldn't be doing this." She eased off another of his buttons. "And my skirt's getting wrinkled."

He slid it down her hips, grateful for elastic waist-lines, and discovered a short lace-trimmed black slip. Incredibly silky as it slipped through his fingers.

She kicked the skirt away and, her mouth finding the gap in his shirt, licked his chest. A deep hunger stirred inside Donovan. He knew better than to do this. He and Francesca had to work together. They didn't agree on anything. They'd have nothing but trouble.

He liked trouble.

His hands glided beneath the camisole, stroking up from Francesca's waist to the rounded swell of her breasts. His mouth sought hers, and she met him halfway, her lips parting to receive him, her tongue taking refuge against his. Her arms encircled his broad back, pulling him closer.

It would be so easy to take her. The shock she'd suffered earlier had left her vulnerable. Donovan knew she would give him anything he wanted, and not blame him afterward.

But he might have to fire her as soon as this job was done. He didn't want her to be left with a lingering sense of betrayal.

Donovan hated being an idealist. He hated pulling away, giving up the feeling of Francesca's body beneath his. He hated going away hungry.

"You'd better get some sleep," he said.

"Hey!" Francesca glared. "Where do you think you're going?"

"I'm your boss. You'd probably sue me for something or other." He crooked her a grin from the far side of the room.

She propped herself sleepily on her elbows. "Donovan, what the heck is going on? This is the first time I've gotten this close to a man in—well, never mind how long. And for all we know, we might get shot tomorrow and never have another chance."

"A risk we'll have to take," he said. "This is business. Let's keep it that way."

"You jerk." She didn't sound like she meant it.

"You'll thank me tomorrow."

"Probably." This time she smiled back. "Oh, go be noble somewhere else."

As he passed through the living room, the dog was beating its tail against the sofa, leaving little ginger-colored hairs.

"Take care of her, Asta," Donovan said.

The dog cocked its head and watched him go.

Chapter Six

Donovan awoke the next morning feeling as if he'd drunk a quart of rotgut, served as a bowling pin all night and then been left lying askew while gutter balls rolled over him.

He hurt like hell, and a couple of aspirin weren't going to do the job. The only cure was action.

By the time he marched up the broad steps of the Newport Beach police station, he had showered, breakfasted and recovered a semihuman facade. Inside, his guts still felt as if they were filled with something between grape jelly and battery acid.

The desk sergeant acknowledged him with a flip of the hand and buzzed him back to Detectives without missing a beat in his phone conversation. "Yes, ma'am, we do have a noise ordinance that includes barking dogs, but— Yes, ma'am— No, we don't usually call out the SWAT team for that, ma'am. Perhaps you could talk to your neighbor first, ma'am...."

The detectives' room was a giant glassed-in rectangle with desks aligned in rows. Efficient, modern and cold. No cubicles for tacking up photographs and cartoons; no private corners for shooting the breeze when you needed to blow off some tension.

Lieutenant Eli Jonas's desk faced the others. As usual, the files and reports on the desk lay in neat stacks. No old coffee cups or gum wrappers littered the surface. You could see the guy was compulsive. It was a good quality in a man responsible for finding the truth that could send a man to prison or set him free.

This early, at seven-thirty, people were still trickling in, a couple of hard workers already at their desks, two detectives comparing lottery tickets as they balanced their coffee down an aisle. Within an hour, Donovan knew, the place would be packed and ready for the morning's briefing.

He figured Eli had to be somewhere around. The guy never slept late. In all the years Donovan had known him, Eli had arrived on the job first and left last. Thank goodness for a patient wife and two kids who considered Daddy their hero.

Here he came now, a doughnut in one hand, a report in the other. Eli was Donovan's age, thirty-six; they'd gone to college together, both prelaw in those days. The product of a middle-class African-American family, Eli had disappointed his parents by choosing police work instead of becoming an attorney, but he'd done a hell of a job.

He spotted Donovan and feigned a grimace. "Well, look what the cat drug in."

"How the heck are you?" Donovan waited till Eli put down the doughnut, and then they shook hands.

"So what're you working on now?" the lieutenant asked, and Donovan told him. He also described the intruder of the previous night.

"You find anything in the car he might have been looking for?" Donovan asked.

Eli shook his head. "No, but maybe it's worth another go-round. The detective on the case is in court today. Maybe we should just wander over to the tow yard and take a look."

Donovan rode with Eli the couple of miles to the towing company's yard. The place was littered with parking violators and hauled wrecks. Police impounds lay out of sight in a locked shed.

The company's owner trudged ahead of them, dangling his keys. "You guys nearly ready to release this one?"

"I thought we were," Eli said. "Now I'm not so sure."

"Hey." The owner stared at the shed door. "Damn. Somebody's picked the lock. I don't get it. Must have been some idiot who thought we kept valuables in there."

"He might still be here," Donovan said.

Eli nodded. "Stand back."

The owner ducked away. Donovan and Eli pressed against the outer walls, and then Eli kicked the door open and leaped inside, gun drawn, yelling, "Police! Come out with your hands up!"

As Donovan rushed in, he saw two frightened eyes peering from the window of a silver sedan. "Oh, hell..." He holstered his gun.

Eli quirked an eyebrow. "You know her?"

He hated to admit it, but he said, "She works for me. Unfortunately."

The lieutenant put his gun away. "Not exactly standard procedure."

"I needed a wife for my undercover act." Donovan jerked open the car door. "Well?"

Francesca slid out, hair partially covering her face. "I was just trying to help."

"What you were doing is called obstruction of justice." Eli put on his sternest face. "Not to mention breaking and entering."

"But I'm studying to be a detective!" Francesca's chin lifted defiantly. "We're not going to let you flatfoots stand in our way!"

"Flatfoots?" Eli's shoulders shook with suppressed laughter. "You watch a lot of old movies or something?"

"It isn't like that in real life." Donovan tried not to notice how Francesca's fuzzy green sweater stopped short of her midriff, and how her slim black skirt barely reached to midthigh. Just inhaling her fragrance sent powerful desires roaring through his veins. "The police aren't our enemy, and we try not to get in their way."

"We go our way and they go theirs," she said stubbornly. "And may the best man win!"

That did it. Eli loosed a guffaw that rattled the shed. "My Lord, this woman has spirit!"

Francesca glared at him until Donovan muttered, under his breath, "Be glad he thinks this is funny. You could be arrested, and you'd deserve it."

The towing company's owner, reassured by Eli's laughter, came in to check, and he favored Francesca with a long look that bordered on a leer. Donovan turned the man firmly toward the door. "This is confidential."

"Okay, okay. I'll be in my office."

When Donovan returned, he found Francesca apologizing to Eli, who accepted with good grace. They learned she'd arrived only a few minutes before and hadn't discovered anything yet.

"Let's divide this baby into three parts," Eli said. "Faster that way."

"I'll take the engine," Francesca volunteered. Catching the lieutenant's dubious look, she added, "I could take this motor apart and rebuild it. Believe me, I know what belongs and what doesn't."

"She's not kidding," Donovan said.

"If you say so." Eli chose the interior; Donovan inherited the trunk.

Making a search sounded easy in theory, but in fact there weren't many obvious places to hide something in a car, which didn't mean there weren't lots of not-so-obvious places. That meant prying up upholstery and unscrewing anything that would yield to the tools Eli had brought along.

It was the lieutenant who made the discovery—a secret compartment built under the back seat. "Don't know how the boys missed this one," he said as he pulled the whole seat up. "It's on special hinges, see?"

"It all depends on what you're looking for." Donovan had to admit he wouldn't have made such an exhaustive search had he not known about the burglar. The crime lab guys would have been looking for fingerprints, hair, fibers, that kind of evidence—not buried treasure.

"Would you believe it?" Eli fiddled with a tiny combination dial. "It's locked. Somebody knew what they were doing when they built this baby. Shoot, it won't budge. We'll have to break in."

"Okay if I try?" Francesca scrambled into the car and knelt, ear to the lock. A few clicks and twirls later, it opened. "Voilà!"

"Wait!" Eli's voice snapped her to a halt as she reached inside. "Don't touch!"

"Sorry." Francesca slithered out.

Eli donned plastic gloves and drew out a stack of bills. "Well, well . . ."

In the harsh light from the shed's bare fixtures, they counted out half a million dollars in cold cash.

Donovan whistled. "Somebody must have wanted that bad."

"But who does it belong to?" Francesca asked.

"Jon Blakely, I guess, but we'll have to keep it as evidence." Eli set about tagging the money. "Evidence of what, I don't know. Why would his wife be carrying an amount like this?"

Donovan considered several possibilities. A drug deal, maybe, but that seemed unlikely. Ransom—but who would Cindy have been ransoming? Or, more probably . . . "Blackmail?" he suggested.

"You see, it wasn't Jon at all!" Francesca beamed. "Someone must have been blackmailing her. She went to make the payoff, there was a fight, and the guy killed her. Then he couldn't find the money, and later he came back looking for it."

"Makes sense." Eli closed up the car and led the way out of the shed. "If she'd had a lover, or done anything that would give her husband the upper hand in a divorce, she'd have been a sitting duck for a blackmailer."

"On the other hand, who installed the safe?" Donovan pointed out. "Blakely must have known about it, but he didn't tell the police."

"So?" Francesca asked challengingly as they emerged, blinking, into the morning light. "Maybe he was so upset he didn't think about it."

Donovan searched for some explanation that would implicate Blakely. Damn it, he knew the man was guilty. He'd seen it in Amanda's pain, and in Blakely's arrogance. Francesca wasn't the only one who could lay claim to intuition.

"Suppose he hired someone to blackmail his own wife? Then lured her to a remote cliff, where she was murdered to make it look like an accident or suicide? Maybe the guy was supposed to take the blackmail money as his payment, but he got scared off before he could find it."

"Farfetched," Eli said. "Blackmail his own wife?"

"She wouldn't know that, of course," Donovan pointed out.

"There's a big hole in your theory." Francesca let out an exasperated breath. "The killer would simply have contacted Jon to get the money later, not come sneaking around the garage."

Eli slipped the bills into a plastic bag. "We'll have to try to trace these." He shook his head. "I wish you'd caught that man last night, my friend. It would certainly have simplified my life."

"We'll keep an eye out for him," Donovan promised.

"I think our man would have figured out by now that the car's still in custody," Eli said. "Plus, you two must have thrown a scare into him. Whoever he is, he'll find some other way to get his payment, if that's what this is."

Half a million dollars. Donovan had seen people killed for a lot less. He didn't plan to be one of them.

When they left the shed, Eli excused himself to discuss security with the yard owner.

"You going to wait around all day?" Francesca asked Donovan. "We've got a job to do."

"By the time a cab could get here, Eli'd be ready to go."

"You chicken or what?" said Francesca.

Donovan favored her with a long, level gaze. It had no effect whatsoever. How come it worked so well for Arnold Schwarzenegger?

"I'll drive," he said.

"You got a motorcycle license?"

He had to admit he didn't.

"Come on." Francesca didn't look back as she marched toward the parking lot.

Donovan had never liked the idea of skimming alongside tractor-trailers on an overgrown bicycle. And, pilot's license notwithstanding, he didn't feel too confident about entrusting his life to the kind of woman who could call a police officer a "flatfoot."

On the other hand, he'd never been a coward, and he wasn't going to start now.

He caught up with Francesca in a few long strides. They wove their way through a maze of broken-down vehicles and flashy cars sporting expensive summonses on their windshields, the three-hundred-dollar kind you got for parking in a handicapped space.

In his present mood, Donovan half hoped someone had towed the motorcycle.

No such luck. Francesca tossed him a spare helmet and straddled the big bike with shining eyes and eagerly parted lips.

Great. The woman got turned on by her cycle, Donovan grumbled to himself as he donned the helmet and swung on behind her.

Francesca glanced back. "Put your arms around me, big guy. I don't bite."

"Thought I might pull you off." He contemplated her slim shape.

"Not in a million years." She revved the engine, and he grabbed her for support as the bike shot forward.

Vibrations zinged through Donovan's body. The hard metal between his knees contrasted startlingly with the soft nakedness of Francesca's stomach. Her skirt—which turned out to be one of these divided affairs that looked like a skirt but was really a pair of shorts—might meet the standards of public decency but it didn't leave a whole lot to the imagination. And that fuzzy sweater seemed to shrink every time he looked at it.

The cycle bounced over a curve, skidded into a left turn and arrowed down the street so fast it felt as if they'd slammed into a wall of wind.

"Hey!" Donovan shouted. "They've got traffic laws around here!"

"They'll have to catch me first!" He could have sworn he heard a crazed edge to Francesca's laughter as she accelerated around a corner.

Donovan gave up trying to bring things under control. At this point, he had to trust Francesca; any interference was likely to send them careening out of control.

They barely touched the pavement as they darted in and out of traffic. Francesca quivered with a kind of ecstasy as they shot between lanes and around obstacles.

Leaning forward, gripping her, Donovan felt her joy rocket through him. Her elation sparked him, ignited him, until his body melted into hers. She'd been right; he'd never experienced anything so close to flying outside an airplane.

His lips tasted the salty sweetness of her neck, and her back arched in response. Damn, he was going to get them both mashed into the nearest building if he wasn't careful. But he wasn't sure he cared.

All too soon they pulled into the police parking lot. "Sorry you left last night?" Francesca asked sweetly as she stopped beside his van.

He swung off the bike. "Is this revenge?"

"Just the bittersweet taste of regret." She tapped her watch; it was almost ten o'clock. "See you in two hours." The cycle roared off.

Two policemen paused on the steps to watch. One uttered a low whistle. Donovan knew what he meant.

He spooned himself into his van and called Tammi on the mobile phone. "Thank goodness!" she declared. "I got a call from Ms. Carruthers. She said she'd meet you at ten at Gary's Gardens. You know, that garden shop near Newport Center."

In the background, Donovan heard the sharp rap of a hammer. "What's going on there?"

"New curtains," Tammi said.

"I never authorized—"

"Francesca suggested I read our lease," his secretary said, interrupting him. "You know what? We were supposed to have draperies in here, not just these dusty old miniblinds. So I called the landlord and he's putting them in."

"I wish you'd checked with me first," Donovan muttered, although he had to admit he didn't mind getting something for nothing. "You don't work for Francesca, you work for me."

"I thought you'd be pleased." Tammi sounded on the verge of tears. "I could send them away, I guess."

"No. No, it's all right. Any other calls?"

She passed on a few more messages, nothing urgent, and Donovan headed for the garden shop.

He'd never had occasion to visit Gary's Gardens before. It looked more like a botanical display than a gardening store, with miniature settings promoting the shop's landscaping service and a cornucopia of fuchsias and impatiens dangling above the outdoor aisles. Even the brightly colored shovels and hoes had been hung in eye-pleasing patterns.

Donovan thought about the small patch of bare dirt behind his condominium. The real estate brochure had described it as a "private garden spot." He'd stuck twenty dollars' worth of geraniums in there once, but they'd died, probably because he'd forgotten to water them.

Amanda Carruthers waited by an ice plant. From her cigarette holder protruded a half-smoked brown stub. "You're late," she said.

"Working for you." He started to tell her about the intruder, but before he got to the cash Amanda cut him off.

"I was right. Jon's definitely involved in something, but what?" she said. "We need to ruffle his feathers and see if we can flush him out. Leave some clues to let him know he's being watched. Why don't you rearrange the papers on his desk? Watch what he does, and see if he tips his hand."

"And maybe, not being a complete fool, he'll figure out that his new employees are responsible," Donovan said. "It's too soon to risk discovery. We haven't even had a chance to search the house."

Amanda stared past a large camellia bush covered with buds. "You do carry a gun, don't you?"

Donovan nodded.

"Jon has one somewhere. Be on your guard." She tossed her spent cigarillo aside and snapped the holder into her purse. "Mr. Lewis, my sister was a trusting young girl. She loved her husband. I don't know how Jon set her up, but it wouldn't have been difficult. Maybe he was doing something illegal and used her as a courier. I don't know. I just know that she died because of him, and I don't want him to get away with it."

A tear wended its way down her pale cheek, leaving her mascara intact. The effect was of a kind of Hollywood vulnerability.

"Whatever he did, he'll pay for it," Donovan promised.

Amanda glanced around, but there was no one in sight except a couple in their sixties who were inspecting citrus trees. "This female partner of yours, she's working out?"

"She's competent," he said.

"Be careful she doesn't fall for Jon. He can be charming when he wants to." Amanda favored him with a small smile. "Although, with a good-looking guy like you around, I doubt he'd have a chance."

For some reason, the compliment made Donovan uneasy. He liked to keep things strictly business with his clients. "I'll keep an eye on her," he said.

"I'll contact you again soon." She disappeared through a drift of pink bougainvillea.

Donovan mulled over the conversation as he returned to his van. Why had Amanda suggested he "ruffle" Blakely? No doubt she wanted revenge and she wanted it fast, but it seemed rash. He hoped she wouldn't decide to interfere on her own.

Donovan grabbed a bite of lunch and arrived at Francesca's apartment shortly before noon.

She opened the door after one ring. She'd gathered her wealth of hair into a tidy bun and traded her skinny sweater outfit for a shirtwaist dress in a small flower print.

"Very appropriate," Donovan said.

Francesca swung the door wider. "I figure I made enough of a fool of myself this morning."

A soft-sided suitcase waited by a blond coffee table. Donovan headed for it.

"Don't you think we should go over procedures before we start?" Francesca asked. "As you like to point out, I'm new at this. What should we be looking for? How should we act?"

Donovan paused. "The first rule is to avoid getting 'made.' Don't do anything suspicious."

She drew him beside her onto the sofa. "Okay. No deerstalker hat, and no peering at Miss Feinstein through a lorgnette."

Donovan smiled, fighting the urge to stroke the hair where it hugged her head. "No Rollerblading in the front hall."

"No throwing water balloons out the windows." Francesca crossed her legs and leaned back. How did she manage to make even a conservative dress look revealing? "As for the housekeeper thing, I watched every episode of *Upstairs, Downstairs* at least twice. But, I mean, how do we dig up clues? Just prowl through drawers?"

"More or less. Housecleaning provides the perfect cover," he said. "Pay attention to what might have fallen behind the furniture. Glance through the trash when you empty it. You'd be surprised what people throw away—notes, bills, medicine bottles, phone numbers. And, yes, check her drawers. If she had a lover, if she was being blackmailed, she might have left a clue."

"How about questioning the staff?" Francesca asked. "Shouldn't we nose around?"

"Leave that to me," Donovan said. "Mostly I want you to stick to your duties. Get the job done. Including the repairs."

"Sounds boring." Francesca wrinkled her nose. "Can't I put the screws to somebody? I want action!"

"This is your first assignment," Donovan reminded her. "Plan to spend most of your time observing." Her pulse fluttered in her throat, and he wondered how it would feel beneath his lips.

"Are you staring at my throat?"

"I can see your heart beating."

"Talk about observing!" She laughed and flicked a thumb across his earlobe. The unexpected touch threw his own pulse into overdrive. "Mr. Detective, you weren't hired to examine me!"

"But you're a lot more appealing than Jon Blakely."

"Am I?" Francesca spidered her fingers across his chest, and Donovan's heart thudded as if he'd just completed a workout at the gym.

"What—?" He had to pause to catch his breath. "What are you doing?"

"Getting used to being your wife. You wouldn't want to arouse suspicion, would you?"

"That's not the only thing you're arousing."

She grinned, enjoying her effect on him. "You're the one who was ogling my jugular."

"I was expressing a purely aesthetic appreciation." Donovan wished Francesca didn't have such a muddling effect on his senses. He needed his wits about him for this job, and all he wanted was to pull her onto his lap and show her exactly how much he appreciated her aesthetics.

"Come here, big guy." Francesca seized him by the lapels and touched her lips to his, taunting him, daring him.

For a fraction of a second, Donovan considered resistance. Then he plunged ahead, taking her mouth with his tongue, driving into her and then pulling out until she grabbed him and made him do it again.

He lowered her to the couch, his mouth never leaving hers. His hand found a smooth expanse of stocking and followed it up to silk and lace.

She'd been right. If they planned to pose as husband and wife, if they were going to live together in one bedroom, what was the point of holding back? Sooner or later passion would claim its due, and Donovan preferred sooner.

Something wet slimed across his ear. He brushed it away. "Francesca?"

"It's him."

Him? Passion collided with alarm. Francesca had some other lover? What the hell was he doing here?

And why was he licking Donovan's ear?

"Oh, Asta." She sighed and slid away. "Pooch, it isn't time to go yet."

Donovan groaned. "You know, I could develop a real dislike for that dog."

"He doesn't mean to interrupt." Francesca tickled her pet's chest. "He's just lonely."

"He isn't the only one."

"He won't be like this the whole time, I promise."

Something in her phrasing caught Donovan's attention. "What whole time? We're going to drop him at a kennel, right?"

"A kennel?" Francesca said. "Don't be ridiculous. He's coming with us."

There had been other unromantic interruptions in the course of Donovan's love life. Once, as a teenager, petting in the balcony of the neighborhood movie theater, he'd dumped an entire tub of buttered popcorn over the railing onto the head of a woman with a screech like a banshee.

And a few years ago, in a vacation cabin in the mountains, he and his then-girlfriend had leaped onto the bed, only to have it collapse in a tangle of sheets and springs, leaving him with a sprained ankle and her with a permanent case of the giggles every time Donovan came near her.

But this was infuriating. Donovan meant to be gentle. He meant to be polite. He meant to be restrained. *"What do you mean we're taking that dog?"* he shouted.

"Calm down." Francesca sat up. "Honestly, you get sidetracked so easily. Would you just forget the dog?"

"Only when you tell me we're taking him to a kennel!" He knew some people considered their dogs to be family, but you didn't bring your children along on an undercover assignment, and you didn't bring your dog, either.

"He could be useful." Francesca walked toward the door. "Shall we go? It really is getting late."

"No." But even as he spoke, Donovan picked up her suitcase. Jon Blakely would be expecting them to show up shortly. "Don't you have some friend you could leave him with? How about your father. He lives in Laguna, doesn't he? Or your sister?"

"Asta and my father don't get along." Francesca led the way downstairs, the dog tagging along. "My sister left yesterday in a camper for a two-week vacation."

"Maybe one of my friends would take him," Donovan said, without much hope. He'd left his longtime friends back in Boston. Most of his chums in California were beer-and-football buddies, not the kind who would baby-sit a pooch.

"Why don't we just take him along and see?" Francesca suggested as she helped Asta into the van. "You might be surprised."

"Very surprised," Donovan muttered, but he didn't see what he could do about it.

Chapter Seven

They heard the shouting as soon as they turned into Blakely's driveway.

A stand of cypress trees blocked the house from view. "Sounds like it's on the lawn," Francesca said. On her lap, Asta whined with excitement.

Donovan pushed the accelerator, shooting them into the parking lot. As he clicked off the engine and left the van at a dead run, he could hear Jon Blakely shouting, "Get off my property!"

A male voice responded in low tones. Donovan couldn't catch the words.

"You have no right!" Even in outrage, Blakely never lost his upper-class accent.

Had the killer dared to return in broad daylight? Was he demanding payment, or trying to extort more money?

Donovan dashed around a corner, then broke stride as he took in the scene. A thirtyish man in a cheap suit had Blakely boxed in by the fountain, thrusting a microphone into his face. The mike was engraved with the call letters of a local radio station.

The reporter wore a sly grin. "Mr. Blakely, it's been two weeks, and the police still say they don't know what happened to your wife. Surely you must have some idea. Come on, now.''

"If I knew, I'd have told the police, wouldn't I?" snapped the thin man.

The reporter pressed on. "Have you heard from any kidnappers, Mr. Blakely? Have you—"

"Oh, sure," Blakely drawled sarcastically. "My wife's been kidnapped but I refused to pay them off. I figured I'd let them kill her for me. Any other stupid questions?"

"How much did you pay to have her killed?"

"Just a minute!" Donovan strode toward the reporter.

"And you are—?" The microphone swung toward him.

"Mr. Blakely's . . . bodyguard." He looked toward the thin man for directions.

"Going to manhandle me?" The reporter chortled. "Is that how you treat the police, too, Mr. Blakely? We hear you're not cooperating in the investigation."

"That's a bald-faced lie!" Jon stormed. "The only people I don't cooperate with are two-bit reporters who try to manufacture news because their ratings are in the basement!"

Scarlet flooded the reporter's face. "You just don't believe in the public's right to know what—"

He never finished the sentence.

A ball of ginger fur whizzed through the air. With a shout, the reporter staggered, groped toward the fountain for support and got a spray of water all over his bargain-basement suit as he tripped and fell onto the grass.

Asta kept going, past the sprawling man and across the lawn at lightning speed. From beneath a stand of trees came a hiss and a yowl, and something gray shot up a cypress.

"Siccing your dogs on me?" the reporter hissed.

"That's not my dog," Blakely said. "Not my cat, either."

Francesca strolled up. "I'm sorry. Asta can't stand cats, and he never lets anything get in his way."

"You'll regret this," the radio man snarled at Blakely.

"The only thing I regret is that you came here in the first place."

The man's mouth twisted with anger. He sputtered incoherently for a moment and then stalked away.

"Good riddance," said Blakely. "Thank you both."

"I'm afraid he's up to no good," Donovan said. "Radio is still powerful in Los Angeles, and he wants revenge."

"Some people are just bad sports. You can't spend your time worrying about them," said Francesca, and went to collect Asta.

Blakely led them into the house. "It's not the legitimate press that bothers me, the major newspapers and networks. It's the little guys with big egos who'll do anything for a sound bite."

Asta whimpered with what sounded like sympathy and laid his head across Jon Blakely's Italian leather shoes.

"By the way," Blakely said, "what is that dog doing here, anyway?"

"He's ours," Francesca said. "He makes a terrific watchdog, don't you think?"

Their employer studied their faces with a mixture of disbelief and amusement. "You brought your dog? Oh, what the heck. Right now we can use all the help we can get."

A chubby young woman peered out of the kitchen. "Is this the new couple? Hello, I'm Marta, the cook."

"I'll leave them in your hands." Blakely nodded to Donovan and Francesca. "I'm afraid I'm late for an appointment at the plant. By the way, I dropped off the station wagon at the garage and picked up a rental, so you won't have to fix it."

"Oh, all right." Donovan tried to look disappointed.

Blakely tossed him some paperwork. "You can take care of swapping the cars tomorrow."

The next few hours sped by as Marta installed them in their private apartment—which had an excellent view of the garages—and left a big plate of leftovers for Asta in the kitchen. The dog chowed down, tail thumping the ground.

As Marta escorted them on a tour of the estate, Donovan was relieved to find that several entire wings had been closed off. Even a full-time handyman couldn't take care of a mansion this size by himself.

"The north wing's for guests, and the east wing is meeting rooms. Mr. Blakely sometimes holds business conferences here, but of course not since Mrs. Blakely's...disappearance," Marta said.

"Did you see her that night?" Donovan asked as they returned to the kitchen.

"I left about seven." Marta frowned. "She seemed, well, unsettled, and I was a little concerned. I thought maybe they'd had another fight."

"Did you hear the phone ring? Did she have any visitors that evening?" Francesca ventured.

A cold voice cut them off. "I don't see what business that is of yours."

Tenley Feinstein glared at them from the sink, where she stood rinsing out a coffee cup.

"I'm sorry," Francesca said. "I just feel so bad about what happened."

"So do we all." The assistant smacked the cup down on the counter. "There's a lot of work to be done."

"Of course. We'll get right to it." Donovan meant to be conciliatory, but Tenley didn't seem to notice.

She led them briskly out of the kitchen. "I want to go over the mechanical plans to the air-conditioning and plumbing systems. There's also an intercom that could use some fine-tuning."

In her office, Donovan accepted the stack of blueprints and tried not to look as overwhelmed as he felt.

"You do know how to fix computers, don't you?" Tenley demanded.

Donovan caught Francesca's subtle nod. "Certainly," he said.

"You need to ream out the powder room toilet first, and then take a look at my IBM," said Miss Feinstein. "Well? What are you waiting for?"

It might not be the best time to ask questions, but Donovan didn't know how often he'd get a chance to query the assistant. "By the way, what happened to the last couple who had our jobs?"

Gray eyes fixed him with a chilly stare. "Why should that concern you?"

"We'd like to know what mistakes to avoid," Francesca put in.

"They were fired for stealing," Tenley said. "I wouldn't call that a mistake."

"I'm surprised," Donovan pressed. "I should think you'd have checked their references."

Tenley didn't miss a beat. "Nobody checked *your* references," she said.

As he left with Francesca, Donovan wondered what lay behind the woman's hostility. Extreme loyalty to her boss, or some agenda of her own?

By six o'clock, Francesca had repaired the toilet and determined that the computer had a software problem. Donovan pretended to supervise, and though Tenley eyed him dubiously once or twice, she didn't object.

When they were finished, the assistant locked her desk, steered them firmly out of the office and departed with a reminder that the gardeners and day maids would arrive at eight the next morning.

"Day maids," Francesca groaned when they were alone. "At least I don't have to do all the cleaning myself."

"Good, because Marta mentioned that the spare vacuum cleaner needs repairing," Donovan said. "You can take care of that in the morning."

"And what will you be doing?" She folded her arms and planted her feet apart. "Something more interesting, I presume?"

"We have to work as a team," he reminded her.

"Teams don't save all the interesting stuff for one partner."

"Until you've got a bit more experience, that's how we're going to work it."

"And when am I going to get experience if I'm off scraping lint out of a vacuum cleaner?" she demanded.

Donovan considered. Tenley had left; Marta was busy in the kitchen; Blakely wasn't expected back until later.

They had no time to waste. And, though Francesca might be inexperienced, he could use an extra set of eyes and fingers. "How about right now?"

"Now?" she echoed.

"What better time?"

"Okay, boss," she said. "Lead the way."

They went upstairs to the private wing that held the master bedroom and twin dressing rooms. On the way, Francesca flipped open a linen closet and retrieved a stack of towels. "We should have a cover in case someone walks in. Towels always need replacing."

Donovan probed an adjacent cabinet and found a can of spray lubricant. "And hinges always need oiling."

"Let's go." She gave him a conspiratorial grin. "I feel like a real gumshoe already!"

"Don't touch anything until I say so."

"Why not?"

"Because you're still learning."

She made a face, then nodded.

They started with Cindy's dressing room, a large, odd-shaped chamber wrapped around a tiled bathroom. Donovan worked with quiet efficiency, aware of Francesca's fascinated gaze. Before moving an object, he made a mental note of its location, and he returned everything to the exact spot.

The cleaning staff had done its work. There wasn't a stray hair on the flowered vanity, not even a dust mouse under the Victorian love seat, and there were no loose bits of paper wadded on the blue carpet. The trash had been emptied in both the dressing room and the bathroom. A hair dryer and curling iron lay tidily in drawers, the cords wrapped in place.

Donovan wondered how the rooms had looked when their mistress lived here. Surely not so impersonal and pristine. He found not even a drip of shampoo on the outside of the bottle.

Jon Blakely hadn't wasted a moment erasing his wife's personality from her own rooms. It seemed like the final insult.

"Find anything?" Francesca asked from where she stood, about two feet behind Donovan, with a clear view over his shoulder.

"Not yet."

He checked through the triple-width mirrored closets. Cindy hadn't left so much as a matchbook cover or a scribbled phone number in a pocket—or rather, her husband hadn't left them. Judging from the plastic wrappings and laundry tags, everything had been cleaned.

"He must have sent it all to the laundry the day after she vanished," Donovan grumbled. "Place feels like it's been sanitized."

"You think Jon did that on purpose?" Francesca asked as he opened a drawer. Silk underwear lay stacked as precisely as if folded by machine.

"Either that, or Cindy was the coldest creature that ever walked the earth," Donovan said. "I'm going to take a look in the bedroom. You finish going through the drawers."

"Check," said Francesca, and gave him a delighted grin, like a child unexpectedly handed a piece of candy.

As he stepped through an arched door, Donovan saw that the vast bedroom contained an oversize oak water bed with a mirrored headboard and matching bureau.

At the far end of the room, a low couch and cabinets had been arranged to form an entertainment nook as large as most people's dens. There was enough audio-visual equipment to stock a discount store.

Donovan slid open one bureau drawer after another and found them all empty. In the entertainment area, he spotted a copy of the current *TV Guide* and a recent issue of *Forbes* magazine. Otherwise, there were no personal items at all.

Did Jon Blakely even sleep here? Maybe he'd taken to bedding down on one of the couches in his office. Did that mean he missed his wife? Or had they been sleeping apart even before her disappearance?

Donovan checked his watch. Nearly six-thirty. Figuring he could steal a few more minutes, he opened the door to Jon Blakely's dressing room.

His first impression was that the place had been burglarized. Clothes lay strewn across the chairs. The closet doors gaped, revealing racks of squashed suits and a jumble of expensive shoes on the floor.

While Cindy had left behind not a single note, this place was littered with them. Receipts and theater tickets dotted the bureau, and memos spilled onto the floor. Donovan picked up several. "Envy Advertising. Handled Westheimer account. 555-5779." "Half-size boxes. Feasibility study?" "Washing machine tie-in. Try Appliance Busters stores."

Some bore dates, all from the past two weeks.

Expensive cologne sat lidless on the vanity, and a cord dangled from a hair dryer. A silver tie clip lay wedged in the crevice of a chair.

A hasty probe of drawers and closet failed to turn up anything useful, just bunched underwear, jumbled socks and scattered cuff links.

How could a man who created such chaos have sterilized his wife's quarters and their mutual bedroom? It seemed like the work of two different people.

Suppose, Donovan mused, Blakely had an accomplice on his own staff, someone as precise as he was messy. Someone with a lot of nerve and intelligence, someone like . . . Tenley Feinstein.

He couldn't quite make himself believe it.

They didn't act like lovers. Also, Tenley didn't strike him as Jon Blakely's type. Too chubby, too middle-class. Not to mention the photograph of children on her desk.

In the dressing room, Donovan found Francesca paging through a rack of coats. "Any luck?"

"It's strange." She abandoned the coatrack. "There's no diary, no letters, no scrapbooks. And no jewelry, either, except a few costume pieces."

"The good stuff's probably in a safe-deposit box," Donovan said.

"She'd keep some at home to wear. And look at this." Francesca indicated two fur coats hanging in the closet. "A fox jacket. Can you believe that? I mean, foxes are practically like dogs. How could anyone—?"

"We weren't hired to judge her." Donovan wanted to get out of here, now that the job was done.

"Okay. What I meant was, there's a fox jacket and a long mink," Francesca said. "Nothing in between. A rich woman who likes furs would own coats for more occasions."

"Cold storage." Donovan shut the closet doors.

"Why? The place is air-conditioned."

He didn't know much about furs. "Maybe they need a deep freeze. She probably had them cleaned and stored for the summer and hadn't picked them up yet."

"That's not all." Francesca hefted a hand-blown glass dish. "Ashtrays. I counted five."

"So?"

"No cigarettes. She cleaned them out, Donovan," Francesca said. "I think she packed. I think she left on purpose."

"Or someone wants us to think she did." He steered her toward the exit. "If Cindy vanished intentionally, why leave the cash in her car? You could buy a lot of fur coats with half a million dollars."

"Maybe she thought she was meeting a lover, and someone double-crossed her."

Donovan guided Francesca into the hall. "Let's go see if supper's ready before Marta comes looking for us."

"I'd still like to know what happened to all her stuff," Francesca said.

So would I, Donovan thought. So would I.

THEY FOUND MARTA setting out food on the kitchen table. She'd fixed a pot roast with potatoes and carrots that reminded Donovan of his mother's cooking.

Marta grumbled good-naturedly throughout the meal about their employer's absence. "It'll be cold by the time he gets home," she said. "Unless he stops and picks up some junk food. I wish he wouldn't eat that stuff. He's getting into his forties now. He ought to be careful."

"How long have you worked here?" Francesca asked.

"Fifteen years. Since he built the house," the cook told them as she refilled their plates.

"Since before he was married." Donovan didn't want to ask directly if Marta had gotten along with Mrs. Blakely. Instead, he said, "It must be hard for two women to share a kitchen."

"Oh, Mrs. Blakely, she never cared about cooking," Marta said. "The thing I didn't like was, she said I didn't work hard enough. She expected me to fill in when one of the maids got sick. I'm a cook, not a cleaning lady! Back when Mr. Blakely was single and he had house-guests all the time, I worked plenty hard."

"Mrs. Blakely didn't entertain much?" Francesca asked.

Marta sniffed. "She'd have some of her Hollywood friends over, tracking in mud and spilling drinks. She used to be an actress, you know, before she got married. But dinner parties, no, only when Mr. Blakely had businesspeople to take care of. Even then, sometimes he took them to restaurants."

It was obvious the late Mrs. Blakely had held a vastly different attitude toward life from her husband, but then, she'd been a good ten years younger. Perhaps her youthful exuberance had been part of what appealed to Jon, making his accustomed routine seem confining and stale.

Opposites might attract, Donovan thought, but a good marriage required a lot of compatibility. Or so he'd heard.

After dinner, while Marta cleared the table, Donovan slipped out the back door. Francesca caught up with him on the patio.

"What're you looking for?"

"I want to check the garages. You should help Marta with the dishes," he said.

"Give me a break!" Francesca paced alongside. "I don't have to play housekeeper all the time, do I?"

"Marta might open up to you while you're working together," Donovan said. "Let something slip that could be useful."

"I never thought of that." Francesca sighed. "Darn. I figured we'd already picked her brain, but you're right, there might be some little detail..." She glanced back.

"Too late," Donovan said. "It would look strange if you went back now."

"Oh, good." Francesca slipped her arm through his. "We can pretend we're an old married couple taking a walk. Don't you love domestic bliss?"

Donovan didn't feel like part of an old married couple. Francesca's light grip on his elbow was sending electric tingles flowing through his nervous system.

He was becoming aware of her all over again here in the quiet evening, aware of her musky perfume and that perpetual quirk of the eyebrow that hinted of mingled skepticism and invitation.

Francesca gave a little skip, her energy clearly brimming over. She darted a conspiratorial smile at Donovan and touched her cheek to his shoulder.

"What a swimming pool!" She gazed down to where a designer had created a naturalistic pond rimmed with large rocks and tumbling vines. "It looks like a mermaid's grotto."

"How about a swim?" Donovan said.

"Now?" Amusement pulled at her lips. "We don't have our suits."

"There's nobody around."

"You're bluffing," she said. "You wouldn't dare."

"Why not?" He pointed down toward the garages. "We've got a good view from here. We can see anyone come and go."

"And then what?" Francesca demanded. "We leap from the pool without a stitch on and go tearing after some robber?"

He caught her by the waist. "I didn't think you were easily embarrassed."

"I'm game if you are," she shot back.

Donovan didn't know why he kept teasing her, except that he loved watching Francesca's eyes dance with that daredevil challenge. He knew what kind of challenge he wanted, and it had nothing to do with skinny-dipping in Jon Blakely's pool.

His arms slid around her, and Francesca stood on tip-toe, her mouth coming up to his. Donovan caught her lips with his own in a lightning attack, followed by a gentle retreat, then a surprise advance that left them both short of breath.

In the twilight, they twined together like vines. "Let's retire for the night," he murmured. "To hell with work."

Below them, a light mounted on the edge of the garage building flicked off.

"Uh-oh," sighed Francesca.

Donovan uttered a low curse, wishing the problem would go away. But it wouldn't, and he couldn't ignore it.

He considered and rejected the possibility that the light might be automatic. Timers were set to turn illumination on at night, not switch it off.

"Maybe Asta did it," Francesca said hopefully.

"Dogs can't turn off lights."

"You never know."

Donovan wished he'd studied the electrical plans Tenley had given him. Where was the light switch? Could it have been done from the house?

Come to think of it, the light had been off last night, when they'd surprised the intruder. Donovan remembered how murky the parking lot had seemed.

"This guy knows his way around," he muttered.

"Shouldn't we call the police?"

"Think about it," Donovan said. "If we were really a pair of live-ins and we saw an exterior light go off, would that make us call the cops?"

"No."

"We're just out for an evening stroll, remember?" He took her arm lightly, ready to grab for his gun at a moment's notice. "Let's see if we can flush him out."

They strolled down the steps. Donovan could feel Francesca's pulse thudding, but she never quickened her pace.

She had a cool head, even in the face of danger, he had to concede. But he wished she were safely back in the kitchen with Marta.

Donovan was ready to concede that a woman could be just as quick and courageous and strong-minded as a man. What he couldn't get rid of was his own overriding instinct to protect her.

"We'd better wait till he comes out," Donovan said in a low voice. "We'll follow him, get a license number."

"Don't you want to catch him?" Francesca asked.

"Depends on whether he's packing." Seeing her confusion, Donovan said, "Carrying a gun. He's probably come prepared tonight. That kind of confrontation we don't need."

She grimaced, but lapsed into silence.

As they neared the garage, Donovan cut a path well behind the building. Since he hadn't heard a car last night or tonight, he assumed the man had arrived on foot through the back of the property. He wouldn't have parked far away, though; he'd have to be prepared for an emergency.

All they had to do was wait. Time was on their side.

The sudden sound of a car turning into the driveway made Donovan stiffen. Even from behind the building he could detect the headlights sweeping toward them.

Jon Blakely had returned at the worst possible moment.

Donovan heard the whine of a remote-controlled garage door opening. "He's going to drive right in there!" Francesca whispered. "He'll run right into the thief!"

"I'd better go in."

"I'm coming with you!"

He pulled her against the building. "Stay here. Hug the wall. Damn it, do it my way, just this once!"

There was a ragged, reluctant intake of breath. Then, "Okay."

As he drew his gun and edged toward the rear door, Donovan's mind raced over possible scenarios. The intruder might attack Jon, he might bolt out the back and run straight into Donovan, or he might hide and wait for the owner to leave.

At the door, Donovan paused to listen for a clue to the interloper's whereabouts, but Jon's car was roaring loud enough to cover the sound of a herd of elephants. No sooner had the engine cut off than the garage door began its noisy descent.

Realizing his gun would require too much explaining to his boss, Donovan tucked it back in the holster, but didn't strap it. As he waited for the sound of Blakely's footsteps, he devised an excuse for his presence. He'd come to investigate the switched-off light, then seen the door open....

"Hey!" From inside the building, Jon's voice exploded with surprise. "What the—?"

Donovan burst into the brightly lit garage stall. He took in the scene instantly: Blakely clutching a briefcase as he pressed back against the rented Cadillac, struggling with a dark-clad man in a stocking mask. The robber's build was solid, muscular, and all too familiar from last night.

Blakely caught sight of Donovan. "Get that wrench!"

Donovan jerked the tool from a hook on the wall. But as he swung around, he heard Blakely's stifled oath and stopped, the wrench still held in midair.

The robber's gun was a big one, a .45. And it was aimed right at Jon Blakely's face.

"Drop it," said the masked man.

Donovan let the wrench fall with a clang to the concrete floor. He remembered Francesca's comment about his own gun. Not big enough. Not in his hand, either.

"Give me the suitcase." The man spoke in a snarl.

"Like hell!" Blakely said.

"Shut up and do it!"

In that brief moment, while the intruder's attention was turned to Blakely, Donovan dived forward. As the gun barrel shifted toward him, he hoped his boss wasn't the kind of man to panic in a crisis.

For a moment, Jon froze. Then, as if it were all happening in slow motion, Donovan saw him form a fist, saw the arm draw back and then punch forward. Donovan dodged, and heard a bullet scream past his ear.

Then came a crunch as Jon's fist connected with the side of the intruder's head.

The gunman shouted with pain, and the gun flew under Jon's car.

Donovan stopped short. Between him and Jon, the man was cornered. No sense getting beat up.

"Get some rope," Jon said. "Behind you."

Donovan grabbed it. The robber shifted and feinted, looking for a way out. But there wasn't one.

And then, with a grinding of gears, the damn garage door opened again. Just bloody opened. And the intruder fled, fast as a rabbit.

Donovan and Jon leaped to give chase, and collided so hard that Donovan saw little flashes of light. "Aw, hell..." He rubbed his bruised forehead.

"Your language is cleaner than our last handyman's. But we never banged our heads together, either." Blakely rubbed his temple. "Who opened the damn door?"

They both looked straight back at Francesca, who was still standing with her hand on the wall-mounted button.

"I thought you were in trouble. . . ." She let the words trail off. "I'm sorry."

Blakely took a deep breath. "You did your best. In any event, your husband saved my life. And this." He picked up the fallen briefcase.

The latch had broken loose. Before Blakely snapped it shut, Donovan caught a glimpse of thousand-dollar bills. A whole lot of them. Maybe half a million dollars' worth.

Chapter Eight

"The police must have given him the money," Francesca said when they were alone in their apartment.

"I don't suppose they felt too comfortable keeping that kind of cash around." Donovan winced as he peeled off his holster. "Now how did our burglar know about it?"

"One thing you have to admit—that crook isn't working for Jon." Francesca began unbuttoning his shirt. "I knew he was innocent."

Donovan was in no mood to make concessions. "We're just here to get the facts for Amanda."

"Does she pay you by the bruise? Because if she does, you're rich." Francesca examined a purple mark on his shoulder, a souvenir from the previous night.

"The only injury I got today was on my forehead," Donovan pointed out.

"Your chest is a lot more interesting." Laughter bubbled through their small, cozy living room.

"Could you please find a piece of ice?" Donovan didn't want to admit how appealing he found the idea of sharing a bedroom with Francesca. He didn't want to yield to the impulse to cup her chin in his hand and kiss the corners of her smile.

They were colleagues, darn it. They could be friends, but they couldn't be lovers. Before he knew it, he'd be afraid to take chances for fear she'd get hurt. He was glad he finally thought of that. Well, not too glad.

"Ice, coming right up." She emerged from the kitchen with some cubes tucked into a plastic bag. Donovan relaxed on the couch and let her press it to his forehead.

The injury went numb. But with Francesca draped along the sofa, with the soft swell of her breasts brushing his arm, the rest of Donovan came alive.

As a fiery hunger raced through his nerve endings, he tried to distract himself. "Where's the dog?" Even a canine interruption would be welcome at this point.

Okay, maybe *welcome* was the wrong word. Expedient. Sensible. And a real pain in the neck.

"Sleeping in the kitchen. Don't worry. He's been known to nap through fireworks on the Fourth of July."

"I thought he was a watchdog."

"The only thing he watches is his supper dish." Francesca sighed. "Unless a burglar brings his cat along, Asta wouldn't do a lick of good."

Donovan really didn't want to talk about the dog. He wanted to trace patterns with his fingers along Francesca's sleek thighs. He had only to bend his neck a little to kiss her. If only every joint and muscle didn't hurt.

"Still, Asta and I have bonded." The words came from far away as the ice was lifted from his forehead and Francesca reached to massage his back. "He doesn't really belong to me, you know. He's my friend."

Donovan heard himself mutter something. Maybe it was "Oh, right," or it could have been "Good night."

"Dogs are a lot smarter than people give them credit for. We call their intelligence 'instinct,' as if that makes it less important...."

Somewhere between the loyalty of guide dogs and the powers of bloodhounds, Donovan fell asleep.

HE AWOKE IN DARKNESS. He was still lying on the couch, and nearby a digital clock flicked silently from 2:15 to 2:16.

From the bedroom came the soft rhythm of Francesca's breathing. The clicking of toenails in the kitchen announced Asta's presence.

Donovan wasn't sure whether he'd awakened because of the dog, or because of his own aches. He could tell he'd never get back to sleep without a double dose of aspirin.

Stifling a groan, he lurched into the bathroom and flicked the switch. The light smashed into Donovan's eyes like a rifle butt, and he turned it off fast.

He found the aspirin bottle by moonlight and downed four pills, then staggered out. He was debating whether to join Francesca in bed when Asta padded in.

The dog crossed the room and scratched on the exterior door.

"What do you want?" As if that weren't obvious! "Can't you just use the bathroom? No, I guess not."

The apartment had its own private exit, and Donovan slogged over to let Asta out. He hoped the pooch would do its business with dispatch. He especially hoped there weren't any cats in the neighborhood.

The apartment lay above a slope, the closest part of the house to the garages. Donovan didn't see anything moving down there, thank goodness.

Then he heard a low growl. He waited, hoping whatever the dog had spotted would go away. A moment later, he sighed with relief when he saw Asta trotting toward him.

"Nothing there, huh?" Donovan said. "Good boy. Good—"

As if to mock him, a garage door churned open below, spilling out a rectangle of clear yellow. An engine roared, and Jon's rented Cadillac backed from the stall.

If Blakely was taking that money to a rendezvous, Donovan needed to be there. In any case, he had to find out what the millionaire was doing out at such an early hour.

He stuffed the dog back inside, grabbed his keys and wallet and dashed down the path, his muscles screaming with every step. He didn't realize until he'd reached the van that he'd forgotten his gun.

Too late to go back now.

The Cadillac was curving down the driveway, its headlights dappling the cypress trees. Donovan put the van into gear.

He managed to get his shirt buttoned one-handed as he tailed the car along night-dimmed streets. The lack of traffic, and the danger of being spotted, made him hang well back, and several times Jon's car vanished. Donovan guessed that his employer was heading for the freeway, and sure enough, he soon picked up the Cadillac again.

Where was Blakely going at this hour? He certainly couldn't conduct legitimate business. On the other hand, he didn't seem the type to hang out with the lowlifes who frequented all-night dives.

Donovan had to admit he'd begun to admire some qualities in the millionaire. Courage, tenacity, and just plain fairness. Another man might have yelled at Francesca for letting the intruder get away, but Jon had acknowledged her honest attempt to help.

Would a man like that really have arranged his wife's murder? The idealistic part of Donovan's character couldn't believe it. Yet there was a lot of money at stake; Jon's estate must be worth tens of millions.

One thing Donovan had learned: Where money was concerned, people would do almost anything. Even someone with courage, tenacity, and a sense of fair play.

He pressed his lips together grimly and stepped on the gas.

Only little blobs of sleepy headlights dotted the freeway at this hour. The occasional truck roared past, reveling in the freedom of the night.

Donovan had come to know the darkness well in his years as a detective. It had served as an accomplice that shielded him as he tailed suspects, a therapist that listened to his troubles, a confessor that absolved him of his sins.

In a way, it was the night that had changed his life.

Donovan found it hard to remember now the young man he had been only six years ago. Mr. Perfect, the up-and-coming lawyer turned prosecutor.

Some of his father's friends had tabbed him as a future politician with all the right credentials, and Donovan hadn't disagreed with them. He'd imagined he was making a difference, righting the world's wrongs while building his own spotless reputation.

Like all prosecutors, he lost some cases that he felt he should have won, but that was par for the course. He even reluctantly accepted the acquittal of Joss Marten, who cold-bloodedly murdered a rival for his girlfriend and then intimidated the witnesses.

Donovan tried to tell himself the jury knew best, that perhaps Joss really had been framed. Or that, at the very least, Joss had vented his rage at society and was no longer a threat.

He would never forget the night a few months later when he had returned from a political fund-raising ball.

The phone was ringing; it was a contact at the police department. Joss Marten had been arrested for murder again. He'd shot a man after an argument, and accidentally killed an innocent bystander.

Two more victims had paid for Donovan's failure to convict Joss Marten.

All night, drifting between wakefulness and fitful dreams, Donovan relived that earlier trial. He thought of the things he might have done differently, and of the tricks Marten and his defense attorney had played. Evidence excluded on technicalities, witnesses who fled the country, a police detective made to look foolish simply because he'd entered a few minor discrepancies in his report.

Afterward, the defense attorney had made a statement to the press. "The system works. It has freed my client."

The system had freed his client, all right, but it hadn't worked. Two more men lay dead that night, men who would have lived had Marten been behind bars.

Donovan spent a lot of sleepless nights after that, pacing aimlessly or driving on the freeway, trying to sort out his thoughts. Finally he realized that he couldn't go on being part of the system.

It meant taking his career back to square one. He moved to California, where Eli recommended him for a job with a private investigator. Three years later, when he qualified for his own license, Donovan poured his savings into starting a business. So far, it had proven precarious even in the best of times.

Sometimes, on nights like this, when he ached all over, Donovan wondered if he'd made a mistake. He could have gone through life as one of the golden people, never getting his hands dirty or worrying about where the next check was coming from.

He couldn't even be sure he'd done more good as a detective than he would have as a prosecutor. But he slept better at night.

Most nights, anyway. Not this one.

Blakely's car veered off the freeway in one of the seedier areas of Santa Ana. Donovan exited, keeping his distance.

He smelled a payoff. Millionaires didn't drive to bad areas at night, possibly toting huge sums of money, if they weren't mixed up in shady business.

The Cadillac jounced over a pothole and slowed; Donovan did the same. It was hard to keep the van out of sight with so few cars around, and he hung back further than he would have liked. Then he had to scoot through a yellow light, or he'd have risked losing Jon altogether.

The Caddy turned abruptly into the parking lot of a bowling alley. A neon sign blinked on and off, announcing a twenty-four-hour coffee shop.

A handful of vehicles sprinkled the cracked pavement, giving Donovan a chance to park unnoticed behind a peeling camper. He watched as the rental car claimed a slot near the entrance.

The Caddy drew stares from three young men lounging around a row of newspaper racks. With their greasy hair and their military-style boots, they didn't look like the bowling-league type to Donovan.

Jon sat in his car for a while. Maybe he was early, or maybe he was just suspicious of the young men. With good reason, Donovan thought.

They were giving the Cadillac a thorough inspection. Then one of them nudged another, and they all planted themselves in place. Waiting, coolly and arrogantly, for Jon to get out.

Donovan tapped his fingers against the steering wheel. He wouldn't be able to go to Blakely's rescue, not without revealing himself and raising a whole lot of unanswerable questions.

All he could do would be to dial 911 at the first sign of danger and hope the police could get here fast enough. On the other hand, maybe those guys just intended to panhandle.

Yeah, and maybe cows could fly.

Five minutes passed and no one moved. A standoff. Donovan was beginning to think Blakely would drive away, when the door to the Cadillac swung open.

The millionaire had dressed down for the occasion, in jeans and a polo shirt. Even from here, though, Donovan could see the expensive logo on the shirt and the designer cut of the jeans.

One of the men crumpled a beer can and tossed it into the bushes.

Jon paused, briefcase in hand. Calculating the distance to the entrance, weighing how fast to walk and how to respond to any interruption.

The guy had a cool head. But that might not be enough.

It wasn't. As Jon stepped forward, the three men fanned out to block his path.

Donovan picked up the car phone.

He saw Jon murmur something and try to move around the men. They moved with him. He took another step, and so did they. One of them, the biggest, ambled forward and favored Jon with an unpleasant grin.

After only the briefest of hesitations, Blakely lowered his head and charged like a bull. Caught off guard, the bully went sprawling. Jon himself stumbled to his knees as a second punk reached into his pocket and flicked open a knife.

Donovan knew the police couldn't get there in time. He leaped out of the van, but there was no way he could would be there fast enough to prevent a tragedy.

He heard the motorcycle before he saw it, thundering toward the bowling alley with its headlight flashing. The assailants shielded their eyes as they turned to look.

The bike slammed straight toward them, the headlight switching on and off. Donovan couldn't see the driver, only a ghostly blur.

The men backed up, but the cycle didn't slow. Damn, it was going to run over the whole lot of them.

The same thought must have occurred to the attackers, who edged away and then broke into full flight. Jon stood his ground a second longer and then dived for his car.

As the cycle boomed past, Donovan got the bizarre impression that it was driven by some unearthly creature. A translucent shape swirled and billowed, like a jellyfish in the open air.

It must be too little sleep and overstressed nerves. Donovan rubbed his eyes to clear them.

The noise slowed as the cycle swung around, past the spot where the men had stood. It grumbled toward Donovan and then halted in a pool of silence.

The odd figure slid to the ground and pulled off its helmet, dark hair spilling free. "What the heck were you doing?" Francesca said. "Jon could have been killed!"

She wore a diaphanous blue robe over a shimmery nightgown. Her slender feet sported tufted open-heeled slippers.

"Have you lost your mind?" Donovan snapped. "You can't go riding around on a motorcycle dressed like that!"

"I'm decent," she said. "Besides, I didn't have time to change. Asta barely woke me up in time to see you leaving."

"I had everything under control." He didn't mean to lie, but it infuriated him to realize how easily Francesca could have been injured. From the corner of his eye, Donovan saw the Cadillac spin away, and lashed out. "Now you've scared him off! I'll never find out who he planned to meet."

"We could go inside and look," Francesca suggested.

"Dressed like that?"

"You could go inside and look."

"Only if you wait in the van. And let me drive you home."

She nodded reluctantly and sat in the van while Donovan took a quick tour of the coffee shop. Whoever Blakely had planned to meet must have given up or been scared off, because the place was empty except for a weary-looking waitress and two teenagers smooching in a booth.

"No luck," he said when he returned. His nerves were still humming from Jon's close encounter and Francesca's startling rescue.

"He probably just wanted to bowl a few games."

"On a scale of one to ten, one being likely and ten being next to impossible, I give it a twelve."

"You never did like Jon! You're just biased!" Francesca grinned as she helped him load the bike into the van, vibrating with excitement from her adventure. Donovan wished she'd exhibit at least a trace of nerves. Didn't she realize she could have been seriously injured?

"What do you think was in the suitcase, his bowling ball?" Donovan snapped.

"There's no call for sarcasm," she said. "He might have just wanted a cup of coffee." A pause. "No, I guess not."

As they drove home, the night's events replayed themselves in Donovan's mind. He couldn't stop thinking that Francesca might have been killed.

"I can't believe—" he began.

"You're not going to scold me again!" She spoke so quickly, she must have been waiting for his remark.

"Well, going around dressed like that—"

"This is perfectly appropriate for nighttime."

"Outdoors?" Donovan's gaze swept over her. "I can practically see through it."

"That's an illusion. Only the robe is transparent." Francesca held her head high. "Anyway, nobody on the freeway seemed to mind. I got cheers."

Donovan shuddered. "You're lucky you didn't get arrested."

"And you're the one who claims the coppers aren't the enemy!"

He was too tired to quarrel. Besides, even if he argued her into a corner, Francesca would never concede victory.

They had exited the freeway when she spoke again. "Are you that angry?"

"Excuse me?"

"You haven't said anything for a long time."

"What's the point?"

"Am I fired?" she asked.

"How can I fire my wife?" Donovan stretched his shoulders, and instantly regretted it as pain arrowed down his back. "I can't believe we have to work tomorrow. I mean today."

"Do you think Jon recognized me?" She reached over and rubbed his neck. "It could make him suspicious, don't you think?"

"Why? I'll bet all his housekeepers ride around on motorcycles in their nighties, scaring the wits out of criminals," Donovan said.

"It might start a trend," she suggested.

Their eyes met, and it was as if a spark had hit tinder. And then they were laughing, howling so hard Donovan could hardly keep the van on the road.

"I must have looked like some kind of nut!" Francesca gasped.

"I thought you were a jellyfish from hell!"

That sent them off into fresh gales, and it was with relief that Donovan at last pulled into a space by the garages. He wasn't sure he could have driven much farther without hitting a tree.

After making sure Jon's car was indeed safely inside, they went back to their apartment. Asta, who had awakened them to the night's activities, lay snoozing on the couch.

Donovan considered rousting him, then decided he and Francesca might as well get used to sharing a bed. They'd simply have to exercise some self-control, that was all.

He hadn't counted on Francesca.

No sooner had Donovan closed the door than she stripped off her bathrobe and the nightgown.

"Whoa!" he said. "What do you think you're doing?"

Moonlight streamed through the window, caressing her sleek skin and her smoothly rounded hips. "You can't see anything. It's dark." Francesca tossed her clothes in the hamper.

"I can see plenty."

"Well, don't look." She headed for the bathroom. "Honestly, Donovan. I need a shower after that little excursion, or I'll never get to sleep. Don't make a big deal out of nothing."

"Now I'm going to need a *cold* shower, or *I'll* never get to sleep!" he retorted.

She paused in the bathroom doorway, a Venus in silhouette. "If we're going to share this apartment, you can't be drooling every time I change clothes. Think of me as one of the guys."

Before he could answer, she closed the door.

Donovan sat in the dark, grinding his teeth. A few minutes ago he'd been too exhausted to do anything but fall into a sound sleep. Now he could think of nothing but the moonlight singing across Francesca's curves.

In his experience, the best way to fight fire was with fire. Besides, he had to teach her to exercise a little modesty, or they'd never get through the next few days.

Donovan shed his clothes, trying not to wince as he moved. The hot water was going to feel great.

Briefly, before he opened the bathroom door, he wondered if he might upset Francesca. But to her he was just one of the guys, right?

Donovan tapped on the shower door, then clicked it open and stepped into the oversize tub.

"Hey!" Soapy water trickled down Francesca's throat and through the valley between her breasts. "What do you think you're doing?"

"Taking a shower," Donovan said. "Pay no attention."

Her dark hair clung to her slender neck. "How can I help it? You're taking up the whole tub!"

"There's plenty of room," he pointed out. "You move to that end and I'll stay over here."

"No way! I'd freeze over there!" She stood defiantly beneath the spray.

"Okay, if that's the way you want it." Donovan squeezed in beside her. He had to admit it wasn't entirely fair, since he was bigger and took up the lion's share of the water, but she'd asked for it.

Francesca regarded his chest. "You're one of those bodybuilders, aren't you?"

"I work out," Donovan admitted as he soaped his arms. "It's all part of keeping in shape for my job."

"Don't tell me you strike poses in front of a mirror at the gym." She shook her head. "Come on, you didn't get that tight stomach by accident. You work at it. Total narcissism, right?"

"I told you, I like being fit." The water soothed away his tension. Well, some of it.

"You must drive women wild."

"You're a woman." He grinned at her. "How come I don't drive you wild?"

"Who says you don't?" She bit her lip. "I didn't mean that."

As a detective, Donovan prided himself on his insight into human nature, but now the realization struck him that where Francesca was concerned he hadn't been paying attention. She projected such an air of detachment that it had never occurred to Donovan she might be bluffing.

It occurred to him now.

"You mean I'm not just one of the guys?" he said.

"If you'll quit hogging the water, I'll rinse off and get out of here."

He decided he'd pushed her far enough. "Okay. If you insist."

Maybe it was a sliver of soap on the bottom of the tub. Or maybe it was luck. As Francesca moved forward, she slipped, and Donovan caught her. Her body touched his; he expected her to pull away, but she didn't.

The woman who gazed up at him was someone new, her eyes bright with longing, her skin seeking his. Francesca poured over him like liquid, bathing him in her sensuality. Donovan needed to touch every inch of her, to arouse and satisfy her.

They knelt together, water flying around them, mouths linked and bodies melting. She murmured endearments, her hair swirling in the water, and arched to kiss him again.

Donovan had known desire before, but never like this. Some part of him had always held back. Not now. Not with Francesca.

He wanted more from her, more than they could share in one moment or one night. He wanted to explore her, to coax her into revelations, and to reveal himself. He wanted dangerous things.

"Kiss me," Francesca whispered. "With your whole self."

He claimed her with a mixture of tenderness and urgency. He felt her around him, yielding and demanding, soaring with him.

They flew through uncharted skies, tantalizing each other onward. As Francesca matched him stroke for stroke, Donovan felt some wild spirit break loose deep inside himself, rocketing with her toward bursts of color in a sapphire sky.

At last they smashed into the heavens, tumbling in each others' arms, clinging and calling out. Donovan could not believe it would ever end.

Yet, in time, he felt the shower spattering on his back. Francesca sighed and sat up, wringing water from her hair.

"Let's do that again," Donovan said.

She laughed. "I know you're in good condition, but it's four o'clock in the morning, and we have to be up in three hours."

"Who cares?" But the unwelcome aches and pains seeped back, and Donovan's eyelids grew heavy. "Did you have to remind me?"

"Come dry my back," she said, and hopped up.

A few minutes later, he had wrapped her in a fuzzy towel and was smoothing away moisture from behind one of her shell-like ears. Donovan wanted to talk about what had happened between them, how everything had changed. Surely she felt it too. "That was special," he said.

Francesca ran her hand across his chest. "You put all those muscles to good use, I'll say that for you."

"It wasn't just physical!"

Her expression softened. "No. I—" She chopped the words off. "I knew I'd enjoy detective work."

"Hey!" Donovan didn't know whether to laugh or snap her with the towel.

Francesca strode into the bedroom and pulled a terry-cloth robe from the closet. "This doesn't change anything, you know."

"The hell it doesn't!"

He would have pursued the matter right then and there, except for one little problem. As Francesca climbed into the bed on the left side, Asta jumped in on the right.

"He always sleeps there," she said before Donovan could protest. "If you throw him out, he'll never give us a moment's peace."

She had withdrawn like a turtle into its shell. Except he'd never seen a turtle with fiery dark eyes and a soul to match.

"You won't get away with this," Donovan said.

"Go get some sleep. You're dead on your feet." She rolled over, away from him.

Donovan decided it wouldn't do any good to shake her into wakefulness and talk about how they were going to work together and what they meant to each other. He'd have to deal with Francesca tomorrow, or maybe the day after that.

Sometime when his eyes weren't drooping. Sometime when random dreams didn't keep fuzzing up his thoughts.

He shoved Asta over and slid into bed. After all, he had only a few hours until the house filled with maids and gardeners and, perhaps, a few more clues to a murder.

Chapter Nine

Donovan awoke to full daylight flooding the room. He groped for the clock on the bedside table and discovered, to his relief, that it was only seven o'clock.

A glance across the bed found it empty and neat, as if Francesca had never slept there. Even the dog had decamped.

As he shaved and dressed, Donovan wondered about the previous night. She'd responded without reservation, and then she'd pulled back. Why? What did Francesca *want*? And why didn't she want it from him?

He couldn't go on working with her under these conditions. It was what he'd always feared, an entanglement that interfered with his concentration.

They had a job to finish here, and Donovan would do his best. Then, unless he and Francesca could work out a less volatile relationship, they would have to part company.

Not at all pleased by that prospect, he went in search of breakfast.

Marta had set out a spread of bacon, eggs and potatoes fit for a king. The cook hummed as she emptied the dishwasher. There was no trace of Francesca.

Donovan noticed that the kitchen, although large and airy, suffered from benign neglect. The cabinets looked dark and dated, the wide tile counters were marked by stained grout, and the flowered wallpaper had faded from repeated washings.

He could see that Cindy Blakely hadn't taken much interest in the kitchen.

"Your wife's an early riser," said the cook. "Help yourself to the food. Mr. Blakely had a tray in his room, and there's plenty left."

Donovan engaged Marta in conversation as he ate. He learned that the gardeners would arrive in an hour and would require supervision, and that the repair shop had called to say the station wagon was fixed. Other than that, the house was in good working order; he should have plenty of time to snoop.

From a side hallway he could hear women chattering in Spanish, and he realized the day maids had arrived. To his surprise, he recognized Francesca's voice among them, also speaking Spanish.

"Your wife's amazing," Marta said. "Where did she learn all those languages?"

Donovan choked on his coffee. All what languages? "She's, er, Italian," he said fumbling. "So, well, Spanish is pretty close."

The cook mopped up his spilled coffee from the table. "Where did she learn German?"

Francesca spoke German? "Germany's, um, not far from Italy," Donovan improvised.

"She speak anything else?" Marta poured him more coffee.

"English." He was relieved when she chuckled.

Somewhere a vacuum cleaner roared to life. "I'll say one thing for Francesca, she's the best-organized housekeeper we've had," Marta said. "She found all sorts of things that need doing. And you know what? She's right. No one's cleaned the molding in the bathrooms in months."

Well organized? Francesca certainly was full of surprises this morning. "We always have spotless molding," Donovan said. "Especially in the bathroom."

"You two make a nice couple," said the cook. "Some people are just suited to each other. Not like... Well, I don't normally gossip."

If she needed urging, Donovan was more than ready. "We're part of the family now," he said. "Mr. and Mrs. Blakely had their problems, I take it? That's too bad."

He sipped his coffee and waited.

"At first, he was wild about her," Marta said. "She was so pretty and lively. Mr. Blakely got lonely up here. She used to go to the theater with him, the opera and the ballet. But after a while her real tastes came out—that screeching music, heavy metal, whatever they call it, and dance places where people show up in their underwear."

Donovan prodded gently, and bit by bit the story came out. First the couple had quarreled over Cindy's partying, her coming and going as she pleased. Then they'd fought over her friends and her extravagant spending.

"That last day, well, they really had at it. You could hear them all over the house." Marta took bowls and a hand mixer from the cabinet. "He accused her of stealing. She said that this was a community-property state, and what belonged to him belonged to her, so she had no reason to steal."

She went on to say that Blakely had accused his wife of taking money and artworks, and she'd hotly denied it. According to Marta, either Cindy was a better actress than anyone believed, or she'd been honestly affronted.

Sympathetic as he felt toward a hapless murder victim, Donovan had to admit that finding half a million dollars in Cindy's car did seem to justify Blakely's accusations. But it didn't answer the question of why she would take the money, when she was legally entitled to so much more.

Donovan had no chance to investigate further during the next few hours as he made sure the gardeners trimmed the bushes and replaced spent petunias. He failed to catch even a glimpse of Blakely.

At lunch, Francesca snatched a sandwich and darted back to work before Donovan could get out more than a greeting. There were, he decided, advantages to sharing rooms. At some point she'd have to face him.

By three o'clock, the gardeners had departed. Tenley had been at the soap plant all day, and Donovan saw his employer heading toward the bedroom wing for what Marta had described as his usual afternoon nap. Donovan guessed that gave him perhaps half an hour to search Jon's office.

He needed a cover, in case he was spotted. He mulled over the possibilities while angling the riding lawn mower into the utility shed.

Paint almost always needed touching-up, but the samples he spotted in the shed didn't look the right color for Blakely's office.

As he walked out, still considering his options, a scraping sound from the side of the house snapped Donovan to attention.

Francesca, a rope wrapped around her waist, was braced overhead, washing a second-floor window. Dark hair formed long tendrils around her neck.

As Donovan stared in disbelief, she lowered herself toward the window to Blakely's office.

"What are you doing?" he yelled. Francesca reacted with a jerk, lost her balance and slipped until she dangled helplessly between the first and second floors.

"You idiot!" was the kindest thing Donovan could find to say as he ran to her rescue. He stood beneath Francesca, gripped her ankles and pushed her up until the rope slackened. She seemed to take forever untying herself, and then, without warning, she flopped right on top of Donovan, knocking them both flat on the ground.

After a breathless moment, Donovan staggered to his feet and reached for her hand. "What the—?"

"You scared me!" Francesca jumped up, ignoring the offer of help. "You ought to be more careful!"

"Me? *I* ought to—?" He swallowed the rest of the retort. "What did you think you were doing?"

"Getting into Jon's study! In case you've forgotten, we didn't come here to chase dust balls!"

"Would you forgive me for pointing out that Blakely's office is on the ground floor?" Donovan heard the irony dripping from his voice, but he couldn't help it. "I hardly see the need for hanging in midair like a trapeze artist."

"I wanted to look authentic. That way, if anyone saw me fooling with the window, they wouldn't get suspicious."

"Some people stand on a ladder to wash their windows," Donovan said.

She followed his gaze up the side of the house. "I couldn't find one. All I found was the rope. Okay, I guess I overdid it. I'll go take it down, and then we can pry the window open."

Donovan slipped the master key ring from his pocket. "Why don't we just open the door?"

It was the first time he'd seen Francesca at a loss. "Oh." She recovered quickly. "How come the housekeeper doesn't have keys like that?"

Donovan shrugged. "The fewer keys floating around, the less chance of one disappearing."

"I suppose that's a practical point of view." Francesca studied the rope drooping overhead and began to laugh. "Oh, Donovan! Can you imagine? I must have looked positively ridiculous. I *felt* positively ridiculous! And I thought I was being so clever."

"Well, you're certainly original," he admitted. "Just get the thing down, will you?"

"I have to run up to the attic. Wait for me?"

"No." They'd already wasted too much time. "It's too risky."

"You don't have to protect me!" Francesca snapped. "Darn it, why are men always like that?"

"Like what?"

"Like you!"

Had any woman ever been so infuriating? "You mean because I saved you from breaking your neck?"

"I wouldn't have fallen if you hadn't startled me!"

"I was just trying to... Never mind." She was right, Donovan realized. He'd wanted to protect her.

Well, so what? Was it a crime for a man's heart to go into a nosedive when he saw his lover nearly fall two stories? Was it hopelessly chauvinistic to want to keep her safe?

In any event, this was no time for an argument. "Get the rope, and then return Blakely's rental car and pick up the station wagon. The key and the address are on the kitchen table."

Francesca opened and closed her mouth a few times, then stalked off.

Pushing away the vague sense that he was being unfair, Donovan went into the house, collecting a supply of light bulbs from a service closet. The darn things were always burning out, even in millionaires' houses; it was as good an excuse as any to go into Blakely's office.

He hadn't counted on Tenley Feinstein.

She wasn't expected back today, and Donovan hadn't heard her come in. But when he stepped into her office en route to Blakely's, he saw that he'd miscalculated.

"Yes?" The single word dripped acid as Tenley swung away from her computer.

"Thought you might need some bulbs changed."

She regarded him over half glasses. He decided she was younger than he'd thought at first, despite the gray in her hair. "If I need you, I'll call you."

"Sure thing." Donovan tried to appear pleasantly thick-skulled as he searched for a way to draw her out. His gaze fell on the photograph decorating her desk. "You have beautiful children."

"My niece and nephew," she said.

"Well, they're cute." If he couldn't search the office, he could at least start getting to know the prickly Ms. Feinstein. "Francesca and I, we really like it here."

"That's quite a conclusion after, what—twenty-four hours?" she said. "I'm glad you're so good-natured. Now why don't you take those light bulbs into the guest wing?"

"Sure thing." Donovan walked away, scolding himself for not having come up with a more brilliant opening. He'd found that in most cases a little conversation could sluice away debris and uncover golden nuggets of information.

But he could hardly ask Tenley Feinstein if she'd helped her boss murder his wife, now could he?

Donovan attended to the guest wing and then called Eli Jonas at the police department. He confirmed that the money from Cindy's car had been turned over to Blakely last night.

"We photographed it and logged it in," the lieutenant said. "Beyond that, I don't want it around. Too much money to be responsible for."

Donovan described the night's activities. "I wonder who Blakely was meeting with all that money, assuming that's what was in the suitcase."

"I don't know, but I did run across another interesting point." Donovan could picture Jonas leaning back in his chair and plopping his feet on the desk. "Blakely filed a theft report about his last housekeeper and her husband, and another one about the ex-chauffeur."

"A real nest of thieves, huh?" Tenley had said the couple was fired for stealing, but there'd been no such comment about the chauffeur. "You think they did it, or is he paranoid?"

"The housekeeper returned a silver service, soup spoons and all. Since she made restitution, he declined to press charges," Eli said.

"How about the chauffeur?"

"Blakely said the man had been pilfering petty cash, taking spare parts, that kind of thing. When we checked, we found out the guy had a record as long as your arm. Thomas Moorehouse. Armed robbery, extortion, that kind of thing."

"Wonder how he got hired," Donovan said.

"Seems he was a chum of Mrs. Blakely's." Eli broke off abruptly. After a moment, he said, "I've got to go. Catch you later, Donny boy."

"Thanks. Thanks a lot."

So Cindy's friends left something to be desired. That might mean she had a kind heart, giving the guy a second chance. Or it might mean she hung out with the wrong kind of people.

An ex-con. Could he have killed Cindy for reasons of his own? Was he the person who'd arranged to meet her on the cliff that fatal night?

If there were shadows in Cindy's past, surely her sister would know. Donovan made a mental note to check with Amanda. But in the meantime he'd been hired to investigate Jon Blakely, not the chauffeur.

He couldn't get into the office today. But tonight, after Ms. Feinstein left, he was going in, no matter what.

"WELL?" FRANCESCA SAID. "Find anything?"

They were sitting on the patio after dinner, playing cards. It had been Francesca's turn to choose the game, and over Donovan's objections she'd picked the children's game Go Fish.

The sun was yawning its last, spiking the deep blue sky with gold and rose. A cacophonous flock of birds settled into trees around the estate.

"Got any tens?" said Donovan.

"Go fish."

He took a three off the deck and discarded a jack. "Tenley Feinstein was guarding the door. I couldn't get in."

"If I'd been there, I would have distracted her," said Francesca. "Aces?"

He handed her a pair.

"Sevens?"

He gave her one.

"Threes?"

He tossed one over. "No wonder you like this game. You must have X-ray eyes."

"I'm lucky." She laid down a book of four sevens. Donovan couldn't believe he was not only playing a child's game, but losing, as well.

"How about you?" he said. "What did you find?"

"Me?" Francesca frowned. "I went to get the car, remember?"

"That's right." Donovan asked for tens again, didn't get any, and drew an ace. He slipped it into his cards, looking forward to besting her next time. "That's the car Blakely's been using. Not to mention the former house-keeper and probably the chauffeur. No telling what might turn up in the cracks."

"I never thought of that." Francesca frowned. "I'm sorry. I'll take care of it as soon as I can. Got any aces?"

"You're cheating!" He tossed her the card.

"I told you, I'm lucky." She nodded toward the parking lot. "There they go."

Donovan turned to see Tenley Feinstein folding herself into her car. The assistant gave a brief nod of acknowledgment to Marta, who was heading for her own battered auto.

"Wonder what Jon's got on tap for tonight?" Francesca murmured.

"You stay out of his office!"

"Why?" she asked challengingly. "You don't need me to do any more fetching and carrying, do you? Come on, Donovan, let's have this out. I want to learn how to investigate, not serve as your flunky."

"Okay, let's lay our cards on the table. Figuratively and literally." He dumped his hand on the discard stack. "One thing you have to get through your head. I'm your boss. You want to learn the ropes, you follow orders."

"I'm not going to learn the ropes supervising the maids." Francesca completed a book of aces and set them neatly on the table before dumping the rest of her cards. "You're not trying to teach me, Donovan. You're trying to protect me."

"I'm trying to keep you from screwing things up! That caper with the rope..."

"You didn't get inside, either," she reminded him. "Don't change the subject. Now that we're lovers, you want to lock me up in a cage and bring me out for show-and-tell. Well, I won't have it!"

"Where'd you get that idea?" She wasn't entirely wrong, but she wasn't entirely right, either. "Just because we're...friends, that doesn't mean I want to own you."

Donovan definitely wanted more of what they'd experienced last night. He wanted to taste the salty sweetness of Francesca's skin and to feel her respond with a shudder of desire. He wanted to fly with her, twisting and turning with her across unexpected heights.

But he would never try to banish the impishness in her eyes or the tenacity in that uplifted chin. He wanted the real Francesca, not some Kewpie-doll version.

"Men can't help it," she said. "When they love you, they hold on too tight. I learned that from my parents. And my own experience, too."

Donovan shuffled the cards and returned them to their case. "I'm not your father or one of your ex-boyfriends, whatever they were like."

For a fleeting moment, Francesca's lips parted and her expression grew gentle. "I know. I know that, Donovan. But in the long run..."

"I don't live for the long run," he said. "Neither do you."

"My dad loved my mother." Fading pink light glowed in her eyes. "And she loved him, more than anything. Except that when she started to fly airplanes, when she needed to spend time away from him, he couldn't handle it. He couldn't let her go and trust that she'd come back. The divorce nearly killed them both. It nearly killed me, too."

"They could have worked it out," Donovan said.

She shook her head. "Mom couldn't live like a prisoner. She couldn't guarantee he'd always be able to reach her by phone. She couldn't promise to come home whenever he felt lonely. Why can't a man let a woman be everything she is, even if it takes her away from him? I have this wildness, Donovan. It's always going to be there."

He had to ask the most painful question of all. "And someday you think you're going to meet a man who's as wild as you are and can make you happy?"

Surprise flickered in her eyes. "If there were ever going to be a man like that, it would be you."

"Then give me a chance."

"There's no point. Look, we can still have fun together. Just don't try to hold on to me," Francesca said.

He wanted to argue that she was judging him without evidence. But, as much as he hated to concede it, she was right.

Donovan could imagine how empty he would feel if she took off for Alaska and he didn't know when she might return. He'd try to talk her out of it. He might even follow her.

And she couldn't accept that much possessiveness.

"How about you?" he said. "Wouldn't you care if I wasn't around when you needed someone to talk to or to share Christmas with?"

Francesca stared at the pool below; its water was touched with peach and scarlet. "I'm not sentimental. I don't live for the future, and I don't regret the past. I enjoy where I am right now."

Donovan hoped she didn't know herself as well as she believed. But he couldn't prove it.

The sky was fading, and from the corner of his eye he saw lights pop on in the wing where Blakely's bedroom was. "Looks like the coast is clear," he said. "The way our host likes to wander around in the middle of the night, this may be the safest time."

Francesca raised an eyebrow in an unspoken question.

"No," Donovan said. "You're not coming."

She let out a long breath. "That's okay. I've got other stuff to do anyway."

"You promise to behave?" He stood up. "I'm still your boss, even if you are kicking me out of bed."

"I'm not kicking you anywhere, and I've sworn off ropes and pulleys forever." Francesca collected the cards and their coffee cups. "I'll clean up. I am the housekeeper, after all. And, by the way, those cards were marked."

"I knew it!" he said.

"They're Cindy's cards," she noted. "If you'd been paying attention, you'd have noticed."

She clattered away with the cups before he could think of a response.

DONOVAN TURNED THE KEY in the lock and stepped inside Blakely's office. He saw at once that, unlike during the interview, the couches and desk were littered with notes, file folders, even a pouch of pipe tobacco.

He swept the room with his flashlight and decided to start at the desk. A thick ledger book sat on the top, and Donovan flipped through it. Maybe it held some cosmic significance, but the columns of numbers and the abbreviations scrawled down the left margin meant nothing to him.

Next he turned to the drawers, and was surprised to find them unlocked. Inside lay neat stacks of stationery supplies. He found nothing useful, not even an address book.

Donovan assumed Blakely kept his personal papers in a safe. He found the safe located—rather tritely, in his opinion—behind one of the paintings.

That hefty combination lock wasn't going to yield to casual fiddling. He doubted even Francesca could get it open.

Donovan muttered an oath and turned to the crumpled notes.

He was leaning down to pick one up when he heard the slap of shoes in the outer office. The step was confident, like that of a man who owned the place.

Blakely had come back, and the minute he turned the knob he'd realize the door was unlocked.

Donovan sank down behind the couch and wished at least he'd brought the bloody light bulbs along. A thin excuse was better than none.

The phone rang.

The shrilling shocked through Donovan's nervous system. He felt himself lift a good inch from the carpet.

One line on the desk phone lit up. Blakely must have taken the call in Tenley's office.

Distantly Donovan heard his employer speaking. "Yes? Where the hell have you been?"

A brief pause. "Well, you saw what happened," Jon snapped. "I had to leave. Now we've got to meet." Another silence. Then: "I don't want to discuss this over the phone. Okay. I'll see you there."

The light went dead. Donovan held his breath until the footsteps retreated.

Blakely must be heading for his rendezvous.

Although his instincts urged him to hurry, Donovan waited several minutes. Then he slipped out of the office, pausing every few steps to listen.

In the kitchen, Donovan glanced out the window, and his heart skipped a beat. Blakely stood directly outside, muttering to himself and turning as if he'd left something behind.

Before Donovan could react, their eyes met.

"Oh, hey," called the millionaire. "I forgot to lock the back door. See to it, will you?"

"Sure thing," said Donovan.

That reminded him to go back and lock the office door, as well. Then he hurried to get Francesca. After all, he'd promised to train her, hadn't he?

In the apartment, Asta sprang to greet Donovan with a low whine. Donovan called for Francesca, but there was no sign of her.

He couldn't wait.

When he opened the outside door, Asta leaped ahead of him.

"Hey!" Donovan called. "Back! Come back!" He might as well have been talking to the wind.

Well, the pooch would just have to stay out until Donovan returned. Or, more likely, until Francesca did.

He saw the garage door lumbering open. Blakely hadn't wasted any time.

Picking his way in the darkness, not daring to use the flashlight, Donovan hurried down to his van. As he opened it, a furry body flashed inside.

"Out!" he whispered sharply.

A tail thumped the seat in response.

Oh, *hell!* This was no time to struggle with Asta. He'd just have to put up with the pooch.

Every muscle taut, Donovan waited as the station wagon backed out. He didn't dare turn on the engine until Jon was safely out of earshot.

Then Asta began to bark.

"Shut up!" Donovan said.

The dog gave him a reproachful look, but fell silent.

The garage door closed with a motorized whir. The station wagon straightened and pulled forward.

Suddenly Asta leaped against the window, toenails clicking on the glass, and uttered three sharp yips. Donovan caught him by the collar and pulled, feeling the dog's body wriggle in defiance.

"Would you cut it out?" He tried to keep his voice low.

Asta groaned as if something were terribly wrong.

Something caught Donovan's eye, something moving in the back compartment of the station wagon. For a confused moment, he wondered if Blakely was transporting a pet.

Then a terrified face pressed against the rear windshield for an instant before disappearing.

Francesca.

Donovan's heart thundered. She must have gone to search the car and panicked when Blakely came in. In his hurry, he probably hadn't even glanced into the back.

Now Francesca, unarmed and unprepared, was on her way with Blakely—perhaps to meet a killer.

Donovan twisted the key in the ignition and threw the van into gear.

Chapter Ten

The cars wove through light traffic onto the freeway. It didn't take long for Donovan to realize that the station wagon was probably heading for the same bowling alley as before.

He had to fight the instinct to force Blakely to the shoulder and rescue Francesca. Intellectually he knew she faced no immediate danger, but, damn it, he worried about her even if she didn't want him to.

By the time they exited the freeway, however, Donovan's fear had taken on an edge of annoyance. Francesca must not have turned on the overhead light while searching the car, or Blakely would have known someone was there.

No, she'd been skulking around with a flashlight like some old-time movie heroine. Why couldn't she just behave sensibly? If she'd gone out there as if nothing were wrong, she could have claimed to have lost some item in the back of the car. Blakely would have accepted the explanation, and no harm done.

Better yet, why not wait until morning, when she'd probably have some reason to drive the car anyway? But Francesca had to be dramatic. Had to put herself in jeopardy.

He put out of his mind the memory of himself ducking behind a couch in Jon's office. He was *supposed* to run risks. She wasn't.

The frustrating part, Donovan discovered as he trailed the station wagon into the parking lot, was that Francesca's voice, or some passable imitation of it, had implanted itself in his mind.

He could hear her responding, "Why shouldn't I run risks? That's part of being a detective! When you try to protect me, you deny me a chance to prove what I can do."

She was right. And that made him even grouchier.

Donovan parked where he could see the station wagon in his mirror. There were no hoods hanging around the newspaper racks tonight, thank goodness.

He watched Blakely get out of the car carrying the suitcase and stride into the coffee shop.

In the jumbled back of the van, Donovan found a couple of baseball caps left over from a Little League team he'd coached a few years back. It was the best he could do for disguises on short notice.

He slid open the door and discovered three things: that the young toughs had reappeared, that Francesca had emerged from the station wagon, and that, once again, he hadn't brought his gun.

Maybe he ought to call the police before plunging to Francesca's aid. But one of the hooligans had taken her arm and was bending over her with a leering expression.

Rage exploded inside Donovan.

He grabbed a baseball bat and thundered across the parking lot, whooping like a banshee. Asta bounded alongside.

The young men took a few steps back. The arm-grabber dragged Francesca with him, holding her in front like a shield.

Donovan crunched to a halt. He couldn't swing the baseball bat, not with Francesca in the way. To make matters worse, he heard a whir that could have been a switchblade opening.

Donovan lowered the bat. "Just let her go and we'll call it even."

Francesca's captor sneered. "How about you toss over your wallet first?"

"Don't give it to him, Donovan!" she said.

"Shut up." The creep jerked on her arm.

"You slimy worm." Donovan took an instinctive step forward.

"What're you planning on doing with that?" One of the others gestured toward the bat. "Going to play Tee-ball with the little kids?"

Donovan knew he couldn't win against all three. But every male fiber in his body cried out to save Francesca. It might be primitive, it might be stupid, but he couldn't face himself in the mirror if he didn't.

He hefted the bat.

"Donovan, don't," Francesca pleaded.

Her captor grinned. "Yeah, listen to the lady."

Francesca let out a low whistle. Asta, tail wagging, trotted over to his mistress and stood panting at her side.

"Anybody scared of Fido?" jeered the hoodlum.

Asta cocked his head and studied the youth. Then the dog lifted his hind leg.

"Hey!" The hooligan edged backward. "What do you think you're doing?"

"Leaving his mark," said Francesca.

"Like hell!" Her captor released her and swung one booted foot back for a kick.

There would never be a better time to intervene. Donovan leaped at the thug.

As he swung the bat, he was vaguely aware of some kind of mist drifting through the air. The wood connected with a satisfying thump, and he heard a shout, and then a lot of coughing. Gasping, wheezing, and more coughing.

Some of it seemed to be coming from his own lungs.

Tears streaked down Donovan's cheeks. He couldn't breathe. He staggered and barely caught his balance.

The kids were running away; he could hear the scuffle of their steps. Painful hacking noises drifted back to him.

"You—" The words choked off.

"Donovan!" Francesca pulled him into a patch of clear air. "You idiot!"

"You Maced me," he gasped.

She stuck a spray tube back into her pocket. "It's not as strong as Mace. It's something I bought from a catalog. Why couldn't you just hold back a minute?"

"I was ... trying ... to help."

She whacked him between the shoulders. A gulp of cold air racketed into Donovan's lungs, and he thought for a moment he might simply detonate.

A warm tongue rasped over his hand.

"Even Asta's worried," said Francesca. "Oh, are these your baseball caps? Somebody dropped them."

Donovan remembered about Blakely. "Disguises," he croaked.

"We'd better hurry!"

He wondered how so much water could pour out of his eyes. He wiped it on his sleeve.

"That stuff really works," Francesca said. "I've never used it before."

"Do me a favor." He wobbled toward the entrance. "Don't use it again."

Toenails clicked alongside. "I'm glad Asta didn't inhale any," Francesca said. "No telling what it does to dogs."

Donovan didn't bother to reply. He just jammed his cap low on his forehead.

The bowling alley was nearly empty at this hour, except for a group of senior citizens.

"There." Francesca tilted her head toward the coffee shop on their right. "He's behind that fern. If we're not careful, he'll see us."

"Anyone with him?" Donovan didn't want to risk facing Blakely directly.

"Not yet."

They rented shoes and balls and found a spot with a view of the coffee shop. Although the lanes themselves were well tended, the walls looked shabby and dented, as if they'd taken the brunt of a great many badly thrown balls.

The only bright spots were a series of paintings across the back wall. A hand-lettered sign read Courtesy Santa Ana-Costa Mesa Landscape League.

In his fuzzy state, Donovan half expected to see surreal paintings in which bowling balls grew on trees, but closer inspection revealed only an assortment of pastoral scenes.

"You going to bowl, or you going to stare at the wall?" Francesca returned from landing a spare. "I'll keep score."

"We aren't here to work on our game, remember?"
Donovan launched his ball onto the gleaming wood. It
wobbled for a few feet, then flopped.

"There's no excuse for gutter balls," Francesca said.

Donovan was trying to think of a biting response
when, from the corner of his eye, he glimpsed a big man
slouching toward Jon's table. The newcomer wore a
shapeless overcoat and a tweed hat that looked familiar.

"Who's that?" Francesca hissed. "It's not the guy
from the garage."

"Of course not." Donovan had already figured their
employer wouldn't drive out at night to meet the thug
who'd tried to rob him. "Let's see if we can angle
over..."

Asta, who had been resting beneath a row of seats,
sprang to his feet, ears and tail laid back. A growl rum-
bled from his throat.

"What's he—"

With a string of sharp barks, Asta flung himself across
the bowling alley, straight toward Blakely and his com-
panion.

"No!" Francesca called. "Asta!"

Jon looked up. Recognition and surprise flashed across
his face as Donovan and Francesca, giving up all attempt to hide, ran after the dog.

Asta scrabbled on the linoleum floor, knocking over
Jon's briefcase, then leaped at the big man with a roar
that made everyone in the bowling alley turn to stare.

The suitcase split open, spilling out photocopies of
ledger pages. They looked like the ones in the account
book Donovan had seen on Jon's desk. There was no sign
of half a million dollars.

Apparently Blakely hadn't come to pay anybody off.

By the time Donovan and Francesca reached Asta, the big man in the overcoat was holding the dog by the nape, dangling him at arm's length. The roar had turned into a whine.

"What have we here?" said the man.

No wonder his figure had looked familiar. His name was Stewart Waters, and he, like Donovan, was a private investigator. They'd shared a few beers together over the years.

"I'm so sorry," Francesca said. "I've never known him to attack anyone."

"Must be the cat hairs." Stewart's grin wavered slightly as he caught sight of Donovan. "I was playing with my Siamese this morning."

He gave no sign of recognition. That was one of the unwritten rules of detective work: You didn't break a fellow P.I.'s cover.

Donovan and Francesca introduced themselves as Jon's employees. "We bowl here a lot," Francesca added.

"I thought you two just moved from out of state." Jon had watched the encounter with a puzzled expression.

"Well, we did . . ." she began.

"We discovered this place a couple of weeks ago." Donovan gestured toward the paintings. "You know how interested we are in art. We were checking out the exhibit and, well, we liked the ambience."

"The ambience?" Stewart couldn't resist a touch of irony.

"Real down-home Americana," Francesca put in. "None of your fake yuppie decor. This is the real thing."

"It's real, all right," Stewart said.

"Sorry about Asta." Donovan collected the dog. "He invited himself along." Then, to Francesca: "I think we should be heading home, dear."

Her mouth tightened as if she were about to argue, but she dutifully said good-night and followed Donovan outside. As they neared the van, she said, "We could have joined them for a cup of coffee."

"You think they were going to discuss business in front of us?"

"We might have picked up *something*. Besides, how can we leave Jon alone with that monster?"

"A little grumpy, but hardly a monster." Donovan told her who the big man was. "I've known him for years. He's rough around the edges, but honest."

Her face brightened. "Then Jon *didn't* kill Cindy! He's hired a detective to find her!"

"He could be trying to find a lot of things. It might have nothing to do with Cindy." Donovan opened the van door for her. "Jon Blakely's life didn't begin two weeks ago. He could have been involved in some other investigation."

"You can't stand to think he might be innocent!" As he slid into the driver's seat, Francesca added, "What is it about that Amanda Carruthers? How come she really got to you? To me, she sounded like a stiff."

"A stiff?"

"You know, so cold she might as well be dead. Isn't that a detective term?"

"Not in my lifetime." Donovan made sure Asta had settled down before he put the van into gear.

"There must be something about her that appeals to you." Francesca ruffled the dog's ears. "It's that air of helplessness, isn't it? You want to protect her. Can't you see you're being manipulated?"

Donovan knew he had a weak spot where attractive women were concerned, but he didn't have a weak head. "Oh, yeah? Manipulated how?"

"Maybe she thinks she'll inherit Cindy's money if Jon's behind bars," Francesca speculated. "Or maybe she's not really Cindy's sister at all, just some opportunist."

"There's a family resemblance."

"Could be a coincidence." Francesca switched on the radio. "I'm too tired to argue."

The oldies station was playing an Anne Murray song. They had begun to relax by the time it ended.

Then a newscaster came on.

"This station has obtained an exclusive confession by millionaire Jonathan Blakely that he arranged the murder of his wife, Cynthia, who disappeared two weeks ago."

Donovan and Francesca jerked to attention.

What they heard next was unmistakably Jon's voice. "Oh, sure. My wife's been kidnapped, but I refused to pay them off. I figured I'd let them kill her for me."

The words, right down to the sarcastic tone, rang a bell with Donovan. "I heard him say that on his own front steps! To that pesky reporter!"

"It was a joke!" Francesca agreed. "Those sleazy— We'd better go back and warn him."

"We can do him a bigger favor by heading off the press." Donovan veered onto the freeway. "I'll give you ten to one they're camped out on the front lawn right now."

The situation turned out be even worse than he feared.

The station must have aired the same report earlier, because by the time they arrived, vans bearing the logos of news stations were pulling into Blakely's driveway.

Minicam crews and photographers roamed the front lawn as if it were a public park, and eye-searing lights pierced the darkness.

A few individuals stood out: a woman with Teflon-perfect hair bathed in a spotlight, declaiming into a microphone; a technician poking in the bushes, as if expecting to find an electrical outlet there; a couple of reporters thrusting their microphones toward the front door as they rang the bell repeatedly.

"Surprise, surprise," muttered Donovan. "Nobody's home."

"I can't believe they couldn't tell the tape was a joke," Francesca said.

"Must be a slow night for news." He wove past the haphazardly parked vehicles. "But that doesn't give them the right to trespass." Donovan picked up the car phone.

"What're you doing?"

"Calling the police." He punched 911.

Before he could press the enter button, Francesca snatched away the handset. "Don't be crazy!"

"They're breaking the law."

"They're doing their job!"

"You're defending them?"

"First of all, if we kick them out, they'll bear a grudge against Jon," Francesca pointed out. "Secondly, having them here gives him a chance to set the record straight."

"If he wants to." Donovan had to agree, though, that siccing the law on the press could be a big mistake.

He found a parking space among the welter of vehicles. Heads turned as they got out, but no one approached.

With their casual clothes, he realized, they might be mistaken for the advance guard of yet another camera crew. "We can slip into our apartment before they realize it," he said.

It might have worked. There was just one problem.

Marlena Marabel, the eccentric human-interest lady hired to spike the ratings at one of the smaller TV stations, had come attired in a garish costume, from her feathered headdress to her flowing tie-dyed chiffon robe. Unfortunately, she'd also brought her very white, very fluffy, very delectable cat.

Donovan could have sworn he saw a gleam in Asta's eye a split second before the dog went airborne.

"You know," Francesca said, "leaving him in a kennel might not have been such a bad idea."

A dozen cameras swung into action as the dog exploded into the middle of Marlena Marabel's broadcast. Yowls and screeches filled the night, fur flew, and then a white ball streaked across the lawn and up the nearest tree.

"My poopsy!" cried Marlena. "My pettikins-wettikins!"

Asta gave a few satisfied barks at the foot of the cypress and trotted back. He sniffed the human interest lady's robe, and she jerked it away.

"Are you all right?" Donovan asked as they hurried up.

"I most certainly am not!" cried Marlena.

"Someone must have stolen the Beware of the Dog sign." Francesca assumed a placating smile. "We had no idea anyone would bring a cat onto Mr. Blakely's property. People around here know it just isn't done."

"Well!" huffed the reporter, but without the same indignation. Perhaps, Donovan reflected, it had finally sunk in that she had no business being here in the first place.

People converged, thrusting microphones, aiming lights.

"You two work here?"

"Did you know Mrs. Blakely?"

"Has Mr. Blakely confessed to you?"

Donovan was about to order them back when Francesca silenced him with a gesture. Still smiling, she told the reporters, "Mr. Blakely isn't home right now. If you'd be so good as to leave your names and phone numbers, I'm sure . . ."

"This is too good to miss!" called a balding, beerbellied man carrying a steno pad.

"Yeah, and we're on deadline!" called someone else.

"Got to make the ten-o'clock news!"

It was hopeless. Francesca turned to Donovan, "Please go make coffee. There's a big pot in the pantry. Bring real cups. We don't want to screw up the environment with CFCs." When he tried to object, she said, "Donovan, we might as well get them in a good mood. It's called running damage control. And I don't dare leave you out here alone, with your quick temper."

For once, he bowed to Francesca's judgment. There didn't seem to be much else to do.

Inside, Donovan locked the front door behind him to keep out any emboldened members of the press. At this point, he wouldn't put anything past them.

Lights from the lawn flashed through the windows, giving the marbled hall an uneasy glare. After the clamor of the reporters, Donovan's footsteps echoed in eerie silence.

A shadow shifted to one side. Donovan turned in time to see a dark-clad figure rush toward him.

He lifted his arm to protect himself, and stumbled as a heavy object crashed across it. As he twisted away, he saw that the attacker was too short to be the thug from the garages.

Donovan braced against the wall, preparing to kick. There was a tense standoff, and then the attacker turned and switched on the lights.

"Mr. Lewis!" The shocked voice belonged to Tenley Feinstein. "Oh, my goodness! I'm sorry. I thought you were one of those hyenas out there!"

She set down the rolling pin and helped him up. It occurred to Donovan that he'd been bested by a woman for the second time in one night, which was a record he wouldn't care to brag about.

"What—what are you doing here?" He tried to keep his voice steady.

"As soon as I heard the radio report, I came back. I couldn't get through on the phone and I thought Mr. Blakely might need me." Tenley made tentative gestures toward his arm. "Should I call a doctor? How about an ambulance?"

"I'll live," he said. "Could I get you to make coffee?"

"Oh—oh, sure."

"A big pot. The one in the pantry."

He dragged himself into the kitchen to watch Tenley work. It was his best chance to talk to her with her guard down.

Tonight, Tenley's prickliness was all directed at the press, not at Donovan. "I can't believe the way they're slandering him. The man didn't kill his wife! It's preposterous."

"Why?" Donovan started toward a chair, then thought the better of it. If he got too comfortable, he might never stand up again, not in his current bruised state.

"Jon isn't violent." It was the first time he'd heard Tenley refer to her employer by his given name. "He might have disliked Cindy, and with good reason. She was nothing but a gold digger, Mr. Lewis. But Jon's too gentle, and just plain too smart, to get mixed up in a murder."

"You mean he'd find some other means to disenfranchise her?" Donovan suggested. "Such as what? Blackmail?"

"Oh, no." Tenley poured water into the coffeemaker. "At least I don't think so. I mean, he might try to find a legal means of proving she wasn't entitled to half his estate. If only he'd signed a prenuptial agreement! I tried to tell him."

So Tenley had mistrusted Cindy from the beginning, Donovan noted. Was she in love with Jon Blakely? Was it possible she would have gone so far as to kill Cindy to protect him? Somehow he couldn't believe it.

He helped Tenley lug the coffeepot out the front door. Reporters swarmed around, helping themselves; a few even thanked him.

By the time Jon's station wagon arrived, the uninvited guests were scattered around the lawn, exchanging cat and dog stories and calling encouragement to Asta, who had resumed guarding the tree.

Jon made it halfway up the front walk before the crews realized he was there. Then they surged into a pushing, shouting mass.

"Did you kill your wife?"

"Where's her body?"

"Who were the kidnappers? Did you hire them?"

Donovan and Francesca cleared a path for Blakely. He climbed to the porch, where he faced his tormentors. "I have a statement."

The questions stopped. "My remarks to that sleazy radio reporter were made in jest," the millionaire said. "I was being sarcastic. I am not a murderer, and if I were, I would not be stupid enough to confess it on the air. I wish I knew what happened to my wife. If anyone finds out, please let me know."

He went inside with Tenley. Donovan and Francesca collected the coffee gear, while Asta reluctantly yielded his post by the tree and wriggled inside between their legs.

"They'll give up soon." Jon's voice drifted back as he strode through the house. "Most of them will, anyway."

"I'll turn on the hoses if they don't!" Tenley said.

It wasn't until they reached the kitchen that Francesca noticed that Donovan was holding his arm. "Don't tell me you got hurt again?"

"Tenley bonked me with a rolling pin. She thought I was breaking in." His adrenaline ebbing, Donovan leaned against the counter.

Francesca touched his arm lightly. "You need to rest. Donovan, you're a tough cookie, but you're still human."

"Think so?" It hurt to make a joke, even a weak one.

"You don't always have to be strong." She slipped her arms around him. "Lean on me."

"I'll knock you over."

"I'm tough."

"Francesca . . ."

Her nose brushed across his cheek, and then she kissed him. Donovan felt himself melt.

"Could we sleep here?"

She chuckled close to his ear. "In the kitchen?"

"Not private enough, huh?"

They kissed again.

"Now would you please lean on me?" she said.

He tried it. Francesca barely wavered as they hobbled through the house to their apartment.

"Where's the dog?" he said.

"In our own kitchenette. Snoring."

He couldn't think clearly. "Which way is the bedroom?"

"Straight ahead, where it's always been."

"You coming?" Donovan asked.

"I'm the only thing holding you up. Of course I'm coming."

They fell across the bed, legs tangling together. Donovan's body couldn't figure out what it wanted more, to go to sleep or to make love to Francesca, but his mind knew what it wanted, and it was letting him know, loud and clear.

"Could you take my clothes off?" he asked.

"Nothing to it," she said.

Moments later, Donovan lay naked, watching Francesca in the moonlight. On her knees beside him, she lifted off her pullover top and unhooked the lacy bra. He cupped the swell of her breasts, feeling the nipples harden against his palm.

She unzipped her skirt and pulled it down across her hips. He treasured the soft contours of her stomach and waist as he eased the skirt the rest of the way off.

Donovan pulled her down onto him.

Pleasure gasped from Francesca's lips as she molded her thighs around him, letting him caress the length of her body. She straddled him like an Amazon, tough and sure.

Donovan steered her with his movements, his mouth, his fingers, and then she seized control and mounted him with a quick, unexpected plunge.

Still inside her, he caught her shoulders and flipped them both, never letting up the urgency of his demands. She struggled for a moment, as if reluctant to yield even in the heat of desire, and then a gasp of pleasure tore from her throat.

Her body quivered before his thrusts and then he felt her arch against him, opening, giving, taking. In that naked moment he lost any sense of space between them, any control, anything but a rush of ecstacy that roared through them both.

Afterward Francesca lay cradled in the curve of Donovan's arm. He gazed down at her face; it was mellow with sleep.

Her eyelashes fluttered against her cheek. There was no trace now of the feisty independence Donovan knew so well.

He wanted to keep her close like this always, but he knew he couldn't tie her down. Francesca might surrender for an evening, but not forever. And he didn't really want her to.

They'd have to come to an agreement of terms.

It was hours later, or days, or maybe only minutes, when Donovan felt a cold nose press into his hand.

He awoke dazedly and saw the hands of the bedside clock edging toward 5:00 a.m.

"Beat it," he muttered to Asta.

The dog growled.

Then Donovan heard another noise, like a window sliding open. If he had to guess, he'd wager it was coming from the laundry room next to the apartment.

Uttering a few harsh words unsuitable for any ears but the dog's, he creaked to a sitting position. Beside him, Francesca didn't even stir.

Donovan couldn't remember ever having taken a job that involved so much physical pain or so little sleep. He decided he would write it into future contracts that he could quit if he were assaulted more than once.

In the meantime, he'd better go see who was breaking into Jon Blakely's house this time.

Chapter Eleven

Donovan prowled into the hallway and blended with a shadow, his eyes on the laundry room door.

A blink later, a man emerged. Early-morning light silhouetted his potbellied figure and gleamed off his bald pate. He was making notes on a steno pad.

"Anything interesting?" Donovan asked.

The reporter's pen flew across the hall. "What? I mean—?"

"Breaking and entering," Donovan said.

The man took a deep breath. "I represent one of the oldest daily newspapers...."

"Not exactly ethical, are you?" Donovan took the man's elbow and steered him away from the apartment. No sense in waking Francesca.

To his relief, Asta sniffed the man and decamped. Not a cat owner, obviously.

The reporter tried a different tack. "Listen, there's something in this for you. A nice crisp twenty."

"Twenty?" Donovan nearly laughed.

"Well, they don't pay me much," the man admitted. "Or—I could get you some free classified ads."

"I'd need them if I cooperated with you." Donovan escorted him toward the front hall. "Because I'd be out of a job, that's for sure. I'll just make a note of your name and what newspaper you're from, in case my employer cares to pursue any action."

"That won't be necessary." Jon's voice drifted down from the landing. Donovan turned to see the millionaire descending the stairs, a maroon robe sashed over printed pajamas.

"This gentleman—" Donovan began.

"Works for the *Orange County Post-Courier*," finished Blakely. "I've run into him before. Come this way."

They followed him into the office. Someone had tidied up the loose notes, Donovan observed.

Blakely picked up the phone.

"Now listen," said the reporter. "There's no need to call the cops."

"I'm not involving the police." Blakely smiled humorlessly. He dialed and waited. "Ah, hello? Turner, how are you? This is Jon Blakely."

The reporter paled.

"Who's Turner?" Donovan asked.

"My publisher."

"Yes, I know what time it is," the thin man said. "We've both been awakened by one of your employees. Fellow by the name of—is it Kevin? Yes, Kevin Fanning. Broke into my house in search of something or other. Certainly." He handed the phone to the reporter. "He wants to talk to you."

What followed was a pathetic series of *Yes, sir*s and *I'm sorry*s. Finally Kevin Fanning apologized to Blakely, took his pad and slunk out into the night.

"Sorry you were awakened." Donovan backed away, hoping to grab a few more exhausted winks before starting the day.

"Join me for a cup of coffee?"

Oh, well. Who needed sleep? "My pleasure."

His boss made a good cup of java, Donovan reflected a short time later. Then he realized that under Francesca's influence he, too, had begun thinking in outdated slang.

In the rosy light, Blakely looked younger than usual, but also sadder, as he toyed with an unlit pipe. "You're a lucky man, Donovan."

"In what way?"

Blakely drew a pouch of tobacco from his pocket. "You're lucky you're not rich."

"I never thought to count it among my blessings."

Blakely sifted some tobacco into the hand-carved bowl of his pipe. "I've always had money. Born with the proverbial silver spoon in my mouth."

"Tough luck." Donovan didn't want to sound unsympathetic, but he couldn't help thinking of his own depleted bank account.

"I never used to think of money as a problem," Jon went on. "I was always good at business, and I always had women. I figured I was invulnerable. Looking back, I suppose I hurt some people, but it didn't occur to me at the time."

"You can't please everybody," Donovan said.

"Then I met Cindy." Blakely stared out the window. Dawn was breaking over his swimming pool. "She turned everything upside down. She seemed so fresh, so innocent. Everything I thought I'd lost."

"You date her long?"

"A few weeks. Not nearly long enough to know each other. But at the time, I figured I was old enough to make up my own mind," Blakely said. "It took me a few years to realize all she wanted was my money, and then I didn't want to believe it. I tried to tell myself she was just . . . foolish.''

''Foolish like a fox?'' Donovan prodded.

''Bit by bit, I got a picture of her that was far from pleasant.'' Blakely patted his pockets for a lighter. ''Cindy used people. She was a better actress offscreen than on, and she knew how to come across sweet and naive. But in the end, our fights got pretty nasty.'' He reached over and pulled a box of kitchen matches from a drawer.

''Fights?'' Donovan said.

It took Jon a few minutes to get the pipe lit. Then he sat for a while, inhaling. ''We fought about all sorts of things,'' he said at last. ''Before we married, she said she wanted children—then she changed her mind. I could understand that, but then I found out she was stealing from me. Why? I'd given her everything she asked for. It was like it gave her pleasure to hurt me.''

''Must have made you angry,'' Donovan suggested.

Jon let out a deep breath. ''I'm not a vindictive man, but sometimes I could have strangled her. She knew just how to provoke.''

The statement struck Donovan as tantamount to a confession. He hoped it wasn't. He'd begun to like Jon Blakely.

''Well, she's gone now. I can't say I'm entirely sorry.'' Blakely drained the last of his coffee. ''Donovan, thanks for catching that pest from the *Post*.''

''My pleasure.'' Donovan stood up as his employer departed.

He wished he could feel gleeful about what he'd learned. He wished he could feel more sympathetic to the hapless Cindy.

And if she had been so manipulative, what about her sister? Could Amanda really be innocent in all this?

Maybe Francesca was right and Amanda had some ignoble motive. The problem was, Francesca had a different theory for every new piece of evidence.

Until the pieces began to fit, Donovan would have to keep slogging along. And Jon Blakely remained the prime suspect.

DONOVAN STARED DOWN into the maelstrom.

Who invented drains, anyway? he grumbled silently. Why couldn't people just pour their dirty water on the front lawn?

"Think you can fix it?" Marta asked.

"No problem," he said automatically, and stuck his fingers into the goo.

Up came a wad of celery strings, hair and miscellaneous food particles. Stifling a grimace, Donovan dumped it into the other sink, where a disposal waited to send it to that great kitchen in the sky.

He ran water into the recalcitrant drain. It gurgled with a sound like a Bronx cheer and refused to yield.

Now what?

"I've got some silver to clean." Marta fetched a metal can of polish from beneath the sink. "Let me know when you're done."

"Sure thing," said Donovan.

Francesca had set herself the task of dusting the closed-off guest rooms as a cover for searching them. She had pointed out that evidence might be stashed anywhere.

Donovan wished she'd stayed nearby. He wished she could tell him how to fix this drain. More than that, he wished he could hold her and finish what they'd started this morning.

As he listened to the water chugging its way down the pipes, Donovan let his thoughts wander back.

He'd returned to the apartment to find Francesca emerging from the shower. His attention had been riveted on the splendid freedom of her body, the unselfconscious way she moved about the bedroom, brushing her hair and selecting her clothes.

She'd come to him as if it were the most natural thing in the world. He'd been sitting on the bed, watching her, and then Francesca had stood before him, bending for a kiss. His mouth had trailed down to the cleft between her breasts, and he'd heard the hunger in her deep sigh.

Then she'd pulled away. "Later, big guy," she'd said, and gone back to brushing her hair.

He'd crossed the room, taken the brush and stroked her long, thick tresses. He'd never noticed before how many colors gleamed in the depths, hints of chestnut and honey among the chocolate. Tendrils curled willfully about her forehead and at the nape of her neck.

When Donovan had nibbled her ear, Francesca had laughingly pushed him away. "I don't see how you can even move today, let alone make love."

"You inspire me."

"I infuriate you."

"Either way, it gets the adrenaline pumping."

"Go take a cold shower." She'd shot him a teasing grin. "It'll do you good."

So it had, he supposed, but a cold shower wasn't what he wanted. Damn it, what was wrong with him today? He wasn't some playboy who spent all his time lusting after women. Usually he had no trouble separating work from pleasure. But then, he'd never had to pretend to be married to a gorgeous dame like...

Dame? He shook his head at the old-fashioned word. He'd done it again. Francesca's influence.

What he needed right now was not her influence, but her expertise. Donovan sighed as he returned his attention to the stubborn drain.

Maybe the storehouse of chemicals under the sink would offer some clue. He sorted through bottles of glass cleaner and tile cleaner, dishwasher detergent, brushes, sponges and... Now what was this? Pressurized air?

For unclogging drains, the label said.

Donovan shook the thing for good measure, stuck the nozzle down the drain and fired.

A huge *whoosh* shot him backward as thick black gunk spewed across the kitchen. A bomb in a barnyard couldn't have created a bigger mess.

The drain uttered a contented gurgle.

Wiping sludge from his forehead, Donovan ran the faucet. The water poured down without a hitch.

"Hey, I did it," he said.

"I'm glad I don't have to clean that," said Tenley Feinstein.

Donovan looked up, startled. He hadn't expected to see the assistant this early, not after such a late night. "You're a hard worker."

"So are you." She actually smiled at him, and then Donovan noticed something different. She wasn't wearing her bifocals today, and she was squinting slightly.

"New contacts?" he guessed.

"I figured it was time I updated my image." The new Tenley hadn't exactly been transformed; she was still short and round and verging on middle age. But she did have lovely violet eyes.

"You look great," Donovan said.

"You look like you need a bath," she said. "I'll go get Marta. I don't think I'd better ask your wife to clean this up, or you'll be in the doghouse for a week."

"Thanks." He wanted to say more, to let Tenley know he appreciated the change in her attitude toward him, but nothing came to mind.

As he showered, Donovan reflected on the change. Had whacking him with a rolling pin vented some long-repressed rage, or had she simply come to accept that he was on Jon's side?

Except that he wasn't. He liked Tenley. He even liked Blakely. But his job was to find evidence of a murder.

As soon as he was dressed, he dialed Stewart Water's office.

"I figured I'd hear from you," said the other detective.

"Thought we should get our signals straight." They couldn't ethically discuss details of their cases, but Donovan intended to pry out as much as he could.

"Who was that chick with you?" Stewart made an appreciative noise. "She taken or what?"

"She's...working for me." Donovan didn't want to use Francesca as bait, but he needed to string Stewart along. No point in staking out his territory yet. "So, let's see, Jon Blakely gave you a copy of his ledger, and the last time I looked, you weren't any accountant."

"She has great legs."

"Jon hired you to find out how his wife was stealing from him and where she put the money, right?" The cash in Cindy's car must have been part of the loot, but maybe there'd been more. "Where'd she stash it? She have some kind of accomplice?"

"Gee, if you could part with the lady's phone number, I might remember something," Stewart countered.

"I'd have to get her permission first," Donovan stalled. "Of course, if you . . ."

From elsewhere on the line came a rustling noise. "What's that?" Stewart snapped, bristling audibly.

"I don't—"

He heard it again. *Thump-thump.* Like a dog wagging its tail along the carpet.

"You're not calling on a secure line? You bonehead!" Stewart slammed down the phone.

Donovan replaced the handset, his blood boiling. He knew he should have driven to a pay phone. Although there was a private line reserved for this apartment, it obviously could be accessed from other phones.

But he'd never expected to be eavesdropped on by his own accomplice.

He stalked out and ran into Francesca in the hallway, hurrying toward him. "I'm sorry." She stood protectively in front of Asta. "I should have put the dog in another room."

"The dog isn't the problem." Donovan rasped out the words. "The problem is, you were spying on your own partner. That's not the way things are done, Francesca."

"I didn't know it was you when I picked up the line," she protested. Their eyes locked, and then she yielded. "You're right. I was curious. I didn't think you'd tell me everything, and I wanted to find out for myself."

"Thanks to you, there's nothing to tell."

"I know," she said. "I'll never do it again."

"Fine. Great," he growled. "Now go act like a housekeeper and stay out of my hair. I've got work to do."

"First I'm fixing you some lunch."

"Why?"

"Because it's noon. Marta's not going to cook. She insisted on cleaning up the kitchen herself, but she was grumbling like crazy. And I want to be sure you eat."

"Why should you care? Does my stomach rumble that loud?" He wanted to stay mad at Francesca, but the expression of concern on her face was making it difficult.

"Because you're a walking basket case!" She caught his elbow and guided him toward the apartment. "Do you know how many times you've been beaten up in the last three days?"

"I've lost count."

"If you don't keep up your strength, you'll land in the hospital." She pulled him through their living room and into the kitchenette. "You big lug, don't you know why I was listening in? I figured you'd go out somewhere and get beaten up again if I didn't stop you. You can't take much more of this, even a tough character like you."

She'd been trying to protect him? Satisfaction swept away Donovan's annoyance.

He wasn't sure where her feelings ranked on a scale from one to ten, with one representing disinterested motherly affection and ten representing passionate adoration. But right now he'd settle for what he could get.

Besides, he was hungry.

Francesca rummaged through the cabinets until she found two cans of chili. Donovan located plates and spoons and set the table.

He knew he was playing with fire, but he couldn't resist. "You don't want to see me battered and bleeding, eh?"

"Of course not." She dumped the chili into a glass bowl and microwaved it. "I mean, if you get killed, how am I going to get trained as a detective?"

He should have expected that.

They ate in silence for a while, and then he said, "Find anything in the guest rooms?"

She shook her head.

"We haven't got much to go on, have we?" Mentally he reviewed the case. "We know Jon hired a detective, probably to investigate Cindy's thefts. And we know she stole half a million dollars and hid it in her car."

"We don't know it was Cindy who did that," Francesca pointed out.

He went on thinking out loud. "It's true that we seem to have an excess of thieves. Cindy. The chauffeur. The former housekeeper."

"And then there's all that stuff missing from Cindy's room." Francesca helped herself to seconds of the chili. She must have a cast-iron stomach, Donovan thought. "Her personal items. She might have taken them with her, if she was planning to run away."

"Or someone might have removed them, to make it look as if she did," Donovan mused. "Or they might have simply been stolen, if we're talking about jewelry and furs."

"Or Jon might have donated them to charity." Then Francesca rejected her own suggestion. "No, of course not. Because he can't be sure his wife is dead."

"Unless he killed her."

"You can't still believe that! You just can't!" She shoved back a handful of hair that threatened to invade her lunch.

"There's a lot we don't know about this household," Donovan reminded her.

"Sure! We don't know when they last sprayed for ants or where they bought the furniture or—or lots of things!" Francesca sputtered. "None of them important!"

"We can't be sure."

"Jon Blakely isn't harboring any deep dark secrets! You might as well accuse Asta of some hideous crime!"

"I don't know much about Asta, either," Donovan said.

After a startled moment, she started to laugh. Her mirth was infectious, and he was about to join in when something stopped him.

In a split second, he identified it as a scream.

Donovan shoved back from the table and barreled through the house, Francesca on his heels. The shriek wavered at near glass-shattering strength, and he calculated that it came from a rear service entrance.

He didn't recognize the voice. It didn't sound like either Tenley or Marta, and there were no day maids on the premises today.

The wild thought flashed through Donovan's brain that it might be Cindy, that she wasn't dead after all and she'd returned and Jon was finishing the job. It was that kind of soul-rending cry.

He and Francesca burst into a small back hall. The first thing he saw was Marta, leaning against the back door and shoving with all her strength.

The second thing he noticed was a thin, pale woman leaning back from the other side. Her foot was caught. The unearthly cry was issuing from her thin lips.

"Marta!" He tugged the cook away. "You're crushing her foot!"

"Keep her out!" Marta demanded. "That thief! That witch! She stole our best service, and now she's back for more!"

The pale woman gasped as the pressure eased. She sagged against the door frame, massaging her foot. She had wispy hair, an angular face, and a grocery sack balanced in the crook of one arm. Donovan guessed her age to be near sixty.

"I'm back for more, all right," she growled. "Here."

She shoved the sack into Donovan's hands. He peered inside and saw a blender, a blow dryer and a plastic bag containing what appeared to be a diamond bracelet.

Francesca took the bag and eyed its contents. "Anyone care to explain?"

Marta drew herself up angrily. "That's Bernice Long. Used to be the housekeeper. See what all she stole! I wondered where that blender had got to!"

"I brought it back, didn't I?" said Bernice.

"I think we should all sit down and get to the bottom of this." Donovan escorted the wary ex-housekeeper inside. She took a few steps and planted herself on the linoleum.

"Just wanted to make it all straight," Bernice said.

"Until something else turns up missing!" Marta folded her arms across her large bosom.

"She deserves some credit for bringing this back," Francesca said soothingly. "Now, Marta, we just want to find out—"

The cook spied the bracelet. "For crying out loud! That's Mrs. Blakely's! What a fit she threw when she couldn't find it! Must be worth thousands!"

"Got five hundred for it at the pawnshop," said Bernice. "Took me this long to get it out of hock, working two shifts as a waitress. I meant to get it all back, and I did."

She seemed genuinely distressed. Why, then, had she stolen from her employers? "You must have needed that money pretty desperately," Donovan said.

The air of indignation faded. "I've got a weakness, I know. It's a wonder my husband hasn't left me. I—I gamble."

Marta narrowed her eyes, but said nothing.

"It was that Thomas," Bernice went on.

"The chauffeur?"

A nod. "Liked to play cards with me. He was the worst poker player I ever saw. Or that's what I thought. Suckered me in, that's what he did. I can see it now." Bernice's shoulders sagged.

"How much did you lose?"

"Three thousand dollars," she said. "I couldn't pay it off fast, not without my husband finding out. Then the threats started. Thomas showed me his gun. Said he had no use for people that didn't pay their debts. He was that kind of man, you knew he could be violent. He started saying he was going to hurt my Joe and me, both."

"So you took a few things and pawned them," Francesca said. "Meaning to redeem them later."

"I was just borrowing," the housekeeper said. "At least that's what I told myself. I know it was wrong. I panicked. And I knew if Mr. Blakely found out I'd been gambling he'd fire us. See, I'd had a little trouble before, and he knew about it, and gave me a chance."

"Betrayed his trust, that's what you did," said Marta.

Francesca's voice stopped them all cold. "The marked cards."

"What?" Bernice said.

"I found a deck of marked cards." Francesca left out the fact that they'd apparently belonged to Cindy.

"He cheated?" The housekeeper took a wavering step backward and caught hold of a chair to steady herself. "I knew he was a sharpie, but I thought—I just figured he had one of those photographic memories, knew which cards had been played."

Marta's frown softened. "He cheated her? And then he had the nerve to threaten her?"

"Nice guy," said Donovan.

Marta took the sack from him. "I'll put these away. No need to saying anything to Mr. Blakely. You've settled your debts with him."

"I'll never gamble again." Bernice shuddered. "That man, that terrible— There's words for people like that, but I can't say them. I'm too much of a lady. At least I used to be."

"You still are." Francesca slipped one arm around the trembling woman. "You've been foolish, but you've learned."

"There's no excuse. I'm too old to be foolish."

"You're never too old to be foolish," said Marta, and the two exchanged a look of reconciliation.

The ex-housekeeper said a muted farewell and departed. Marta collected the bag and set about replacing the items, clucking to herself all the while.

Francesca and Donovan went back to finish their lunch.

"Everything we turn up makes Cindy look worse," he admitted as they shared a can of fruit salad. "Where'd you find those marked cards, anyway?"

"In the station wagon, when I picked it up. I opened the glove compartment to be sure the registration slip was still there, and they fell out," Francesca said.

"What makes you think they were Cindy's?"

"She'd written her name on the box."

Donovan had to concede that the damsel in distress was turning into more of a dragon in disguise, but he couldn't see what she could have had to gain by cheating the housekeeper. "Thomas would have used the station wagon, not Cindy. He must have taken her cards and marked them."

"For once, I agree," Francesca said. "Except for one thing. He was one of Cindy's old friends, right? Which means she knew about his background, that he'd been in trouble. I wonder exactly how well she did know him."

"I'd better talk to her sister, if I can reach her." Donovan cleared away his plate. "That chauffeur is a wild card. Maybe Amanda knows something."

The phone rang. Donovan reached for it, but Francesca beat him to the punch. "I gave this number to my parents."

"This is Francesca." She stopped and listened, her dark eyes clouding. "Of course. I'll be there as fast as I can. Thanks, Victor."

She hung up. "That was my father's assistant. Dad took a bad fall in his studio." Her voice was shaking.

"I'll drive you." For once, as Donovan helped her out the door, Francesca didn't even protest.

Chapter Twelve

The engine in the van sputtered, turned over and died. Donovan cursed it and tried again, with the same results.

"Must be the battery," he said.

Francesca pointed at the fuel gauge. The needle stood at empty. "Let's take the station wagon."

Donovan backed it out, and they headed for Laguna Beach. It was only a short drive, but every traffic light was conspiring against them, and there were a lot more of them than Donovan remembered.

Once this scenic drive along Pacific Coast Highway had been an uninterrupted stretch of wildlands and ocean. Now a resort was taking shape on the coastal bluffs, and tract homes sprouted inland where birds used to nest. Every generation invented the world anew, he supposed, but he wished this one was a little less hyperactive.

"What hospital?" Donovan asked as they crested a hill.

"He wouldn't go to the hospital. He hates them," Francesca said. "He's at home, over his studio."

"That's crazy."

"That's Dad."

"How bad is he hurt?"

"Bad enough for him to let Victor call me." Her hands clenched in her lap. "He tried to reach my sister, but she's on vacation. Can't you pass that truck?"

Donovan stepped on the accelerator and eased around the slowpoke.

A short time later, they drove between the clusters of art galleries, surf shops and candy stores that marked Laguna Beach. Inland, on the coastal bluffs, lay the home of Mrs. Farthington Cornsworth, where Donovan had first met Francesca. Could that really have been only four days ago?

When they reached Bruno Adamo's gallery, Francesca directed Donovan to turn left onto a side street and pull into an alley. The station wagon was still rolling when she jumped out and dashed toward a side door.

By the time Donovan parked and stepped into the workshop, she'd vanished from sight. He found himself alone in a cavernous space punctuated by giant metal sculptures.

Clear sun washed through a skylight, bathing clay models, worktables, welding equipment and a dusty concrete floor. Donovan preferred realistic art, but he had to admire the skill that had gone into these soaring metal shapes. In spirit, they reminded him of the airplane in Francesca's living room.

One piece dominated the room, a sculpture about fifteen feet high. Three wings arched from the base, one reaching toward the ceiling, another leveling off, a third drooping. Donovan supposed a critic could find all kinds of meanings here: sky, sea and earth, or youth, middle age and old age. Or did they represent love, with its inspired beginning, complacent middle and sorrowful end?

Donovan doubted he'd ever grow complacent about Francesca. Did that mean he didn't have to fear a sorrowful end?

As he circled the statue, he saw a metal ladder lying twisted across a workbench. Bruno Adamo must have fallen while working on the piece.

Donovan was about to go look for Francesca when the outer door banged open and a woman stood framed there. For one confusing moment, he thought it was Francesca, that she must have gone out through another exit and returned. Then he saw that the woman, although about Francesca's height and build, was a good twenty years older.

"Victor?" she demanded, her eyes narrowing.

"Donovan," he said. "I'm a friend of your daughter's."

The woman strode across the floor and shook his hand briskly. "Letitia Adamo-Bernini," she said. "Where's Bruno?"

"I assume he's—" Donovan realized there were three inner doors, and he had no idea which one Francesca had taken.

"Upstairs, no doubt. In his own bed, that idiot." Letitia marched toward the door on the left. "He ought to be in the hospital. It's all part of this obsession he has with control."

There seemed no need to answer, so Donovan silently followed her up a flight of steps.

They entered a living room stuffed with sculptures and paintings, far too many for the space, a crazy quilt of styles, from neo-impressionist to postmodern.

"Doesn't look very controlled to me," Donovan observed.

"Oh, Bruno buys things to help his friends," Letitia said. "Then he forgets about them. He only controls what he thinks is important." She pushed open the far door. "Bruno? You moron!"

Several rooms must have been combined into one, because the bedroom was nearly twice as large as the living room. A scarlet-and-orange Cessna hung from the ceiling.

In an enormous round bed, a man lay against the pillows. His leonine head was topped by a thick shock of dark hair. A splinted arm lay across the batik bedcover.

Francesca sat beside him, her mouth parted in surprise as she regarded her mother. At a bedside table, a thin young man was brewing tea.

"Mom!" Francesca said. "How'd you get here so fast?"

"Victor!" Rage flushed Bruno Adamo's face. "I told you not to call her!"

"I didn't . . ." began the timid response.

"I heard it on the radio in Los Angeles." Letitia fixed her frown on Victor, who took a step back and nearly overturned the teapot. "Did you call the paramedics? That explains it. The press monitors their radio frequencies, you know. For some reason, Bruno, people think you're important."

"Because I am! As everyone knows but you. A prophet is always without honor in his own country!"

"You hardly qualify as a prophet!"

"I am featured in collections around the world. Paris! Tokyo! Moscow!"

"Who? Who in Moscow?"

"Never mind who! If I am not in Moscow, I soon will be!"

Donovan felt like an interloper, but no one seemed to notice. In his own family, people spoke in well-modulated tones, their conflicts expressed in hints and understatements. He wasn't sure what the rules of the Adamo family might be. Maybe there weren't any.

"But what were you doing in L.A., Mom?" Francesca asked. "I thought you were in Alaska."

"Flew in last night, spur of the moment. I wanted to do some shopping." Letitia picked up a vial from the bedside table. "Aspirin? You're kidding!"

"It's for the pain," Victor ventured.

"I know that!" Letitia smacked the bottle down. "The man's got a broken arm, not a headache! Well, Bruno? Where's your cast? You can't go around in that splint for a month, now can you?"

"Bruno refused to get in the ambulance," Victor said. "And the doctor won't come here. He needs X rays, he said. I have to take Bruno to the hospital."

"The hell you will!" bellowed Bruno. "If a splint was good enough for Michelangelo, it's good enough for me!"

"Michelangelo broke his arm?" Francesca asked.

"If he did, this would have been good enough!" roared her father.

"If you didn't have a brain like an ox, you'd realize that things change for the better in five hundred years!" Letitia turned to Donovan. "Can you believe this? Have you ever met such a stubborn ignoramus?"

"Not quite." He looked at Francesca. She took aim with a loose pillow, then changed her mind and put it back on the bed, plumping it up.

"Look, Mom," she said. "Dad's not hurt as bad as I thought, but he did break his arm. Go easy, will you?"

"Listen to your daughter," the sculptor said. "You are a hard-hearted woman. Where is the softness of which the poets speak? Where is the delicacy of a real woman?"

Letitia sighed. "You should have remarried, Bruno. You need somebody to take care of you."

"I'm here," said Victor.

"You're an apprentice, not a nurse." Letitia studied her ex-husband. "You shouldn't live alone. You've gained weight. That's probably why the ladder collapsed."

"It fell because I was leaning too far, that's why!" The sculptor winced. "What agony! What tragedy! Now I'll never get that commission finished on time."

"I suppose I could carry out your plans," said Letitia. "If you let the doctor put a cast on your arm."

"They didn't commission you, they commissioned me!"

"Have it your own way, you mule! Francesca, take care of your father. I can't!"

Donovan stepped back as Letitia stormed by. He wouldn't have put it past her to bowl him over if he hadn't gotten out of the way fast enough.

"Can you believe this?" Francesca asked when her mother was gone. "Seven years they've been divorced, and they still fight."

"It's your mother's fault." The color seeped from Bruno's face as he lay back. "She doesn't know how to treat a man."

"I'd say she does pretty well." Francesca smiled. "Dad, you can't really declare war on modern medicine."

"To wear a cast is to be in prison! I have more mobility in my hand without it." Bruno tried to wiggle his fingers, groaned and gave up.

Donovan remembered what Letitia had said about control. In a hospital, Bruno would be at the mercy of other people's rules and decisions. "He needs a doctor who makes house calls."

"In this day and age?" Francesca asked. "Well, maybe there is such a thing. Victor, would you check the Yellow Pages?"

The assistant moved hesitantly toward the door, then smiled to himself as if he'd hit upon a scheme. "I'll bet I can get one of those doctors who visits the old-age homes."

"What?" cried Bruno. "Old-age homes?"

"They do make house calls," Victor explained. "And they're used to cranky patients."

"I am not cranky!"

"Tell him to be sure to bring a bedpan," said Francesca.

Bruno glared at his daughter. "I am not an invalid!"

"I don't know," Donovan joined in. "He doesn't look strong enough to go anywhere, not without a stretcher. Better arrange for a live-in nurse, too."

"You will do no such thing!" Bruno shoved back the covers with his free arm and swung out of bed, revealing a Chinese robe embroidered with peacocks. "I'm not having any nurse in my own house! Better to go to a hospital—at least I can leave when I want to!"

He stalked into the living room and down the stairs, leaving the others to chase behind.

"He's going to the hospital in his bathrobe?" Donovan asked.

Francesca hurried along. "It's on his terms or not at all."

"Don't make problems," begged Victor. "Besides, it's a beautiful robe. One of his former students sent it from Hong Kong."

In the studio, they found Letitia confronting her ex-husband. "You've come to your senses!"

"I'm getting it over with! You people won't stop bedeviling me until I do!" Listing a bit from the pain, Bruno careened out the door.

Victor and Letitia scooped him into a dented delivery van. "We'll follow you," Francesca called.

"Go away!" came her father's voice. "Too much fuss! I can manage by myself!"

His daughter stopped by the station wagon, watching the van rattle off. "He might need me."

"You think so?" Donovan said.

Francesca's mouth curved ruefully. "No. Mom will take care of him. Aren't they great together?"

"I thought they hated each other."

"They do. And they're nuts about each other. That's how love ought to be." Francesca stepped into the station wagon.

"You're kidding." Donovan might have pursued the subject, but as he walked around the car he glanced in the back and saw a sliver of red protruding from beneath a seat. "What's that?"

Francesca followed his gaze and extracted a tiny address book. "I can't believe it. I searched this thing inch by— Oh." She flushed. "Donovan, I'm sorry. I completely forgot. I'd done everything but the back seat when Blakely interrupted me, and I never finished."

He didn't waste time on recriminations. "What's inside?"

What they found were names, phone numbers and a few addresses. Most of them appeared to be shops and services—a furrier, a hairdresser, a manicurist. Cindy worked out at the Slenderella Spa, bought cosmetics from a woman named Mina, and employed her own seamstress.

Only one name didn't appear to be business-related. A Marjorie Jakes was listed with no designation, only an address in Redondo Beach, an oceanside community an hour's drive to the north.

"Must be a friend," Donovan said.

"Only one?" Francesca frowned. "Cindy couldn't have been *that* disagreeable."

"I vote we drop in on the lady unannounced. Friend or not, we might learn something."

After calling Tenley to excuse their absence—attributing it to Bruno's injury—they were on their way.

Donovan found it hard not to keep glancing at Francesca. The bright afternoon sun touched her cheeks with pink and brought out golden flecks in her eyes. She glowed with energy and anticipation of the interview ahead.

Donovan didn't want to attend to business. He wanted to find a private place where he and Francesca could come together with all the fire and fury her parents wasted on quarreling. He wanted to see those sharp eyes transformed with desire and to feel her well-toned body thrusting against his.

Damn it, he didn't want to own Francesca; he just wanted to be with her. To protect her when she needed it, and to let her take care of him when *he* needed it.

He'd always had a dream of righting life's wrongs, of going forth like a knight to rescue damsels in distress. Okay, so Francesca didn't exactly fit the helpless-maiden role. She could ride alongside him and wield her own sword; that would be fine, too.

But her refusal to allow him to get close wasn't a matter of equality, he knew. What she required was freedom. Donovan wished he understood why anyone would want to be free when she could be part of a winning team.

Until he could change Francesca's mind, he knew enough to keep his distance, sneaking looks at her while pretending to check the traffic, memorizing the play of sunlight across her face without letting her notice.

He had no trouble finding the house in Redondo Beach. Just a block from the ocean, the funky cottage was faced with rough-hewn shingles and gingerbread trim. A lemon tree struggled for life in a half barrel on the front patio.

"Not up to Cindy's usual standards," Francesca observed as they parked.

"You'd better stay in the station wagon."

"Why?"

Donovan forced himself to remember that what seemed obvious to him might not be so clear to a trainee. "If Thomas was one of Cindy's friends, who knows what kind of people live here? Maybe even Thomas himself. They might not be too glad to see us."

He'd dressed casually today, in jeans and a work shirt, but Donovan knew that his clipped hair and square-jawed face gave him an inescapable establishment look. Lawyer, cop, you name it. Not the type a creep like Thomas would cotton to.

"If there's going to be action, count me in." Francesca hopped out of the car and went up the walk so fast he had to run after her.

"You give new meaning to the word *stubborn!*"

"How about you, you chauvinist?"

"I'm just—"

"Trying to keep me out of trouble!"

Yes, yes, yes! But he knew better than to say so.

She rapped on the door before Donovan could stop her. He shoved her to one side.

"Hey!" Francesca stumbled and grabbed a light fixture for support.

"If someone fires a gun through this door—"

"Then how come you're standing right in front of it?"

Because he'd been more concerned about her welfare than his own, which was a good way to get killed. Donovan edged away, but not quickly enough. The door flew open, and something screamed in his face. It was a weird otherworldly howl that sprouted goose bumps along his scalp.

"Muffin! Hush!" A young woman with a round, freckled face quieted the cat in her arms. "I'm sorry. Did she scare you?"

"Not at all," lied Donovan. "Are you Marjorie Jakes?"

The woman finger-combed her sandy hair, which only made the unruly tufts spring up at odd angles. "Yes. Yes, I am. Oh, dear. I know I'm behind in the rent, but I've lost my roommate. You're not going to kick me out, are you?"

Donovan showed his private investigator's license. "We're looking into the disappearance of Cindy Blakely."

"Oh, you're from the police." Marjorie opened the door, and he decided not to correct her assumption. "I've been expecting you."

They stepped into a room decorated in early Goodwill: mismatched calico curtains, a worn orange sofa, shag carpeting in a faded brown. "You're a friend of Cindy's?" Francesca asked.

Marjorie blinked in surprise. "I thought you knew. I'm her roommate."

"Roommate?" Donovan took in the shabby surroundings. "Excuse me, but Mrs. Blakely lived in Newport Beach. With her husband."

"Oh, sure." The woman waved one hand vaguely, still clutching the cat with the other. "Um, would you like something to drink? I think I've got some raspberry soda. No? Okay, well . . . see, she used to live here, before she got married."

"That was five years ago," Francesca said. "You still think of her as your roommate? You must have been close."

"I don't think anybody was close to Cindy." Marjorie shrugged apologetically. "She always seemed to be watching you, like she was trying to figure out if you could be useful."

"She isn't the roommate you were referring to, the one you just lost?" Donovan asked.

Marjorie nodded. "Uh, yes." The cat struggled loose and rubbed against Donovan's ankles. "She kept paying her half of the rent. Like, she wanted to have her own place, you know. . . ." Her voice trailed off.

"For five years?" Francesca said. "That's strange. Didn't you think so?"

"I don't know. I needed the money, and this way I basically got the house to myself," Marjorie said. "Anyway, at first I thought she just wanted a place closer to Los Angeles, to stay over after some late party, or the theater or something."

"Her husband came here?" Donovan asked.

"No. I only met him once or twice, when they were dating. Seemed like a nice guy." Marjorie sighed. "And then, well, she used to bring that man here, that Thomas.

I didn't like him. He even dropped in once by himself and tried to date me. I threw him out, but I never told Cindy. Maybe if I had..."

"You think Thomas killed her?" Donovan asked.

"She's really dead? I thought she was just missing."

"We haven't found a body." Some things still didn't make sense. "Cindy could have afforded an apartment of her own. Why would she share this place?"

"She kept a lot of stuff here," Marjorie said. "Expensive clothes, some jewelry, furs. She said she felt safer having somebody in the house. Although lately I've been gone a lot. Come on, I'll show you her room."

The woman led them through a narrow hallway into a bedroom. The decor matched—or rather mismatched—the rest of the house: a sagging double bed, a cheap dresser, and a double-width closet with warped sliding doors.

Donovan checked the drawers and closet and found them empty. "When's the last time you saw her?"

"That's the funny thing." Marjorie bit her lip. "She hadn't come by for over a month. And then, about two weeks ago, I was out of town with a play—I'm an actress, when I can get work. Anyway, I came home and her stuff was cleaned out."

"A break-in?" Donovan suggested.

She shook her head. "Nothing of mine was touched. It's like she just moved out. Only, the funny thing was, when I caught up on my old newspapers, I discovered she'd disappeared—been killed, whatever—right before I left town."

"So somebody came by after she was dead," Donovan said. "Assuming that she *is* dead."

Marjorie shivered. "It gave me the creeps. I had all the locks changed after that. I guess it must have been that jerk Thomas, huh?"

"It's a good thing you weren't here, or you might have been hurt," Francesca told her sympathetically. "Any of your neighbors see anything?"

"I asked around, but no." Marjorie escorted them back to the living room. "There was one odd thing, though."

"What was that?" Donovan asked.

She indicated a CD player sitting on an orange crate. "We had some of our CDs mixed together. Whoever came in took Cindy's, but not mine. How would Thomas have known which was which?"

Donovan was trying not to overreact, but his brain was racing through the possibilities. If Cindy wasn't dead, where was she? With Thomas? Lost, dazed, injured or kidnapped? Or none of the above? "You might have gotten the dates mixed up. She might have come here before she disappeared."

"If you were busy getting ready to leave town, you might not have noticed her things were gone," Francesca added.

"Well, maybe..." Marjorie didn't look convinced.

They were about to leave when another thought occurred to Donovan. "Could it have been her sister who picked up her things?"

"Amanda?" Marjorie shoved her hands into her jeans pockets. She reminded Donovan of a teenager, although she must have been near thirty. "I guess. I mean, I only met her once. She lives, I don't know, in South America or something. But it's possible. I never thought of that."

They thanked her and left. "That was peculiar," Francesca said when they were back in the car.

"That Cindy kept a place of her own? Or that her things disappeared? Frankly, I agree—on both counts." Donovan checked his map. It was getting toward rush hour, but he didn't see any alternate route back to Newport.

"She was so underhanded, I wouldn't put anything past her." Francesca glared through the windshield. "Or that sister of hers, either. If Amanda did pick up Cindy's things, why didn't she tell you about this place? Seems like she must have known a lot about her sister that she didn't tell you."

"I'm the one who's supposed to do the investigating." But Donovan couldn't help adding, "I wish everything we turn up wouldn't add another complication. If Cindy *is* still alive, we're running in circles while her life is in danger."

"You and your rescue-the-fair-maiden instincts!" snapped Francesca. "Cindy was an opportunist and a louse. Cheating on her husband, and probably stealing from him, too. And I'll bet her sister's no better. You ought to quit trying to be a hero to Amanda and figure out what she's up to."

He wasn't sure which annoyed him more, Francesca's stubbornness or the nagging realization that she might be right. "It's my job to do what my client asked, which is find out all I can about Cindy's disappearance and Jon Blakely's role in it."

"If you'd read even a single old detective novel, you wouldn't be so trusting," Francesca said.

"Would you cut that out? Old detective novels!"

"She's playing you for a fool!"

That was going too far. "Are you sure jealousy isn't clouding your judgment?"

Outrage blazing from every pore, Francesca folded her arms. "You flatter yourself! Jealousy indeed!"

The car inched onto the crowded freeway. "That's why you hate her, isn't it?" Donovan went on. "Frannie, I'm not interested in Amanda in anything but a professional capacity."

"Frannie? Did you call me Frannie?" She quivered with indignation all the way up to her ears. "I am not Francis the talking mule, thank you!"

Donovan's annoyance dissolved into laughter. "Francesca, we're both being ridiculous."

"Oh, yeah?" As her mouth flew open in denial, he leaned over and caught her in a kiss. "You'll get us both killed!" Or at least that was what she seemed to be saying, but the words got caught.

He pulled back fast, before she could slap him. "I've read about fire snapping out of people's eyes, but I've never seen it before."

Pointedly ignoring him, Francesca switched on the radio, and for two and a half hours they crept along the freeway, listening to a mind-numbing amalgam of news, music and talk-show chatter.

His mind returning to the job at hand, Donovan wondered if he'd missed a clue somewhere. A piece that would pull together the puzzle of Cindy's missing possessions, both at Marjorie's and at Jon's; of the attacker in the garages; of the half-million dollars that Cindy might or might not have stolen; of Thomas's conniving; and of Cindy's vanishing in the middle of a divorce that might have netted her half of her husband's estate.

Only when he settled this case, Donovan realized, could he concentrate on squaring things with Francesca. Only then could he take the time to convince her that sticking around didn't have to mean getting stuck.

And, one way or another, he intended to do just that.

IT WAS DARK by the time they pulled into the garage building. The automatic light threw shadows into the corners, and the corridor beyond lay in gloom.

Francesca voiced Donovan's own concern. "What if that man comes back?"

He killed the motor and sat listening. He heard nothing suspicious but, of course, their noisy entry would have given an assailant plenty of warning.

"Stay here," he cautioned.

"What makes you think I'm going to sit back and let some thug shoot you?" Francesca flung her door open.

Under the noise of the squeaking hinges, Donovan heard a dull metallic clank, as if someone had accidentally kicked a pipe. Then silence.

Francesca shot him a look of alarm. Donovan gestured to her to stay where she was, and this time, thank goodness, she obeyed.

He slipped toward the corridor. His best guess was that the sound had come from the repair bay.

There was no chance of surprise. The prudent course might be to dive into the station wagon and drive to safety, but then the intruder would escape.

If there was even a slight chance that Cindy was being held somewhere against her will, that she was still alive and could be saved, Donovan had to do his best.

The repair bay lay adjacent to the station wagon's slot. Donovan edged toward the door, muscles tensed. He tried not to focus on his own miserable track record with this particular opponent.

Maybe this time he'd get a sliver of luck. And the way his adrenaline was pumping, that was all he'd need.

Donovan stiffened, hearing a brushing noise. A shoe moving over concrete. The intruder wasn't sitting around waiting to be cornered.

Donovan checked the ceiling, hoping for a bare rafter. If it was low enough, he could hoist himself up and hang there, waiting for an unwary foe to pass beneath. But he saw nothing in the way of handholds, just an oversize spiderweb rippling in a draft.

He dropped to the floor and pressed against one wall. The intruder wouldn't be looking for him here. In the darkness, the man might not notice him even with a flashlight.

Donovan crouched there, waiting.

He heard a faint intake of breath and caught a whiff of cigar smoke—or rather its harsh aftermath. The guy was closer than he'd thought.

Come on, come on! Why was the guy hesitating? The air pulsated with breath and body heat. Donovan felt like a trapped animal, knowing that to bolt was to risk death, but unable to stand the suspense a moment longer.

Do something. Anything!

Fabric crinkled. The guy was moving. No, bending, getting so close there was no way he could miss—

The cold nose of a gun poked against Donovan's forehead. "One wrong move and you're a wall decoration."

The voice belonged to Amanda.

Chapter Thirteen

Something rushed them from behind. The pistol swung away, and Donovan heard shouting in the darkness.

"Francesca!" he called. "It's Amanda!"

There was no response except the rasp of heavy breathing and a thudding noise off to one side.

He scrabbled and found a light switch. The painful brilliance washed the world white, but after a moment Donovan made out Francesca shoving Amanda against a wall. The gun lay on the floor.

"It wasn't even loaded!" Amanda pulled away indignantly. Her white-blond hair sagged from its French twist, and twin dots of scarlet enlivened her pale cheeks. "How the hell did I know it was Donovan, and who are you?"

"My assistant." He moved between the two women. "I needed a wife for this job, remember?"

"Oh. Yes." Amanda pulled her white fur jacket tighter against the chilly air. Her pale silk slacks were smudged with grease.

"What were you doing sneaking around here any-way?" Francesca demanded.

Instead of answering, Amanda bent toward the gun. Francesca grabbed it first and handed it to Donovan. To humor her, he checked the barrel, and found that it was indeed empty.

"Clean as a whistle." He tossed the cheap little Saturday night special to Amanda. "Carrying an unloaded gun isn't exactly a wise idea. The fellow you come up against is likely to overreact."

"It was just a precaution." She stuck the gun in her purse. "I was looking for you. I tapped at your apartment door, but nobody answered, and some dog started barking, so I thought I'd check out here."

"In the dark?" Francesca asked.

"I couldn't risk a light. If Jon found me..." She grimaced.

As Donovan's eyes adjusted to the harsh light, he saw that a purplish bruise darkened one of Amanda's temples. "Who hit you?"

"Jon." She brushed a lock of hair forward over the injury.

"He wouldn't!" Francesca protested.

The blond woman smiled bitterly. "Oh, he's a smooth character, but he can be violent. He barged into my hotel room this afternoon. You see, my lawyer's been trying to find Cindy's will. She told me recently that she'd changed it, leaving everything to me instead of Jon. Well, he was furious. He accused me of trying to steal half his estate."

"Any idea how he found you?" Donovan tried to view Amanda objectively, to detect whether she was lying, but the sight of that ugly bruise made him too angry.

"He—he must have heard from someone that I was in town, and called the hotels." Amanda cleared her throat. "I live in Peru. But that's not what I came here about."

Francesca kept pressing her. "Are you the one who picked up her stuff at Marjorie's house?"

Surprise flickered across Amanda's face, but she recovered quickly. "Yes. I thought about staying there, but Marjorie was out of town, and it might have been a shock, coming home and discovering me on the premises." Amanda drew a cigarillo from her purse with unsteady fingers. Donovan leaned forward to light it for her.

"We'd better run over what we've found," he offered.

"No time. I came to bring you this." Amanda held out a slip of paper. "I've been going through Cindy's things, and I found the combination to Jon's office safe. Don't ask me how she came by it."

"That must be how she got all the money," Francesca said.

"What money?" Confusion wrinkled Amanda's forehead. "No, you see, he never kept money or valuables in it. The safe is for papers, things he doesn't want to lose in case of fire, or things he doesn't want lying around for anyone to see."

It seemed to Donovan that Amanda knew an awful lot about her brother-in-law. Cindy must have written long, gossipy letters.

The pale woman let out a heartfelt puff of smoke. "If there's a paper trail to the hit man, it's likely to be there. That's my last hope, Mr. Lewis. I can't afford to stay in town much longer, and frankly, I'm frightened."

"Of Jon?" Francesca's voice dripped with disbelief. "Come on, who really hit you? That creep Thomas?"

Amanda's mouth twisted. "Honestly, Mr. Lewis, couldn't you find an employee who knows how to keep her mouth shut?"

"I apologize." Donovan grabbed Francesca's wrist and signaled her to desist. "You really think you're in danger?"

"He showed me a gun. Said he knew how to use it—in fact, that's why I bought this one." The woman tapped off a layer of ash with quick, nervous movements. "He's obsessed with money. He'd rather shoot me than let me inherit even one penny. That's the kind of man he is."

Francesca opened her mouth to argue, but Donovan cut her off. "Ms. Carruthers, we'll get into that safe tonight. Then I'm going to wrap things up. You'll be getting a written report."

She stubbed out the cigarillo on a bench. "Just—just look in there. Then at least I'll feel I've done the best I can for Cindy."

Outside, Amanda refused his offer to walk her to her car. "I parked up the street. I know my way. Thanks, Mr. Lewis. I'll talk to you soon." She disappeared into the darkness.

"She's lying, of course," Francesca said.

Donovan had to admit he couldn't visualize Jon as a violent man, but sometimes people surprised you. "Exactly which item don't you believe?"

"Everything. I don't know."

"We'll be done with this job soon." He escorted her into their apartment. "In fact, if this combination works, we may be done this evening."

Asta, snoozing on the couch, didn't even wake up when Donovan bent to retrieve his pistol from its hiding place under the sofa.

"You're not taking that!" Francesca stared in disbelief. "It's bad enough breaking into the man's safe. And then to take a gun!"

"Amanda says he's packing. If he is, he's liable to shoot rather than ask questions," Donovan said. "I'd rather be alive and in jail than laid out in the morgue."

"I'm not going." Francesca planted herself firmly in the doorway. "And neither are you."

"You're fired," he said.

"Excuse me?"

"You heard me. If you intend to work for me, you'll do as I say. Besides," he added, "if Jon is innocent, we won't find anything, will we? So you'll be helping clear his name."

"In a twisted way, I suppose you're right." After a moment of internal debate, she added, "Okay. Let's go."

"You weren't planning on marching in there right now, were you?" Donovan asked as he covered his shoulder holster with a jacket.

"Why not?" She followed his gaze to the wall clock. "Oh, it's only eight. Jon's still up."

"Jon's not here. Francesca, if you're going to be a detective, you have to pay attention. His car was gone. Didn't you notice the empty stall?"

"No," she admitted. "Well, if he's gone..."

"But Tenley's car isn't."

"Oh." Francesca grinned ruefully. "At least that gives me time to check on my dad."

"Good idea."

She made a call to Laguna Beach and learned that Bruno was in the hospital, happily terrorizing the nurses. Her mother had left, hoarse from arguing, but had promised to resume the battle the following day.

Francesca thanked Victor and hung up. Donovan, whose stomach reminded him they hadn't eaten since lunch, hauled her out of the apartment and down the hall to the main kitchen.

Marta had left thick glazed pork chops in the refrigerator, with apple rings and green beans. Donovan was so hungry he could have devoured the leftovers cold, but Francesca insisted on heating them in the microwave.

They were nearly finished eating when Tenley came by and sagged into a chair. "Gosh, it's late. I just wanted to finish a few things. Jon's been so stressed out, I wanted to make his life a little easier."

"He doesn't deserve you," Donovan said.

"Yes, he does." Tenley stretched wearily. "I just wish he'd notice. Well, anyway, he went to a play at the Performing Arts Center. He was going to leave a couple of extra tickets for you, knowing how you like the theater, but I can't find them. He must have decided to turn them in at the box office."

"What a thoughtful man," said Francesca. "I'm sorry we're so late."

"How's your father?"

"Much better."

Tenley fixed herself a cup of coffee, chatted for a few more minutes and then left. Despite the late hour, she seemed reluctant to abandon her post, and she bustled around her desk for a few minutes before they heard the outer door close.

"She's in love with him," Francesca said as she cleared the table.

"Probably," Donovan conceded. "But he'll never marry her."

"Why not?"

"He's one of Newport's elite, and she's a clerical worker."

"What a snobbish attitude!"

"I'm not saying it's *my* attitude, I'm saying it's his."

"Nonsense!" Francesca slammed dishes into the sink. "He married Cindy, and she was a lowlife if I ever heard of one!"

"Yes, but she was an actress, and performers—successful ones, anyway—are Hollywood's elite. Don't forget, we've had a president who was a former actor." Donovan knew he was baiting Francesca, but he enjoyed watching the sparks fly. He was beginning to understand why her parents liked to fight so much. Francesca was never quite so intense as during an argument—except, of course, when they lay in each others' arms. . . .

Francesca bristled. "Jon is *not* that kind of man! And by the way, Donovan, how come I'm doing the dishes?"

"Because you cleared the table." He could see he was in dangerous territory. "All right, I'll do them."

"About time, too." She yielded her place at the sink. "I've had enough of this housekeeping business."

By the time he'd finished, Tenley's car had purred down the driveway and the house lay in a pool of stillness.

"You stand watch," Donovan said.

"Why?"

"Keep an eye on the driveway. He might hate the production and come home early."

Francesca muttered something he couldn't catch, but she followed orders.

Just in case, Donovan took a flashlight with him into Jon's office. Tenley must have straightened up; the place was as neat as an operating room.

He swung the painting aside and regarded the safe. If, as Amanda had said, it was intended more for fire protection than to keep out burglars, it was no wonder Jon hadn't taken pains to hide it.

Following the numbers on the paper, Donovan spun the dial. Nothing happened on the first try, but combination locks were notoriously finicky. He figured he'd probably turned a notch too far.

Nothing happened the second time, either.

Had Amanda written the thing down wrong? Or could this be the wrong code entirely?

After ten minutes, perspiration was trickling down Donovan's neck. He'd tried every variation he could think of.

He found Francesca in the living room. "You're the lock-picker. Maybe you can figure it out."

She came without argument, obviously relieved to be part of the action. "She might have left out a digit."

"That only leaves about two million possible combinations," Donovan growled. "We'll never get the damn thing open."

"Don't be such a pessimist." Francesca grinned as they entered the office.

"You're enjoying this!"

"I'm a jewel thief, remember?" She snatched away the slip of paper.

Donovan stood back, grinding his teeth and wishing he could pound the lock into submission. He wanted this case cleared up, one way or the other.

The truth, he admitted to himself, was that he liked Jon Blakely, and from everything he'd heard he didn't like Cindy very much. Part of him didn't want Jon to be guilty, and part of him feared the guy might be one of those Dr. Jekyll types, as bad as Amanda described and worse.

It was entirely possible the man was a clever sociopath. Donovan had met a few such monsters when he'd prosecuted them in his former career. They could be charming and personable, intelligent and seemingly sincere. And deadly.

If that was what he was, Jon would have suspected Donovan and Francesca the moment he saw them in the bowling alley, if not before. He might have arranged tonight's supposed outing as a setup.

Cold sweat creased Donovan's hands as he held the flashlight for Francesca. He knew he was psyching himself out, letting the enforced waiting and the nerve-racking clicks of the combination lock wear on his nerves. But, damn it, what if Jon had purposely left them this opening? What if he was hiding on the premises even now, with his gun?

Donovan reached into his shoulder holster and started to draw out his .38.

"Got it!" Francesca said, and opened the safe.

After all the suspense, Donovan found himself disappointed that no cache of jewels tumbled glittering into the beam of light. All he saw were a few folders and some rubber-banded packets.

As Francesca started to reach in, Donovan caught her wrist. "Could be booby-trapped," he said.

"You're paranoid!"

"That's my job." He steered her firmly away. Finding a yardstick by the desk, he leaned out and poked it into the safe. From this distance, he had to admit, if the thing was mined it would blow him to smithereens, but at least Francesca might be spared.

Nothing happened.

"See?" She started forward, just as a sharp rumble echoed from far off in the house. It stopped almost as quickly as it had begun, a dull clacking like a big box of dice being shaken.

"What the—?"

Francesca laughed. "It's the ice-maker in the refrigerator. Good thing you have a housekeeper along to explain."

Donovan tried to shrug off the incident. He knew his nerves were strung taut. This whole case bothered him. People weren't what they seemed, and matters kept twisting in unexpected directions.

He felt as if he'd fallen into a maze lined with distorted mirrors. The fun house had stopped being fun a long time ago.

"Look at this." Francesca pulled some paper loose from around a packet. "It's money. Thousand-dollar bills. Guess he hasn't had time to run by the bank yet."

Donovan reached past her and pulled out several folders. He opened one and spotted Stewart Waters's letterhead, along with a series of dates. "Looks like he's been having his wife investigated for quite a few months."

They leaned against the back of the sofa, Francesca peering over his shoulder. Donovan flipped through, speed-reading the reports. Apparently Cindy had squirreled away several hundred thousand dollars in bank accounts and stock investments under her own name, in addition to the property she held jointly with Jon.

"Sneaky," he said, "but not entirely unreasonable. She might have been afraid he'd cut her off and she'd need the money for a long legal battle."

"What about the half-million dollars?" Francesca tapped a packet against her knee. "Why didn't she just put it in the bank? Not to mention that she couldn't have built that secret compartment in the car herself."

He read on. "There's more. Apparently Jon noticed works of art are missing from the house, small carvings, miniature paintings, things like that. Cindy's been selling them on the black market. Only a fraction of their value, but that still comes to—" he mentally added up some figures "—three-quarters of a million dollars."

Francesca whistled. "Wow."

Donovan began to understand Jon's anger. A wife was entitled to half her husband's estate, and if she wanted to tuck away her own funds, she did have that right. But to sell off her husband's prized art collection was ugly.

"Ordinarily, I'd suspect she needed the money for some problem, gambling or drugs," he said. "But then she wouldn't have those fat bank accounts."

"She's just greedy." Francesca shook her head angrily. "And stupid, when you think that she could have made a lot more in a divorce settlement."

They weren't going to resolve the matter now. Donovan stood to replace the folders. "Anyway," he said, "there's nothing in here about a hit man."

Outside, something scraped against the house.

Francesca shot him a frightened look. Donovan shoved everything into the safe. "Get down!"

Something snuffled beneath the window.

"What is it?" Her voice wavered.

"Sounds like an animal." Donovan strode to the window and slid it open. "If it's that dog of yours..."

"I don't see how he could have..."

Donovan leaned out and was greeted by a whine that mutated into a snarl. "Asta!" He slammed the window shut. "Just what we needed. No more dogs on jobs, Francesca!"

"You don't understand. He couldn't have—"

"I saw him with my own eyes. Want to look?" He stomped back toward the safe and banged his toe against a chair. "Would you turn the bloody light on?"

"Donovan, listen to me!" Francesca didn't move. "Asta was in our apartment. All the doors were locked. Remember? How did he get outside?"

"I don't know. Through a window."

"Which window? They're kept shut, too."

Donovan's breath caught as he realized the significance. If Asta had gotten out, then someone must have opened a door or a window. Which meant there was someone else in the house.

"I think we'd better get out of here," he said.

"I think you'd better, too," said a masculine voice from the doorway.

Light streamed through the room. It took Donovan a minute to make out the man's face, but then he didn't have to. He'd already recognized the voice.

Jon Blakely had caught them. And for the second time that evening there was a gun pointed straight at Donovan.

Chapter Fourteen

This time, there was one key difference, and it lay heavy across Donovan's chest. His own holster.

"Duck!" he yelled to Francesca, and dived to one side as he jerked out the .38.

"Donovan, no!" She leaped toward him.

"Stay back!" He took aim. Jon seemed to have gone numb in the doorway; the pistol still targeted Donovan, but it was trembling.

"Don't shoot!" Francesca hit Donovan's arm, and the gun went off. "No!"

"What—?" Jon staggered against the door frame, dropping his gun. There was something wrong with the way it hit and bounced, as if it were too light to be real.

Francesca raced to support the millionaire. "It's a cigarette lighter! I've seen him use it before."

"My—my wife gave it to me for our anniversary." Jon touched his neck gingerly.

"I'm sorry. I didn't know." Donovan holstered his gun, confused. Why had Blakely threatened them with a cigarette lighter? Amanda had been so certain he carried a real weapon.

"Are you all right? I'll call the paramedics," Francesca was saying.

Jon blinked, coming out of his daze. "No. It just . . . grazed me."

Donovan checked the red line along the man's neck. "It looks superficial, but you should get it cleaned."

The thin man took in the sight of the open safe. "I didn't expect to find you two doing something like this. What are you, robbers?"

Donovan produced his private investigator's license and braced himself for an outburst, but Jon's expression remained more puzzled than angry.

"Detectives? Who hired you?" The man winced as he shifted position.

"I'm sorry. I can't reveal my client."

Francesca skewered Donovan with a scowl. "Doggone your professional ethics! We're working for Amanda."

"Amanda Carruthers? Really?" He leaned against a chair, and two tickets fell from his pocket.

"You came back to bring us those!" Francesca rescued the tickets. "You were doing us a favor, and here we were breaking into your stuff. I'm so sorry."

"Someone paged me and left a message with my service. Said you two wanted to see me. I figured Tenley had told you about the tickets, and the curtain was delayed anyway, so I came back." Jon straightened. "I was really beginning to like you two."

Donovan found it difficult to look the man in the eye. He wished now that he'd trusted Jon a little more. On the other hand, just because the safe's contents had proved harmless didn't mean Blakely was innocent. "Of course, you have the right to press charges, but I hope we can clear this up privately."

"I still don't understand about Amanda," Jon said. "What could she hope to—?"

Before Donovan could answer, a female voice spoke from behind them. "They're working for me, Jon."

It was Amanda's raspy voice, but Jon's next words stopped Donovan cold. "Cindy!"

"What?" Francesca's shock mirrored Donovan's.

As he took in the blond woman, whose auburn roots were already beginning to show, a hundred scattered puzzle pieces fell into place. The family resemblance. The clues that Cindy might still be alive. Amanda's evasiveness about where she could be reached.

But what had she hoped to accomplish? Was she trying to frame her husband for a murder she knew hadn't happened? Donovan had heard of bitter divorces, but having to spend the rest of one's life pretending to be dead seemed a high price to pay for revenge.

Cindy brushed past Jon, her gun aimed at Donovan. He slid his hand toward the holster.

"I wouldn't," the blond woman said. "It's loaded this time." She reached inside Donovan's jacket and pulled out his .38.

Francesca shifted toward Cindy, about to pounce.

"I wouldn't do that, lady," said a male voice from the dark reaches of the outer office.

Donovan recognized the hulking figure, the stocky build, those gym-honed muscles. The attacker from the garage. The infamous Thomas.

The former chauffeur stepped forward, and light washed over his pale eyes. "Cindy, get over here. You turn your back on somebody, they're likely to jump you."

"Yeah, okay, Thomas." The blonde hurried to his side.

Donovan sneaked a glance around the room. A silver letter opener lay on an end table a few feet away, but he knew better than to make any sudden movements.

As Cindy passed by, Jon glimpsed his wife's bruised face. He studied her with a mixture of bewilderment and bitterness. "You preferred *that* to me?"

Cindy's classic features twisted as she confronted her husband. "At least he's a real man! He knows how to fight for what he wants. He didn't inherit everything he owns. And he doesn't waste his time on charity balls and opera and all that snob stuff."

"And he beats you up." Jon clenched his jaw. "A real man."

Donovan sidled toward the letter opener. No one noticed.

"He loves me!" Cindy handed the .38 to Thomas and wrapped an arm around his waist. "Yeah, he loses his temper sometimes. He's got to work on that. He didn't have all the advantages growing up like you did. So what?"

Her accent, even her facial expressions, were so different from those she'd affected as Amanda that Donovan almost couldn't believe this was the same person. Then he remembered that Cindy was an actress. Too bad she hadn't put her talents to better use.

"Frankly, I think you two deserve each other." Francesca stopped in midsentence. "My God!"

"What?" Jon said.

"They're wearing gloves!"

"So?" the millionaire asked.

Donovan didn't need an explanation. For him, the final piece of the puzzle had fallen into place.

Cindy wasn't setting her husband up to be convicted of murder; she was setting him up to be killed. It was Cindy who'd given Jon the gun-shaped lighter. It was Cindy who'd arranged for Donovan to break into the safe and warned him that Jon was armed and dangerous. It was Cindy who'd paged Blakely tonight and left the message that sent him back to the house.

If Donovan had killed her husband for her, Cindy would have been a very wealthy widow.

She must have had the plan in mind when she vanished. Such an elaborate setup, such a calculated murder, made him realize the depths of her ruthlessness. Or, perhaps, of Thomas's.

There was one other problem: Once the plot failed and they decided to finish off Jon themselves, they couldn't let Donovan and Francesca escape. That was the significance of the gloves.

Cindy and Thomas had come prepared. If they had thought this whole thing out, and Donovan suspected they had, they intended to make it look as if Donovan and Jon had shot each other. And, blast them, they'd have to kill Francesca, too.

Donovan's fingers closed over the letter opener.

"Move toward the safe," Thomas told Francesca. "That's right. We gotta break you three up a little. Make the scene more believable so the cops don't get suspicious."

"What are you doing?" Jon still didn't get it.

"You should appreciate this," jeered Cindy. "The way you love drama. We're putting on a little play of our own."

Francesca bent down.

"Hey, what—?" Thomas said.

Francesca wrenched off one of her shoes and hurled it at Thomas. He dodged, and the shoe smashed against Cindy's injured temple, raising a shriek of pain.

Francesca started to attack, but Donovan shoved her aside. "Get Cindy!" he called, and plunged the letter opener toward the chauffeur's heart.

The tactic should have worked. Thomas held the gun in his right hand; Donovan attacked from the left. With Francesca's distraction, he would have succeeded except for one thing.

Thomas didn't even try to swing the gun into position to fire. He simply thrust his muscular left arm straight out, fist first.

It was what used to be called a sucker punch. Donovan's own momentum magnified the impact as he took the blow straight on the chin.

The universe was reborn in a big bang of stars and exploding matter. Donovan reeled backward, lost in space. He had the sensation of falling, although that seemed impossible in zero gravity, and then the percussive effect of his head connecting with the floor dumped his consciousness into a black hole.

He awoke to a fuzzy, lash-shaded vision of Francesca kneeling over him. She didn't notice he was awake, and it occurred to Donovan that he might be dead, except that he didn't think corpses got headaches.

He realized she was speaking. He didn't think he could be hearing her correctly, because what she was saying was "Donovan! Please, please don't die! Damn it, you big lug, I love you. Don't leave me!"

Just like in the movies, he thought, before another wave of dark matter carried him out of the galaxy.

He dropped back to earth a few eons later—though it must actually have been only a moment—to hear Thomas ordering Francesca to hand over the cash.

"What cash?" said a blurred voice that he thought belonged to Amanda. Cindy. Whoever she was.

"You ought to know," Jon said. "Half a million bucks that you had hidden in your car. That you stole from the safe in the garage."

"I didn't even know you had a safe in the garage."

"It was in case of a kidnapping." Irony darkened Jon's words. "I was afraid someone might hold you for ransom and I'd need the cash in a hurry."

Cindy sucked in her breath. "Thomas. You never told me."

"Just adding to our nest egg, darling," said the unfazed chauffeur. "Spur-of-the-moment thing."

"Is that how you built the hiding place into the back of her car?" Jon said. "On the spur of the moment? What else did you smuggle out on your little test drives to check the transmission?"

Donovan's vision cleared, but he decided not to move yet. Of course, he couldn't assume movement was actually possible, not while he was still floating inside the rings of Saturn.

"The artwork too?" Cindy asked. "When Jon accused me of taking it, I thought he was crazy."

"Why not?" said Thomas. "You always said you hated the stuff."

For the first time, Donovan heard an apologetic note in Jon's voice. "You weren't stealing then, Cindy. I'm sorry."

"Shut up!" Cindy snapped. Then, to Thomas: "You were ripping me off!"

"As you said, I know how to take care of myself," he returned.

"Why didn't you sneak the money out earlier, like the art? Or take it out of the car before you abandoned it?" That must be Francesca.

"I knew Jonny boy would miss it quick, not like those little knickknacks," Thomas said. "And then, that night, Cindy was hanging all over me. Wouldn't wait in my truck like I asked. I meant to come back later, but the police got it first."

"I was running away with you and you were stealing from me?" Cindy said. "What else didn't you tell me about?"

"Not much."

Not much. Just cheating the housekeeper at cards and then threatening her if she didn't pay up, and encouraging her to steal from Cindy. But that seemed minor to Donovan, compared to the other things Thomas had in mind.

Like planning to kill Francesca. And Jon. And him, if he wasn't already dead.

"I can't believe you'd treat me like this," Cindy said.

"You're not going to hold it against me, are you, sweetheart?" Without waiting for an answer, Thomas added, "Now, Mr. Blakely—" he gave "Mr." a sardonic emphasis "—you stand right here in the doorway. See, you've just come home and surprised the burglars." The chauffeur smiled down at the .38, at the gun covered with Donovan's fingerprints.

"Cindy, think!" Jon urged. "The man's been cheating you all along. You're planning to marry him? If you inherit my money, your life won't be worth zip. You'll be worth far more to him dead than alive!"

"He wouldn't kill me." But Cindy didn't sounded very confident.

From where he lay, Donovan heard a low whistle. It sounded like Francesca calling Asta for dinner, except that the dog was outside. Unless somebody'd left a door open again. Anyway, the dog wasn't going to help them even if it showed up. Asta was about as far from being an attack dog as Francesca was from being a real detective.

Donovan knew he ought to rouse himself. Ought to get up and do something. At least not let himself be gunned down lying here like an invalid.

Donovan's brain sent a clear signal to his legs, which sent back the neurological equivalent of a Bronx cheer. Nothing moved.

He could hear Thomas giving directions, and the people overhead reluctantly shuffling about. Donovan tried to lift his head and shout at them to fight back. The planet Venus collided with the sun in a shower of boiling light, and he sank deeper into the carpet.

"You aren't really going to let him do this, are you, Cindy?" said Francesca from somewhere out in the Milky Way.

"I trust him" was the response.

"Even you deserve better than this jerk," Jon said.

There followed a thud and a grunt as Thomas repaid the insult with a blow.

If there had ever been a person in need of rescuing, it was the hapless millionaire. And Donovan blamed himself for having made everything worse.

He'd been so stubborn, so egotistical, that he'd rejected Francesca's ideas and refused to trust his own instincts. Now they were all going to die for his mistakes.

If he could just manage to move . . .

Something barked. Not something; a dog, getting closer and louder. A real angry bite-em snarl, the kind Asta reserved for cats.

"What the hell is that?" snapped Thomas. "Since when does Blakely have a dog?"

The terrier rushed into the room with the fury of a seasoned rat-catcher who'd just cornered a Norway brown. But Donovan didn't think Thomas was the kind of rat that Asta had in mind.

"Get down, you mutt!" The chauffeur took aim at the dog.

"Don't you dare!" yelled Francesca, who sounded more upset for Asta than she'd been about her own life. She swept the dog into her arms.

As the snarling got louder, the truth swept over Donovan.

Asta wasn't menacing them because he wanted to protect his mistress. He hadn't come here because of Thomas or Cindy at all.

The terrier had one target in mind: Donovan's pants. The pants upon which Marjorie's cat had so graciously bestowed a sprinkling of feline hairs.

The realization that he might at any moment be bitten in a thousand painful places shot life into Donovan's nerve endings. His brain snapped to attention, awake at last.

And at that precise moment Thomas made his only error of the evening. He took a step back, away from Asta, right over Donovan.

In that single vulnerable moment, Donovan did the one thing no self-respecting he-man would ever do unless the woman he loved faced death and a ravening terrier was about to sink its teeth into his calf.

He kicked straight up. And Thomas the chauffeur took a sucker punch where it hurt the most.

Donovan could only imagine the shades of magenta and chartreuse that suffused the man's unlovely face. There was a moment of supreme calm, broken only by the dog's perplexed whine, and then Thomas staggered away with a strangled cough and collapsed, his head making a loud whacking sound against the leg of the couch.

A glow of relief surged through Donovan. It lasted until he heard a triumphant yelp as Asta wriggled free of Francesca's grasp.

"Keep him—" Donovan tried to sit up.

Asta took a long, happy howl and sank his teeth into Donovan's leg.

"Off me!" He scrabbled away, trying to shake the terrier loose.

"You're alive!" cried Francesca, happily pulling off the dog.

Thomas groaned.

"I'll get him." Jon grabbed some packing twine from a drawer, jumped onto the chauffeur and bound his hands so neatly one might have thought he'd spent his life roping steers rather than rattling papers.

They'd done it. With Asta's unwitting help, they'd toppled the mastermind of their own murders. The realization made Donovan's leg throb a bit less.

Except, his still-dazed brain reminded him, for one small detail.

"Hold it." Cindy's Saturday night special wavered from one to another. "Back off, Jon. Don't try to get his gun."

The millionaire tied a final knot and stood up. "You can't tell me you're really a murderer at heart, Cindy. An opportunist, maybe, but not a killer."

"Oh, yeah? Watch this." She bit her lip.

"Aren't you going to stop her?" Francesca asked Donovan.

"Me?" Sitting up was having an odd effect on his kinesthetic sense. He could have sworn the room was doing the Wave.

"All right, I'll stop her!"

"No!" He caught Francesca's wrist. "She's my client. I'll do it."

"Hand over the cash," Cindy said.

Francesca retrieved the bundles from the safe. "Here."

Cindy scooped them under one arm. "Now let Thomas go."

"You sure you know how to shoot that?" Jon indicated the gun.

"I know what a trigger is." Cindy backed toward the exit.

"Just leave," Donovan told her. "You've got enough money to stake yourself to a new life. The police probably won't even look for you as long as they've got the real perpetrator."

"Untie him!" The barrel pointed at Jon.

He stood his ground. "How much is this lying jerk worth to you, Cindy? We had some good times, I thought. Maybe we could have worked things out if Thomas hadn't come into the picture."

"Thomas was always in the picture!" Cindy cried. "He was the one who made me marry you. It was all his idea! And then I got him the job as chauffeur."

Blakely paled. "You really did take me for a fool. I always tried to give you the benefit of the doubt."

"I told you Jon was a nice guy," Francesca murmured to Donovan. "Now would you do something about her?"

He gripped the arm of the couch and wrenched himself upright. "It's the typical abused-woman syndrome." He had to keep everybody distracted until his sense of balance caught up with gravity. "She identifies with her abuser. She believes he loves her, that he'll reform."

"Hogwash!" Francesca clenched her fists. "She's a grown woman and she's responsible for her own actions."

"Would you two shut up?" said Cindy.

The furniture slowed its orbit around the room. Donovan was pretty sure that if he lunged directly between the two Cindys dancing across his vision, he'd run into the real one. "Okay. I can move now."

Thomas groaned. "Damn it, Cindy! Would you just shoot them?"

"I thought maybe we wouldn't have to do that."

Donovan heard a noise in the outer office. It might have been Asta; the dog seemed to have disappeared. But it sounded like a breath of surprise, inhaled so quickly it was almost imperceptible. He must be hallucinating.

"Do it. Now!" Thomas said. "Get Blakely first, you idiot! Fire!"

As Cindy braced herself, Donovan knew there would be no more dogs to the rescue and no more sucker punches. Either he took the bullet alone and gave Jon a chance to grab Cindy, or they all died.

"Shoot me instead!" He hurled himself at Cindy and saw the pistol swing toward him at point-blank range.

Chapter Fifteen

Donovan thought his muddled brain was playing tricks on him.

Just as he expected to feel the impact of a shot, Cindy sprouted another pair of arms. The new hands knocked the gun upward as it discharged, and the bullet slammed harmlessly into the ceiling.

Donovan caught himself in midstride, heaving his body against the door frame to avoid colliding with this new octopus version of Cindy. As he did so, he saw there was someone struggling with her from behind.

"Tenley!" Jon helped his assistant pull Cindy into a chair and tie her wrists.

"I checked with the service in case there were any important calls." Tenley looped the twine tighter than was really necessary. "When I heard that message about someone wanting to talk to you, I got worried. It seemed like a trick."

"You saved my life," Jon said.

Donovan's knees, released from their momentary jolt of adrenaline, began to sag. He wobbled to the couch.

"I'm glad I got here in time." Tenley surveyed Thomas lying on the floor and Cindy glaring up through a loose strand of bleached hair. "I'm afraid even to ask what happened." She picked up the phone. "First things first."

When the police had been notified, Tenley made coffee in the office pot. She was taking the situation with remarkable aplomb, Donovan thought, or maybe she was just in shock.

"This is the part they always leave out on TV," Francesca noted as she gratefully accepted a cup. "Waiting around with the bad guys trussed up like hogs."

"You don't have to insult us," said Cindy. "Thomas? We're going to get out of this, aren't we? You always said you'd take care of me."

"Go hire a lawyer," snapped her boyfriend. "You can afford one."

Cindy burst into tears.

Tenley turned to Donovan. "Do you need a doctor? You've got a nasty bruise."

"I'm fine. Really." He wasn't seeing double images anymore, after all.

"And Jon got shot," Francesca said. Tenley looked to her boss in alarm.

The millionaire indicated his graze. "Not worth bothering about."

His assistant took a deep breath. "If you say so."

"That's what I like about you, Tenley," said Jon. "You don't waste time fussing."

"I hope that's not all you like about her," Francesca said. "She's been in love with you for ages."

"Francesca!" Tenley blushed.

"In love?" Jon gazed at his assistant, his thin, anxious face warming as if he'd shed ten years. "Why didn't I see it? I've always depended on you, Tenley. I took you for granted. But now—"

"Spare us," sneered Thomas.

"A lot you'd understand!" Cindy snapped at the chauffeur. "You creep!" And she burst into a fresh bout of weeping.

Whatever Thomas might have said next was cut off by the doorbell. The police had arrived.

It took over an hour to fill out the reports. The sequence of events was so complicated that the officers had trouble keeping things straight.

"Now, what happened to this Amanda Carruthers?" the sergeant asked. "The real one?"

"I only met her once, at our wedding," Blakely said. "She operates an orphanage in Peru. She sends Cindy photographs once in a while."

"A real saint," Cindy muttered. "I never could stand her."

"Too bad you didn't take her as a role model," said Francesca.

"You should see the pictures of her orphanage!" Cindy grimaced. "Cracked walls, bare cots. Who'd want to live like that?"

Donovan tactfully refrained from pointing out that she'd just given a good description of a jail cell. Only a jail cell didn't come with loving children and a sense of higher purpose.

As the police hustled the culprits away, Francesca watched with a mixture of dislike and pity. "What's going to happen to her?"

Donovan rubbed his chin, where the pain was fading to a dull ache. "She'll probably get a reduced sentence for testifying against Thomas."

"But she tried to kill you!"

"She could make a case for self-defense." Donovan shrugged. "Sometimes you take the lesser of two evils. At least they'll put Thomas away for a long time."

Jon closed the safe and escorted them out of the office. "I want to thank you two."

"For what?" said Francesca. "We did a lot of Cindy's dirty work for her."

"She tricked you just like she tricked me," he said. "And then, tonight, I'm glad I had the two of you on my side. Donovan, you nearly got yourself killed a couple of times. You're a brave man."

Donovan wished the praise could salve his conscience, but it didn't. "I should have seen through her from the beginning."

"Then you wouldn't have had a chance to bring us together." Tenley smiled at her boss. "That's more than enough reason to thank you."

Donovan and Francesca wished the two of them well, then went to clear out their apartment. Only when they were halfway down the hall did Donovan remember about Asta.

"When Cindy's gun went off, he ran out of there in a panic," Francesca said. "Didn't you notice?"

"I was too busy looking at the octopus," he said, and ignored the quizzical arch of her eyebrows. He was too tired for any more explanations tonight.

In the apartment, they found the terrier snoozing, head on paws. Francesca patted Asta's nose. "He's wonderful, isn't he? I don't know what I'd do without him."

Donovan rubbed his bitten calf. The dog hadn't broken the skin, but it hurt like crazy. "You ought to train him not to chase cats."

"I've got an easier solution," she said. "Wash your pants."

He couldn't think of a reply in his current condition, so they set about packing. As he folded his shirts, Donovan felt a twist of sadness, like at the end of a delightful vacation when he had to go back to the realities of dirty laundry and piled-up mail.

He didn't want this time to end. He wanted to stay here forever, breathing in Francesca's nearness.

Donovan felt the air shimmer each time she passed. She must have daubed on some more perfume. Or else he'd suddenly become more attuned to her scent. It followed him, teased him, challenged him.

And yet he could feel Francesca slipping from his reach, moment by moment. She seemed oblivious of Donovan as she tucked her cosmetics in a bag and collected her bottle of shampoo. It was as if their closeness had ended with the job and she was mentally moving on to whatever came next.

He couldn't imagine how he could have known a woman so intimately and shared such close quarters with her and still feel as if she were unattainable. Just as she had that first night in Laguna Beach, Francesca had transformed herself into a phantom, always just around the next corner, elusive as a dream.

Donovan had never been good at the subtleties of relationships. He liked to lay his cards on the table. But he knew that if he told Francesca he loved her, she'd flee.

"You've done a good job for your first assignment," he said cautiously, folding slacks into his suitcase. "You still need supervision, of course, but you're getting the hang of it."

"Oh, I am, am I?" Francesca crammed a wispy lace something-or-other into her suitcase. With her face averted, he couldn't get a clue as to her emotions.

"I think we could work out an apprenticeship." Donovan spoke as steadily as he could. Darn it, why did he have to handle the most delicate situation of his life while still smarting from a fight? His bones ached and his muscles throbbed.

"I'll need to think about it," said Francesca.

"Oh?" What was there to think about? She wanted to be a detective, didn't she? "For how long?"

"Till I see what else comes up." Francesca dumped shoes into her bag.

It was more than a man could take. "Darn it, Francesca!" Donovan thumped his fist against the headboard. "Who else do you think is going to hire you?"

"Stewart Waters seemed interested." She rolled up a pink blouse.

"Interested in hanky-panky!"

"Is that all you think men see in me? Is that all you see?" This time she met his gaze.

"Do you really think you can find a better job?" Donovan asked her, his tone challenging. "Or are you just running away?"

"I never run away." Her dark eyes slid from his.

"Then what happened to 'Don't leave me. I love you, you big lug'?"

"You weren't supposed to hear that!" She tossed her hair back. "You were knocked out!"

"But you do love me! And you're so damn scared I'm going to tie you down that you'd throw it away. Why, Francesca?"

"When I nearly lost you, it scared me. The world seemed so dark and empty." Her mouth softened. "I don't want to need anyone that much. I don't want to be afraid of life. I don't want to live with the fear that you'll be taken away from me."

He sank onto the bed. "What about taking risks? Nobody gets a guarantee, Francesca."

"But it was like somebody tied a noose around my neck." She sat beside him and rested her head on his shoulder. "Like I couldn't breathe."

"You'd still be free to come and go." Donovan wasn't sure how much he meant that, but he swore silently to do his best.

"I'd worry over you like a mother hen. I'd drive us both crazy, and we'd end up hating each other." Francesca nuzzled his neck. "You smell like sweat and gunpowder. It's fabulous."

Out of nowhere, a sense of exhilaration flamed through Donovan. The night's events faded to a single realization: He and the woman he loved had survived. They'd triumphed. They'd met death head-on, and they'd won.

It was the joy of a knight who's slain the kingdom's most vicious dragon and rescued his fair lady from the tower. Never mind that he hadn't exactly rescued Francesca, or that the dragon's attorney would probably drag the case through the courts for years. For now, the good guys had won.

"You want to work for Stewart Waters?" he said. "Fine. Just make sure you don't do this with him."

He slipped his hands beneath the soft fullness of Francesca's sweater as his mouth closed over hers. She didn't even try to pull away. She melted like butter.

Her tongue met Donovan's as her nipples peaked beneath his palms. She was giving herself this time without reservation. Whatever barriers might spring up another day, right now she belonged to him.

He traced her cheeks and earlobes with his mouth, tasting salt and desire. Her arms encircled him, demanding, urging, and a deep, primordial groan welled up from inside him.

Pulling Francesca across the bed, he disrobed her inch by inch, reveling in her eager response. Newly freed from danger, she'd come alive in every cell.

They merged with a passion close to desperation. Donovan teased her with long kisses and let Francesca lure him to the edge of desire again and again.

He heard himself murmuring, and heard her whispering back, tender phrases he couldn't remember even an instant later. Endearments, torments, they all meant the same thing: that they needed each other too much for words.

And then they were caught in a fierce current, rushing forward, lost in foam and thunder until their need for each other swept them over the falls and they cascaded down, clinging together, into warm and sleepy depths.

Donovan wanted to talk afterward, to make Francesca promise to stay. But he'd sunk too deep into the pool, and it was so pleasant lazing in the warmth. His mind yielded to exhaustion, and he slept.

WHEN HE AWOKE, Francesca was gone. Donovan knew without checking that she'd taken her suitcase, although how she'd balanced it on her motorcycle would remain one of life's unsolved mysteries.

Why had she left without saying goodbye? Was she really that frightened of loving him?

Dawn hadn't yet lightened the eastern sky when he walked out into the lettuce-crisp air, hefted his bags into the van and started the engine.

Donovan's eyes prickled from too little sleep, and his muscles had stiffened. What he needed was a dip in a whirlpool spa and a long massage. Preferably at the hands of a dark-haired woman with playful eyes and an exotic perfume.

His condominium hadn't weathered the past few days with any grace. Donovan found a sheaf of papers stuck in the mailbox, all junk and bills. Inside, the air smelled stuffy, and a carton of milk had turned sour in the refrigerator.

He fried some canned corned-beef hash and ate it standing at the kitchen counter. The condo was innocuous in design, off-white in color and still nearly empty after three years. From here, he could see the living room, underwhelmed by a wicker love seat and some batik cushions. There wasn't even a trace of a nail hole on the walls.

What the place really needed was an airplane hanging from the ceiling.

Donovan knew Francesca's name wasn't in the phone book, because he'd checked when he tried to recover the stolen necklace. Yet he sensed it would be a mistake to turn up on her doorstep unannounced. It might even drive her farther away.

On a hunch, he looked in the listings under Asta and found a number for one F. Asta. He dialed it.

Francesca's voice on the answering machine sounded tired and rushed. "Hi, it's me. I'm out of town for a while. If this is an emergency or you owe me money, you can talk to my father." She left the number.

Donovan called it, and Victor answered. Bruno, it turned out, was being released from the hospital that afternoon.

"Letitia left this morning." Victor sounded resigned, maybe a little relieved. "She and Bruno had another screaming fight, and she threw a plate at him. So she's off to Alaska."

In what he hoped was an offhand manner, Donovan asked, "You haven't seen Francesca, have you?"

"Today? No," Victor said. "Is she missing?"

"Not really." Donovan heard the gruffness in his voice, and added quickly, "If you see her, don't mention that I called. She doesn't like people checking up on her."

"Tell me about it." Victor sighed. "Like father, like daughter."

They rang off. Donovan ran water over the frying pan and stood weighing his options.

As a private detective, he knew he could find Francesca sooner or later. But would that be wise?

It's a test. Let her go and she'll come back.

What if she didn't? What if she'd already left for Alaska, or accepted a job from Stewart Waters, or taken a slow boat to China?

Yeah, well, I've gotten along this long without a dame.

It was the word *dame* that really got to him. One of Francesca's old-movie words. She'd managed to squeeze into his thought processes and corrupt his vocabulary. Even if he never saw her again, Donovan realized, Francesca had become a part of him.

DONOVAN OPENED his office door and then closed it again. He'd obviously gone to the wrong place.

Nope, the lettering on the door spelled out his name. He peered inside again.

His outer office didn't have bold geometric-patterned curtains. It didn't smell of lemon cleanser and furniture polish. It featured Tammi's battered desk front and center, not a low couch and coffee table, with a high-tech desk wedged to one side.

What had the bloody landlord been up to while he was gone? The lease wouldn't run out for another six months, and he'd paid the rent this month. Hadn't he?

With a sigh, Donovan stepped inside.

"Oh, there you are!" Tammi beamed at him from behind the high-tech desk. She had done something to her hair; it was shorter, or lighter, or both. And she'd put on a wool skirt and a coordinated blazer.

"You look nice," Donovan ventured.

"Thanks! Here's your mail." She handed him a stack. "The phone messages are on your desk. I can't believe it—we've got ten people needing your services and they all sound like they can afford you! It must be that ad Francesca placed in the *Orange Coast Style*. By the way, where is she?"

"Who knows? Where'd you get the new desk?"

"From the want ads. They made a trade for the old desk and some typing help, and since I didn't have much to do while you were gone, I thought it was a good deal, don't you?"

"Very enterprising." Donovan flipped through the mail as he went inside. He was pleased to discover three requests for help and surprised to find solicitations from several financial advisors seeking to invest his funds, as if he actually had any.

He looked up and cursed silently. Damn, Tammi had even fooled around with his inner sanctum. Gone were the spiderwebs and the well-preserved wedges of dust in the corners. A modernistic pole lamp sprouted beside his desk, and the file cabinet—he couldn't quite believe it— had been painted white. Not that he'd liked army-surplus green, but it had had that gritty, down-to-earth feeling.

This was all Francesca's influence. The least she could have done was to stick around and have to live with it.

Donovan riffled through the phone messages. He could tell from the exchanges that most of the callers lived in affluent communities: Newport Beach, Huntington

Beach, Irvine. He had to admit, there was something to this business of advertising in the right places.

He wondered if he ought to track down Letitia and find out where Francesca was. Or maybe put in a call to Stewart and fish around in case she'd gone there.

Let her go and she'll come back.

If this was a test, Donovan didn't like it. Every fiber of his being demanded that he take action and seize control of the situation.

Tammi stuck her head in. "You hungry? I'm going out for stamps and I could pick up a hamburger."

"Great. I'm starved."

"Back in half an hour."

He plopped his feet on the desk—at least she hadn't replaced *that*—and leaned back. The chair squeaked just as it always had, and Donovan began to feel better.

Then Francesca walked in the door.

Chapter Sixteen

Donovan didn't hear her come into the outer office, didn't have a moment to prepare until she appeared right in front of him.

She'd twisted her hair into a sophisticated bun and put on more makeup than usual. She wore golden-yellow leggings and an angular jacket that might have come from the pages of the *Los Angeles Times* weekly fashion reports, which Donovan glanced at whenever he needed a chuckle.

The style didn't look funny on Francesca, however. She gave it a smart air. Yet there was still something Donovan didn't like. Dressed up like that, she seemed distant, not rumpled and touchable the way she'd been at Blakely's house.

"Surprise," she said.

"Come for your paycheck?"

"You don't have to pay me." She fiddled with the strap on her triangular purse. "Donovan, I feel bad about walking out without a word. That was cowardly. It's not like me."

Let her go and she'll come back. "Find another job?"

"I didn't even try." Sunlight danced through her hair. "I need to go away for a while."

"Why?" he said.

"Donovan, you're more than I bargained for. I mean, my feelings are more than I bargained for. There's this disgusting desire to be—" Francesca spit out the word "—domestic. The next thing you know, I'd find myself moving into your apartment, lining your kitchen drawers and burning chicken casseroles."

"I can burn my own casseroles."

"You know what I mean."

"I'll pay you anyway," he said, and reached for his checkbook.

"No, really—"

A tap on the outer door made them both turn.

"Excuse me?" came a shaky voice. "Is this the detective agency?"

"Come in." Francesca stepped aside.

Donovan glimpsed the scarf first, one of those ugly, expensive designer prints, then the metallic cane clutched in a liver-spotted hand.

From the curve of her back and the wrinkles webbing her face, he guessed the woman's age at over eighty. Keen gray eyes took his measure as Francesca helped the visitor into a chair.

The tan printed blouse and slacks fit right in with the scarf; he knew that if he saw the label he'd recognize the name. This lady shopped in the best stores.

Donovan hoped he could help her. From a selfish point of view, he assumed she could pay her bills. But, more importantly, if there was anyone he liked to rescue almost as much as beautiful young women, it was sweet old ladies.

"I'm Donovan Lewis." He leaned forward for a handshake and found her grip firm. "What can I do for you?"

"I'm Sally Wickworth." She spoke with a clipped finishing school accent that reminded him of Katharine Hepburn. "Does this young woman work for you? I don't care to tell my story in front of strangers."

"She assists me on special cases," Donovan said. "Mrs. Wickworth, this is Francesca Adamo."

The woman tilted her head in acknowledgment. "Very well. I am in a most embarrassing situation. My husband was wealthy, very wealthy. I will not tell you how wealthy, because you would not believe me. After he died, I swore I would never remarry."

The dry voice cracked, and Donovan offered her something to drink, but Mrs. Wickworth shook her head impatiently and went on. "Then, a few months ago, I met a gentleman. At least I thought he was a gentleman. On a cruise, as a matter of fact. I went with my friend, Jane Rhys. Well, that's neither here nor there."

From a shipboard romance, the relationship had blossomed. As Mrs. Wickworth described her beau, he sounded dapper, a few years younger than her, and almost as wealthy.

"When he made me a business proposition, I was actually flattered. Can you imagine that? There's no fool like an old fool. He had an opportunity to expand his business, but he needed venture capital. It was all to be done properly, with lawyers and contracts, and he offered me a most attractive rate of interest."

Francesca listened intently, although Donovan couldn't imagine what interested her so much.

"By now, you've guessed the rest," said Sally Wickworth. "He got his hands on my money, and off he went. He was clever, all right, using the identity of a man who really did exist and owned a legitimate business. But he wasn't the real Marvin Morant."

"You want me to find him and get your money back?" Donovan said.

She waved a hand dismissively. "The money—pooh! I don't care about that. But we can't have him going around conning people and breaking their hearts. Just find him for me, and I'll take care of the rest."

Donovan mentioned his fee, which didn't faze her, and discussed his procedures. "Depending on a variety of factors, it could take from a few days to months."

"I don't care. I can wait."

Francesca spoke for the first time. "Mrs. Wickworth, if I may ask, was there anyone else involved with him? An accomplice?"

The gray head nodded reluctantly. "Some woman. A secretarial person, I believe."

"Surely your lawyer must have checked this man out," Francesca asked.

A frown deepened the wrinkles around Mrs. Wickworth's mouth. "He was quite good at his scam. It's my belief he had some actual connection with the Morant company. Perhaps he's one of those black-sheep relatives people always seem to have."

She hoisted herself forward. "I'll have my lawyer send along the papers. I heard you were involved in finding that Cindy Blakely person. I'm sure you'll do as well for me." A brisk nod, and she stood up.

When he returned from helping Sally Wickworth down the stairs, Donovan found Francesca studying him with a frown. "Is there a problem?"

"You're not really going to take the case, are you?" she said.

Donovan gazed at her in perplexity. "I like helping damsels in distress. You know that."

"In distress, yes." She folded her arms and glared. "*That* was no woman in distress."

"Seduced and abandoned? Robbed of her dreams and her venture capital?"

"Hardly." Her foot tapped against the linoleum. "Isn't it obvious?" Her brown eyes blazed at him. "Any woman can see this is a simple case of jealousy. She was trying to buy the man by lending him money, and then he ran off with another woman, that 'secretarial person.'"

"Wait a minute." He couldn't believe, after the experience she'd gained on the Blakely job, that Francesca would draw such a wild conclusion. "There was absolutely nothing in what she said—"

"But her body language!" Francesca said. "She's a domineering person, and one of her prey managed to escape. Now she wants him back!"

"That should be easy enough to check out," Donovan said. "He either is or isn't this Marvin Morant."

"Maybe he never claimed to be! Maybe she forged the papers!"

"That's the most ridiculous—"

Francesca tossed his checkbook to him. "Put that away. I'll do it for nothing. For the pure satisfaction."

"I pay my employees, and that includes social security and benefits." Then Donovan remembered he didn't offer any benefits. "Workers' compensation, anyway." Trying not to show his delight, he added, "You're really going to work with me on this one?"

"I have to, don't I?" Francesca slipped the purse off her shoulder and tossed it onto a chair. "Just to keep you from acting like a complete idiot."

An angry rejoinder sprang to Donovan's lips. He knew what the hell he was doing. He didn't need Francesca to tell him his business.

And there were other things he longed to say. That he wanted nothing more out of life than to keep her around, even if she did spin absurd theories. Even if she did dangle from buildings and put on outrageous costumes. Even if she did make him so mad he might someday pound a hole in his desk.

Most of all, he wanted to tell her that he loved her. That he cherished every ridiculous excess of fashion dripping from her slender frame, that he adored that annoyed pucker between her eyebrows, that he couldn't wait to hear what harebrained idea she was going to come up with next.

He wanted to say all those things and more.

Instead, he gave her his most impersonal nod. "With the load of cases I've got these next few months, I could use the help. But I expect you to follow orders, understand?"

"As long as you don't order me to do anything stupid." Francesca strolled toward the outer office. "And, Donovan, you've got to put in a decent communications system. Rotary phones? This isn't the Dark Ages!"

He inhaled the lingering enticement of her perfume, as he thought of a dozen clever retorts.

New York Times Bestselling Author

Sandra Brown

Tomorrow's Promise

She cherished the memory of love but was consumed by a new passion too fierce to ignore.

For Keely Preston, the memory of her husband Mark has been frozen in time since the day he was listed as missing in action. And now, twelve years later, twenty-six men listed as MIA have been found.

Keely's torn between hope for Mark and despair for herself. Because now, after all the years of waiting, she has met another man!

Don't miss TOMORROW'S PROMISE by SANDRA BROWN.

Available in June wherever Harlequin books are sold.

TP

THREE UNFORGETTABLE HEROINES
THREE AWARD-WINNING AUTHORS

MAVERICK HEARTS

A unique collection of historical short stories that capture the spirit of America's last frontier.

HEATHER GRAHAM POZZESSERE—over 10 million copies of her books in print worldwide
Lonesome Rider—The story of an Eastern widow and the renegade half-breed who becomes her protector.

PATRICIA POTTER—an author whose books are consistently Waldenbooks bestsellers
Against the Wind—Two people, battered by heartache, prove that love can heal all.

JOAN JOHNSTON—award-winning Western historical author with 17 books to her credit
One Simple Wish—A woman with a past discovers that dreams really do come true.

Join us for an exciting journey West with
UNTAMED
Available in July, wherever Harlequin books are sold.

MAV93

Harlequin is proud to present our best authors and their best books. Always the best for your reading pleasure!

Throughout 1993, Harlequin will bring you exciting books by some of the top names in contemporary romance!

In July
look for
The Ties That Bind by

JAYNE ANN KRENTZ

Shannon wanted him seven days a week....

Dark, compelling, mysterious Garth Sheridan was no mere boy next door—even if he did rent the cottage beside Shannon Raine's.

She was intrigued by the hard-nosed exec, but for Shannon it was all or nothing. Either break the undeniable bonds between them... or tear down the barriers surrounding Garth and discover the truth.

Don't miss THE TIES THAT BIND ... wherever Harlequin books are sold.

BOB3

**Relive the romance...
Harlequin and Silhouette
are proud to present**

by Request

A program of collections of three complete novels by the most requested authors with the most requested themes. Be sure to look for one volume each month with three complete novels by top name authors.

In June: **NINE MONTHS** Penny Jordan
Stella Cameron
Janice Kaiser

Three women pregnant and alone. But a lot can happen in nine months!

In July: **DADDY'S HOME** Kristin James
Naomi Horton
Mary Lynn Baxter

Daddy's Home... and his presence is long overdue!

In August: **FORGOTTEN PAST** Barbara Kaye
Pamela Browning
Nancy Martin

Do you dare to create a future if you've forgotten the past?

Available at your favorite retail outlet.

REQ-G

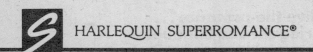

HARLEQUIN SUPERROMANCE®

HARLEQUIN SUPERROMANCE WANTS TO INTRODUCE YOU TO A DARING NEW CONCEPT IN ROMANCE...

WOMEN WHO DARE!
Bright, bold, beautiful ...
Brave and caring, strong and passionate ...
They're women who know their own minds
and will dare anything ... **for love!**

One title per month in 1993, written by popular Superromance authors, will highlight our special heroines as they face unusual, challenging and sometimes dangerous situations.

Purchase your ticket for daring adventure next month with:
#554 THE MARRIAGE TICKET by Sharon Brondos
Available in July wherever Harlequin Superromance novels are sold.